MIDNIGHT TAXI
THE COMPLETE CASES OF
SMOOTH KYLE, VOLUME 1

MIDNIGHT TAXI
THE COMPLETE CASES OF SMOOTH KYLE, VOLUME 1

BORDEN CHASE

ILLUSTRATED BY
SAMUEL CAHAN

POPULAR PUBLICATIONS · 2024

TABLE OF CONTENTS

MIDNIGHT TAXI

Smooth Kyle, Federal Operative, was once a hack driver, so the role suited him well in his fight against a New York narcotic ring

1

ROLLING AGAIN

HE HOOKED BOTH thumbs in his belt and stared at the dirty brick front of the garage. Same old dump—same noises, same smells. It might have been yesterday rather than ten years ago that Peter Kyle had rolled his cab into place and walked down the ramp.

The Ninth Avenue elevated trains still rumbled along the dust covered structure. Beneath, scampering in and out between pushcarts piled high with fruit and vegetables, were a dozen or more poorly dressed youngsters. Same shrill voices, torn and patched clothes and impudent grins that made them lovable in spite of their dirty faces. Yes, Hell's Kitchen at four in the afternoon was just as he had known it when he unpinned his hack badge for what he thought was the last time.

And then Peter Kyle smiled. He had noticed one slight difference. Propped against the garage wall, legs sprawled out upon the sidewalk and his head resting slackly against a barrel of refuse, was Old Squint. His mouth was open and he snored—and it was the first time Kyle had ever seen him without Slumpy the Bum.

He reached down, prodded the limp shoulder and was rewarded by a growled curse and a vacant stare from a pair of bleary gray eyes. The lids flicked. A thousand wrinkles gathered about them.

" 'Lo, Smooth," said Old Squint. "Gotta dime?"

Slug fired, sure of a kill

Kyle flipped a coin into the filthy upturned palm. Here, at least, was one who remembered him and called him by a nickname that had been known in every taxi garage in New York. Smooth Kyle—it was like a page from yesterday. A day when he had "rolled 'em hard and rolled 'em fast"—swinging a hack through the midnight streets of Manhattan—taking in the dimes and dollars and taking a chump whenever the opportunity arose.

"How are they treating you, Squint?" he asked and moved back a little. Squint smelled better at a distance.

"Lousy," said the derelict. "Ain't no money out any more. When a guy books less'n two pounds on a Saturday night he don't flip no dimes away."

That tore it. The present disintegrated—Peter Kyle dropped like a plummet into another world. A world of screaming brakes, clicking taxi meters and cursing drivers who talked a jargon unintelligible to the riders who leaned back against the soft cushions of their cabs. Five dollars became a pound—a taxi cab was a load, a crate or a rig—old tires were chewing gum and a meter was a clock.

"Where's Slumpy the Bum?" he asked.

"The morgue wagon got him. Must 'a' been the booze, Smooth. Slumpy's stomach wasn't never much good."

"Tough luck," said Kyle and started up the ramp.

A wave of smoke rolled down to meet him. A score of cabs vomited acrid fumes from their exhausts, motors roared and coughed, rubber shrieked against concrete as the drivers tested the brakes, men shouted and mechanics cursed. A short, dark faced man with a protruding stomach leaned against the door of a small office close to the top of the ramp. He rolled a well-chewed cigar between his teeth and watched the confusion before him through half closed eyes. When he caught sight of Kyle the cigar slipped from his mouth and splashed upon the floor.

"Smooth! Well, I'll be damned!" he grunted.

"You will—sure as hell," laughed Smooth. "But don't let it worry you. How's chances to roll one of your crates tonight?"

"Where you been—doin' time?"

Smooth grinned and searched his pockets for a cigarette. The owner of the garage had answered his own question. If Harry Tone, one of the wisest of taxi fleet operators, wanted to think that Smooth Kyle had been in jail for the past ten years it was all right with Smooth. Others would probably think the same.

"How about a rig?" he asked.

"What'd they get you for?"

"Playing marbles," said Smooth.

"And now do I go to work?"

"I'd like to put you on, Smooth. But things is different now. The cops are runnin' this racket and they're crackin' down plenty hard. Everything's got to be on the up and up. Got a hack badge?"

SMOOTH DREW A square of metal from his pocket and a glazed card upon which was his picture and name. He extended them to Tone and the garage owner examined them closely. He held the picture to the light and compared the printed features with those of the man before him: a heavy jaw, wide-set eyes that laughed, a good forehead and thin lips. The likeness checked. He fingered the hack badge.

"Phonies?"

"They're legit," said Smooth. "Call the Commissioner if you think I'm kidding."

"How'd you get 'em? The cops ain't handin' out badges to ex-cons these days, Smooth."

"Listen, Harry," said Smooth, "I'm asking you if I take out one of your rigs tonight. But I'm not asking how you get your fast clocks passed—that's your business. Suppose you lay off my affairs."

"Smooth as ever, eh?" laughed Tone, and copied the badge number in a greasy notebook. "Okay, pal. Take Number Twenty—over there in the corner. It's a new rig and I expect big money."

"You'll get it," said Smooth, and he pinned the badge to the lapel of his coat.

He crossed the oil stained floor of the garage and climbed in behind the wheel of a new taxi. Tone handed him a ruled card on which to note the time and destination of each call and lifted the motor hood to check the oil. Smooth wrote the readings of the meter upon the card, twisted the ignition switch and started the motor.

"Gas and water okay?" he asked.

"Yeah. Roll it out—and bring in the shekels."

Smooth drove to the ramp and tested the brakes. He glanced about at the faces of his fellow hackmen but recognized none. Each year sees a new crop of drivers coming in to replace the old timers who have moved on and he had counted on this. Hackmen, as a rule, do not pry into the affairs of their fellow workers. They seldom ask questions and are little interested in the life of the average man who works with them. But Smooth was not average. In his day he was known as a high booker, a driver who rolled more money than most, and one who could be depended upon to take any bonus offered by the fleet owners for efficiency.

He drove up Ninth Avenue, stopped in front of a drug store and entered a telephone booth. He dialed a midtown number and waited.

"McNeary," said a voice in the receiver.

"Kyle," he answered. "Forty-fourth and Broadway, in front of the Claridge in five minutes."

"Right."

SMOOTH GRINNED AND hung up. He swung the cab east, crossed Eighth Avenue and Times Square and drew to a stop on a hack stand in front of the hotel. A gray haired man dressed in a blue, double breasted suit was standing at an orange drink counter on the corner. He finished his drink, flipped a coin to the attendant and paused as though in doubt near Smooth's taxi.

"Want a cab?" asked Smooth.

There was a nod and the gray haired stranger stepped into the car.

"Same old Smooth," said a voice at the hackman's shoulder. "Grabbing one off the back end of the line."

Smooth turned. Another driver was standing behind him, hands in his coat pocket and grinning in amusement.

"Hello, Lucky," said Smooth. "Still shoving a hack?"

"Yeah, still at it. See you later."

"Stick around," said Smooth as he threw the flag and swung from the curb. "I'll be back."

The cab rolled into the stream of traffic and Smooth leaned back, waiting for instructions.

"Up through the park," said the passenger. "Sixth Avenue entrance."

"Right."

They swung north beneath the elevated and Smooth was busy with his driving until they were spinning along the quiet roads of Central Park. He glanced about, saw there were no other cars close by and winked into the mirror above his head. An answering wink came from the gray haired passenger.

"Didn't take you long to get a job."

"Why should it?" grinned Smooth. "I'm a damn good hackman."

"You're not bad at a lot of things if the reports from Washington mean anything."

"They tell me McNeary is a tough boss. That right?"

"Well—I'm not so bad as they make me, Kyle. I expect results and I don't like mistakes. Do your job and we'll hit it off great. Did they tell you anything about this assignment?"

"Not much," said Smooth. "I used to drive a hack in this town and I was told to renew my license and report to the Chief of the New York Division. And that's what I've done."

"How about references for the license?" asked McNeary. "Do the police know who you are?"

"Of course not. I spent fifty bucks on a couple of politicians and got the best references they had. They think I've been away for my health—and maybe the country's, too. The cops are satisfied with the references, and that's that."

They had stopped for a traffic light and a blue sedan rolled close beside them. The driver seemed to be staring casually at the scenery but Smooth noticed his eyes were fixed quite steadily upon McNeary and himself. He stalled the cab when the lights changed and allowed the sedan to move ahead. When it was a few yards distant he stepped on the starter and followed.

"Do you know that guy?" he asked quietly and he was careful not to move his lips. The driver of the blue sedan was studying him through the mirror above his seat.

"Yes," said McNeary. "That's Vince Cartwright, gangster and killer. We want him. Somebody must have pointed me out and his men have been trailing me for weeks. Thought I shook them today but it seems not."

"He'll be watching me now. That was a tough break."

"Don't worry about it," said McNeary, and passed a sheet of paper to Smooth. "Here's your instructions. Read them and don't call me unless you have to."

"Fair enough," said Smooth. "And now what?"

"Pull alongside Cartwright. I'm going to take him in."

THERE WAS A puzzled frown on Smooth's face as he

stepped down on the gas. But he had heard enough about this grim faced Federal man not to question his orders. McNeary was tough. He ran his division with an iron hand, expected absolute obedience from his agents, but he backed them to the limit when he got it. Smooth knew that powerful pressure had been brought to bear in Washington to break McNeary and drive him from the service. His agents were uncovering scandals that were front page news, sending politicians on the run and arresting criminals who had enjoyed immunity for years. And as his men fought for him, so did McNeary fight for his men.

They had reached the curving incline that led past the upper lake in the park before Smooth sent his car crowding against the blue sedan. For a moment there were no other cars close by and Smooth took this opportunity to cut in.

"Pull over, punk!" yelled Cartwright. "If you scratch that fender I'll blind you. You lousy hackmen are all alike."

Smooth flicked the wheel. The cab edged closer. It drew ahead and cut toward the curb. There was a scream of rubber and the blue sedan jerked to a stop.

"You dirty—"

"Get 'em up, Vince," snapped McNeary.

He jumped from the cab, gun in hand and eyes steady upon Cartwright.

"Like hell, copper!"

Cartwright ducked below the body of his car. His hand held a kicking automatic that blazed at the Federal man. Slugs breezed past the cab and Smooth ducked. A car, rounding the curve behind them, swung far to the opposite side of the roadway. A woman screamed and covered her face. Her companion gripped the wheel tightly and stepped on the gas. Farther back, another car slid to a sudden stop. There were shouts and curses. And then McNeary's gun jerked.

There were three closely spaced shots and the fire from the blue sedan was silenced.

"Nice shooting, Chief," said Smooth quietly.

"Get out of here—quick!" barked McNeary. "I'll handle this. Fade."

Smooth rolled. His cab hurtled down the incline, rounded the curve at the bottom and streaked west. He spun the wheel, twisted out onto Central Park West and doubled north. Up and across One Hundred and Tenth Street to Broadway and then down town at a leisurely pace. Cars whirled past him; people hurried from subway exits; newsdealers yelled the headlines of evening papers; two girls stood at the corner of Ninetieth Street hopefully eyeing the passing cars and ignoring the taxis.

A gangster, wanted by the Federal men, had decided to shoot it out. He had died just a few blocks away, but upper Broadway was quite unaware of the fact. That was New York—the town in which Smooth Kyle had learned to drag a living from the streets.

He was glad to get back, glad to be part of that swift beating pulse of his home town. The past few years had taken him the breadth of the country—Cleveland, Chicago, Dallas, and then up into Los Angeles and San Francisco. He had followed the path of the novice in the Bureau of Narcotics, learning the trade, taking orders, covering small assignments where there was little chance for excitement and less for glory. It had been a hard grind but as a result he had been detailed to the New York District with a fine recommendation. His first hour's work promised him his fill of action. And it would be in a town where he knew every street and alley—knew them as only a hackman can.

He stopped before a cafeteria on West Seventy-second Street and walked through to the men's room. He locked the door, lit a cigarette and studied the instructions given to him by McNeary. A strange place for privacy, but Smooth wanted no one reading over his shoulder this evening.

The orders were brief. He was on a job that would make him if he succeeded. If he failed—a sack in the river. A syndicate of narcotic sellers had formed a ring that threaded its way throughout the country. Washington had been given credible reports that New York was the headquarters. That put it up to McNeary, and Smooth's job was to secure information—definite evidence that would break up the ring.

He touched a match to the corner of the paper and watched it burn to a black ash. He gulped a cup of coffee at the restaurant counter and drove toward Forty-fourth Street. Going down Eighth Avenue a hail brought him to a quick stop and a moment later he was on a trip to Washington Heights. He threaded his way through traffic, jockeying into narrow spaces in the stream of north-bound cars, gaining a brief instant on each change of lights and disregarding the speed law completely. To all intents he was a hackman doing a night's work. He accepted a dime tip in addition to the fare at the end of the ride and said: "Thank you." And he sent his cab south again, his ears alert for a hail.

A traffic cop yelled at him on Broadway for passing a light. Another hackman cursed him roundly for stealing a call. There was an argument at Columbus Circle with a truck driver about a scratched fender and another with a pedestrian who did not look before he stepped into the street. Yes, Smooth Kyle was rolling again, grabbing the dimes and dollars.

2

"SUCKER!"

IT WAS AFTER ten o'clock when he drew to a stop at the hack stand on Forty-fourth Street—lunch time for the men who drive at night. The first rush of business had thinned out and there would be no calls until "show-break"—eleven o'clock, when the theaters were emptying their throngs.

He checked over his trip card and counted his bookings. Seven dollars—not bad, he thought, even for the old days. There was still money in New York if a man knew where to look for it. And there were men who sold cocaine and heroin if they could be found. But there was time enough for that. His first job was to establish himself as a hackman, live the part, forget for the time that he was a Government agent and acquire the attitude of the men on the cabs.

He saw a group of them standing beside the first taxi on the line. There was something about their faces that set them apart as different from the average man on the street. Maybe it was their eyes—tired and all-wise. After a man's eyes have looked at the follies and sins of New York each night from sunset until sunrise they are apt to get tired— and very wise. Each face was cynical and distrustful. But when a hackman has seen a spender throwing money away by the handful and then has been left waiting at the front door of a hotel while this same spender slips out the back to avoid paying a two dollar fare, he can't be blamed for his cynicism.

To these men, the average person who made up the night life in Manhattan was a chump. The hackmen had no respect for the New Yorker who would toss five dollars to a head waiter for a table in a drafty corner and argue if the meter dropped an extra dime on the trip home. Nor did he think much of the out-of-towner who winked knowingly and asked to be shown the sights—"not the usual places, you know. Er—maybe we could find some girls?"

Each of the tight lipped men had heard that story many times. Most of them had shrugged and shook their heads. Some had made the mistake of steering the Romeos to a hideaway and had been stripped of their hack badges by the police when the inevitable squawk came from the sucker who had lost his roll. Yes, they were wise, cynical and silent, these taxi drivers. And Smooth slipped back into the life with little effort.

There was a slight jar as another cab pulled into place behind him and touched bumpers. Smooth looked back and saw Lucky Carmine climb from his seat, stretch wearily and walk toward him.

"How's tricks, Lucky?" Smooth said and extended his hand.

Lucky gripped his fingers and stepped back. He cocked his head to one side and studied Smooth.

"They didn't wear you down much, feller," he said at length. "Or do I guess wrong?"

Smooth grinned contentedly. Lucky was answering his

own questions, too. He seemed to take it for granted that Smooth had been doing time in some jail and had just been released.

"Why tag me for an ex-con?" Smooth asked. "Can't a guy quit this racket without going to the pen?"

"Not guys like you," said Lucky. "You're a natural on a hack or I never saw one. Hell—it seems like yesterday when I was watching you take the chumps. Remember when we worked the Village together?"

"Good old prohibition," laughed Smooth. "Those were the days."

"You must have made plenty. I never could figure your racket, Smooth. But it sure was a hot one to get you a long stretch."

"Well, that makes us even. I knew you were smart and I knew you didn't get all your dimes on the front end of a cab—but that's as close as I could guess."

Lucky drew a few bills from his coat pocket and folded them neatly, thumbing the edges in a quick count. He slipped them into an inside pocket of his vest and glanced at a handful of change.

"Coffee money," he said. "That's all there is on the street now. Wanna eat?"

SMOOTH FOLLOWED HIM into a nearby cafeteria and selected a meal. They carried their plates to a marble-topped table and ate without troubling to remove their overcoats. Each studied the other and in the eyes of both was admiration—the grudging admiration of a smart New Yorker who sees a man equally wise.

Lucky knew his way around. There was little that happened on Broadway or any other section of town that got past this thin shouldered, dapper little hackman. He knew the clip joints, knew where the traveling crap games were playing, he was smart enough to keep rolling when a gun went off in a dark alley and he never talked to the wrong people.

Smooth said little until the cigarettes were going and both had started their second cup of coffee. Then he leaned his elbows on the table, drifted a thin stream of smoke toward the ceiling and stared at Lucky.

"Where's the late money?"* he asked. "I'm licked after showbreak. All the old spots must have folded up with repeal. I didn't see any of them while I was cruising."

"There ain't any late money, Smooth. You won't find a pound on the street between midnight and morning. But if you want a piece of advice, you can have it."

"Give," said Smooth.

"Get rid of that rod."

With an involuntary movement Smooth hunched his shoulders to allow more slack across the front of his coat. They were wide shoulders and his coat was snug fitting, not yet dragged from shape by the pull of the cab seat. He flicked the ash from his cigarette and grinned.

"Good eyes, Lucky. How'd you spot it?"

"Any time I can't see a shoulder holster, you'll know I'm gettin' old," said Lucky. "You must be screwy."

"Maybe. But I need money. It's a cinch I'll never get it shovin' a cab these days—not the kind I need. And now

---

* Late money. Any calls after midnight are late money and a hackman must know where to go to dig them up. Night clubs, bars, midnight shows, Harlem late spots, Greenwich Village, or gambling houses are usually where "late money" is found.

suppose you forget the roscoe and wise me to the Big Town, as of today."

"Aw—you're out of my class," said Lucky. "Me—I'm playing it legit.* Forty percent of the clock, tips, and a few stickups—that's all. Maybe I roll a lush or two, but that's tops. My lungs are goin' sour and I'm figurin' on hittin' the sticks in a year or two. A stretch in the pen would kill me, so I'm not bein' stupid. Besides, I like straight hackin'."

"Is this the same bucker** that shot it out with Fay's men on the docks?" asked Smooth with a slow smile. "Lucky—you've gone soft."

"Maybe—but I'm keepin' out of jail."

A HARD FACED youngster with a bundle of papers stepped into the restaurant and made his way slowly past the tables.

"Mornin' paper—*News, Mirror* and *Trib!*" he cried, and flashed a folded sheet before the two hackmen. "Vince Cartwright gets it in de belly. Wanna paper, fellers?"

Lucky flipped him a nickel and grabbed the sheet. He spread it on the table and glanced quickly at the headlines and sub-heads. Smooth twisted in his chair to read with him.

"Know him?" he asked.

"Yeah," answered Lucky. "Just to say hello, that's all. Not a bad guy, but what a sucker to shoot it out with the Feds."

---

* Hackman's jargon. Playing it legit means being honest. Taxi drivers get forty percent commission on their earnings. A stickup is a call done with the meter in non-recording position—*i.e.,* with the flag, or stick, up. Rolling a lush is overcharging a drunk or emptying his pockets before depositing him at the end of the trip.
** A bucker was a driver whose cab was equipped with a double tariff meter that was painted red. These are no longer permitted. Larry Fay, a New York gangster who was killed in a night club, once put out a fleet of cabs. He took over the railroad terminals, steamship lines and some of the hotel stands where the buckers worked, and the buckers put up a terrific fight before being driven from the streets. Fay's cabs were painted gray with a gold swastika on the door.

"Who got him?"

"Bloke by the name of McNeary. That guy's poison in this town." He read silently for a moment and then grinned. "Listen to this. An eyewitness to the shootin' says the Federal Agent was ridin' in a taxi and the driver scrammed when the shootin' started. What did they expect him to do—sing a lullaby?"

"Ever see McNeary?" asked Smooth.

"Never want to," laughed Lucky. "It's none of my business. C'mon, let's get outta here."

They paid their checks and walked to their cabs. A traffic officer motioned them to roll. They nodded and swung from the curb.

Smooth turned north on Sixth Avenue. He picked up a straggler near Fifty-ninth Street and made a short trip uptown. The theaters were empty when he again drove back into the district and groups of cars were parked near some of the stage doors. Rolling slowly and glancing at times from one curb to the other, he noticed a girl standing in the shadows of a theater alley. She lifted her arm and signalled. Smooth pulled to the curb.

He opened the cab door and the girl hurried across the sidewalk, glancing quickly at a man who stood close to an expensive car near by.

"Uptown," she said and put one foot on the running board.

"Wait a minute, Dorothy!"

The voice was harsh, nasal. Smooth turned to see the man who had been standing near the parked car grasp the girl by the arm.

"Please," she said. "I'm going home."

"Aw, why don't you be nice? Loosen up—relax! We're goin' places and do things."

"Do you want a cab?" Smooth asked the girl.

"Yes—yes, I do," she said and tried to jerk her arm loose. "Slug—let go of me."

"Yes, Slug," said Smooth. "Be a nice boy—let go."

"Scram, punk!" said Slug.

SMOOTH SLIPPED FROM the seat and stepped forward. His left hand gripped the lapels of Slug's coat and jerked down. His right circled in a short arc and landed on Slug's chin. He helped the astonished girl into the cab and closed the door.

"What was the address?" he asked as the taxi started.

"Oh—"

"Sorry to be rough," said Smooth. "But things are so bad lately it would have been poor business to let him steal a call. Now—where to?"

"Eighty-third and West End Avenue," she said. "Hurry—he'll follow us and hurt you. I know he will."

Smooth smiled but said nothing. He was studying the girl in the mirror above the windshield. She was crouched forward on the seat as though to lend speed to the taxi. Her head turned at times as she glanced through the rear window and Smooth nearly passed a light admiring the sheen of her dark hair. Her hands opened and closed nervously and Smooth thought he had never seen fingers so small or so beautifully formed. Once, when her eyes met with his in the mirror, she smiled—a scared, pretty little smile that drew an answering grin from Smooth.

"Aren't you afraid?" she asked.

"Not much," he answered. "But I'm wondering why you are. Who's your playmate?"

"That's Slug Conners—and he's no friend of mine. He's one of a bunch of gorillas that have been driving the girls in the show half mad. His boss is the backer and the mob seem to think that gives them the privilege of annoying the girls. I'm just about fed up with the whole thing and I handed in my notice tonight. They can get another lead. Three more performances and I'm through."

"And then what?"

"I don't know. Another musical comedy, probably."

"Think I'll take tomorrow night off and catch that show. You must look great from the front. Do you sing?"

"You're not very flattering," she said. "I thought all New York had seen Dorothy Manning."

"Are you Dorothy Manning?" he asked in surprise. "Say—I saw you in Chicago, but you didn't look so—"

"So small?" she said.

"No—well—oh, I don't know. Forget it." He glanced at a street marker. "Eighty-third?"

"Just down from the corner. Here—this is it." She opened her purse and handed him a bill. "It's all yours. And—thanks."

Smooth glanced at the bill and saw it was a five. He folded it carefully, stuck it in his vest pocket and reached back to open the door.

"I'll bring the change tomorrow," he said. " 'Night."

She hurried across the sidewalk and Smooth did not move until the apartment door had closed behind her. He glanced down the street and saw a car turn the corner. It slowed and drew to a stop. Smooth pulled away from the curb, and the car followed.

He circled the block and spun along Riverside Drive. Behind him the car followed at a distance of one block, pausing for traffic lights whenever Smooth did, increasing its pace or slowing to keep its distance from the taxi.

AT THE ENTRANCE to a viaduct that leads across One Hundred and Twenty-fifth Street, Smooth swung right and took a cobble road that led down to the Ferry House. It was a narrow street, sharply inclined, and it curved in under the great supports of the structure along the river front. A single street light on the corner provided scanty illumination and there was a hush in this little backwater that seemed unnatural to Manhattan. Smooth noticed there were no pedestrians about and he pulled up beside one of the steel uprights.

He slid from the cab seat and lifted the hood, apparently tinkering with the motor. Behind him, a car drew to a stop and the driver left the motor running and crossed toward the taxi.

"Thanks for the setup, dope!"

"Hello, Slug," said Smooth. "When did you wake up?"

Slug was facing him across the hood of the cab, peering intently into Smooth's eyes. His hand was thrust stiffly into his right coat pocket and he swayed from the hips.

"Did I ever see you in Cleveland?" he asked suddenly.

"Maybe," said Smooth. "What about it?"

"It don't matter, now. You're going to get one in the chest. Want to pray or cry a little?"

"You mean you're goin' to kill me?" asked Smooth. "Why? What's the idea?"

"Just to teach you a lesson, Wise Guy. For a hackman, you're plenty dumb—sockin' Slug Conners in the chin!" There was a gun in his hand now and it flipped indolently toward Smooth. If the hackman had opened his mouth to cry out, it would have gone off. Conners was drawing the last ounce of enjoyment from a few moments' torture before finishing Smooth. And as he studied the taxi driver his mind was racing back to a time when he had seen this man in Cleveland. Suddenly he stiffened.

"I make you now!" he yelled and the gun leveled. "A Fed. A stinkin' copper! You—"

Smooth dropped to his knees as the automatic stuttered above his head. His gun was out and making crimson flashes in the darkness. Slug yelled. He crumpled against the taxi and knocked the lifted section of the hood back into place. His arms slid along the hot metal, the gun rattled against a fender and dropped to the ground. Slug followed it and his legs jerked for an instant.

"Sucker!" said Smooth and clamped the hood tight.

He drove east.

3

IN THE KNOW

IT WAS MIDNIGHT and the neighborhood movie theaters on upper Broadway had emptied their throngs into the near-by restaurants. Occasionally a couple hurried through one of the deserted side streets. The night was cool, brisk with a sharpness that comes in late October. Smooth turned up the collar of his coat, settled himself comfortably in the seat and started to cruise. Down Broadway, across and up West End Avenue, doubling and twisting through side streets and then over to Central Park West.

He had rolled for the better part of an hour, ignoring the occasional hails of pedestrians waiting at street corners. His eyes swept the entrance of each apartment house he passed, and at times he slowed or came to a stop. At length he circled a block twice on the upper West Side and drew close to the marquee of an ornate apartment fronting on the park. A doorman, resplendent in gold braid and visored cap, stood before the wide glass doors leading in from the street. At times he swung his arms or stamped his feet upon the pavement. And Smooth grinned when he saw this military figure spring to attention and touch his cap to an incoming couple.

Smooth slid from the seat and stood beside the cab door.

"Pull that crate outta here!" barked the doorman. "There's a cab line at the corner—play that."

"Okay, general," said Smooth, and drew a dollar from his pocket. "Will you mind this for me?"

"What the—"

"Hello, Mullans. I've been looking for you all night."

"Oh, *hello,* Smooth. Where you been all the while?"

"Bouncing around. How about you—still frontin' for Big Joe?"

"What's your guess?"

Smooth nodded and winked. Mullans was one of the old timers with a big paying specialty at his finger tips. For years he had been in the employ of Big Joe Silva, a gambler who catered to the wealthy New Yorkers with money to lose. To Smooth, the sight of Mullans in doorman's uniform was certain knowledge that a big money game was in progress somewhere within the apartment. For Mullans could recognize at a glance each and every member of the New York detective squads. His memory of Big Joe's customers was equally sound. And as a result of this memory, Big Joe had run a profitable game for years.

It was a foolproof proposition. When Big Joe rented a floor or the penthouse of an apartment building, within a few days Mullans was installed as doorman and with him worked Eddie Drinker as hall boy. If a customer appeared, he was welcomed with a bow from Mullans. Seeing this, Eddie immediately passed the signal along to the gambling rooms.

At times a squad of detectives endeavored to visit Big Joe's apartment, but invariably the guests had departed and the paraphernalia had been disposed of when the raiders were admitted. Mullans had merely winked to Eddie and a very different signal had been passed along.

But Mullans was human. He could not resist the urge to add a few quick dollars to a salary far in excess of that paid the average doorman. He had a graft of his own that fitted in very nicely with his nightly duties. Gamblers were big tippers when the wheels had been kind to them. A man with a few thousands of quickly won dollars in his pockets was apt to toss a hackman the change of a five dollar bill at the end of a trip home. Mullans knew this and so did the taxi men, and as a result the doorman had built himself a following of night drivers that paid him well for the privilege of taking calls from this apartment.

OCCASIONALLY AN OUTSIDER, a driver who had not paid his dues to Mullans, drifted into the line. He was urged to "keep rolling" and if this failed the men had a very simple cure for such persistence. A phonograph needle was slipped into each of his tires and when he got away on his first call, four flat shoes ended it within a mile. When the flats were removed to be repaired, the needles drew back into the treads and were not noticed by the repair men. As a result, within an hour there were four more flats. Yes, the men who played Mullans' line knew how to keep it exclusive.

"What's new?" asked Smooth. "Any of the old crowd playing this stand?"

"A few," said Mullans. "Slim Bernstein, Chisler Bond and sometimes Lucky Carmine—that's about all."

"How about the customers? Any spenders?"

"Not like there used to be, the—"

A taxi slid to a stop before the marquee and a man,

neatly attired in evening clothes, paid off the driver and
waved to Mullans. The doorman bowed, swung back the
door and murmured, " 'Evening, Mr. Rudd." He closed the
door and winked to Smooth.

"Remember him?"

"Yes," said Smooth. "That's Bet-a-Grand Rudd, isn't it?
I used to ride him but he was 'on the junk.' Didn't think
he'd still be kicking around."

"Oh, he took the cure a couple of times, but he's still usin'
dope. A good guy, though."

"Save him for me," said Smooth. "It's worth a pound to
you if I get him. He used to be a damn good customer and
I need a few right now."

"Okay. He never plays more than an hour or two. Roll
down to the line and I'll call you. But it's up to you to
square yourself with the boys."

Smooth nodded and circled the block. This was the
break he had been counting on—his first contact with
the narcotic mob. He had no illusions about Bet-a-Grand
Rudd. This gambler might be in no way connected with
the ring but he was one of their customers and as such he
would serve Smooth's purpose.

He pulled to the rear of the hack line and leaned against
the door of his cab. The driver of the car ahead stared at
him for a moment and flicked a thumb in a gesture of
dismissal. Smooth thumbed his nose and lit a cigarette.

"Roll, bum!" said the driver, and walked slowly toward
Smooth. "Find another corner for that load."

Smooth flipped a burnt match at the driver and looked
him over slowly. He was one of the new crop and he was

trying to be hard. Another cab swung into line and Smooth grinned when he saw Lucky Carmine step to the sidewalk.

"Didn't take you long to find a good spot," said Lucky. "Competition is gettin' tough when Smooth Kyle starts rolling."

"No thanks to you, Lucky," laughed Smooth.

"You know him?" asked the driver who had been measuring Smooth.

"Take a walk, chump," said Lucky softly. "This guy was shovin' a hack when you were usin' safety pins for suspenders."

HE TURNED TO Smooth and they talked quietly, pausing at times to pull up their cabs as calls sent the drivers ahead of them away into the night. When Smooth was first out he turned his call over to Lucky and waited for a signal from the doorman. It came at length and he swung up to the marquee. Bet-a-Grand Rudd passed a bill to Mullans and stepped into the cab.

"Bleecker Street, corner of Sullivan," he said. "And while we're going there, tell me about yourself, Smooth."

"Glad you remember me, Mr. Rudd," said Smooth.

"Best driver I ever had. Glad you're back. Meet me tomorrow in the old place and I'll give you a good call."

"Thanks," said Smooth, and launched into a fictitious account of his activities for the past few years.

Rudd listened, asking questions at times and talking of the old days when Smooth had driven him about New York. The car sped quietly along through the dark streets, skirted the theatrical district and headed for Greenwich Village. As they threaded through the narrow alleys of the Bohemian quarter, Smooth wondered what errand brought his rider to this section of town in the early morning hours. When they reached their destination, Rudd made no move to get out but sat quietly in the cab, looking along Bleecker Street.

A dark faced man stepped from the shadows of a doorway and opened the cab door. He said nothing but handed Rudd a small paper package, accepted a bill in return, closed the door and walked quickly along the street.

"Uptown," said Rudd, and Smooth stepped on the gas.

There was no doubt in his mind as to what that package contained. But he made no effort to stop the man who had delivered it to Rudd. In fact, Smooth had glanced but once at the messenger, a single hasty look that had catalogued the face securely in his mind. This was one of the small fry, a runner who made deliveries and collected the price of a small quantity of cocaine. He in turn would contact some one else in a chain of intermediaries and that money would change hands many times before it reached the head of the organization.

It was the old routine of the dope racket. Somewhere in the chain there would be a few breaks that would be impossible to bridge. The men who dealt in this commodity knew the danger of the stuff they handled. The small fry were invariably addicts and must be assured of their supply of cocaine. When the police made an arrest it was unnecessary to apply third degree methods to these weaklings. A few days' isolation with no drugs was enough to make them tell everything they knew. Consequently the heads of the organization were careful to let them know nothing that could cause trouble.

Smooth congratulated himself upon a good night's work

but he was not foolish enough to suppose that he had gone far in the completion of his assignment. In fact, McNeary probably knew that messenger's name and had his record at Division Headquarters, but Smooth cared little about that. As Rudd's driver he had been okayed to a certain degree as one who was "in the know." That, thought Smooth, was a good deal more progress than any other agent would have made in one night.

4

AT THE THEATER

IT WAS NOT quite three in the afternoon when Smooth walked up the ramp of the West Side garage and entered Harry Tone's office. The taxi owner was checking over the cards turned in by the men who had driven the cars on the previous night. His ever present cigar was turning slowly between his teeth and a blue cloud hung low over his head. Outside, the wide expanse of garage floor was empty save for two cars standing near the mechanic's bench. A Negro was scraping clots of dried grease from the concrete and sweeping them toward a pile in the corner. A few hackmen were grouped about the bulletin board, idly reading the notices and waiting for the day drivers to bring in the cars.

Smooth draped one leg over the corner of the desk and waited for Tone to finish his figuring. When Harry looked up, Smooth pointed to his own card and winked.

"Nice money, eh?" he said.

"Beginner's luck," grunted Tone. "Why so early?"

"I've gotta be on the street at three o'clock. Is there a rig ready to roll?"

"Yeah. But why so early?" Tone repeated stubbornly. "Got a steady rider?"

"A good one."

"Okay. Ask the mechanic. I think he's got one ready. Take a card and check the gas."

Smooth nodded, crossed the garage and flipped a half dollar to the mechanic. This greasy faced individual pocketed the coin, slammed down the hood of a cab and pointed to the seat. Smooth climbed in and twisted the switch.

"Gas, oil and water?" he said.

"Yeah—roll it out."

At three fifteen Smooth stopped in front of a hotel in West Forty-seventh Street. Bet-a-Grand Rudd was standing on the steps and he smiled when he saw Smooth.

"Remember the route?" he asked.

"I think so," said Smooth and headed for Eighth Avenue.

At a word from Rudd, he stopped in front of a cigar store and two dapper, sleek faced men hurried to the cab. Each had a bundle of slips folded compactly against a roll of bills and held in place with a rubber band. They handed these to Rudd and accepted other bundles in return. The transaction was completed in an instant and both turned to walk away when Rudd spoke.

"Hey, Matt," he said sharply. "If I catch you holding out again, you're through. Get me?"

One man stopped, turned as though about to argue, but apparently thought better of it and nodded. Smooth let in the clutch and they pulled away. Within an hour they had made dozens of such stops. Threading like the lines of a giant web, Rudd's men spread over the city, taking and paying bets on the horses and turning the play over to the book maker.

IT WAS A profitable hour for Smooth. He met and spoke to a score of men who were skirting the fringes of the law.

None were hardened criminals nor were they big shots. But each was living on his wits and coming in contact with others who had drifted farther over the thin line that divides the law abiding citizen from the crook.

"Can I pick you up at Big Joe's place tonight?" Smooth asked when they had finished the circle and stopped at the hotel.

"Yes," said Rudd. "Er—make it about two or a little after."

He handed Kyle a bill and waved away the change. Smooth grinned his thanks and threw the flag up. He was about to draw away from the curb but paused when Rudd lifted a hand.

"You can do me a favor, if you want," said Rudd.

"Glad to."

"Remember that stop at Bleecker and Sullivan last night?"

Smooth's hands were tight on the wheel. The knuckles were white as he nodded. The break was coming sooner than he expected, and it was a struggle to hold a disinterested grin when Rudd handed him another bill.

"Meet the same guy," said Rudd, "and give him this. He'll slip you a deck and you can bring it to me at Joe's."

Smooth winked and accepted the money. He rolled uptown and stopped at a drug store. A moment later he was talking over the phone to the Chief of the New York Division.

"Sorry to bother you, McNeary," he said. "But I need help."

"Now what?"

"Got a man who can cut junk?"

"Yeah. Why?"

"Bring him with you and meet me at Columbus Circle. Two o'clock near the monument."

"What's the idea?" asked McNeary.

"I'll tell you later," said Smooth, and flipped the receiver onto the hook.

He climbed in behind the wheel of his cab, threw the flag and went for a ride in the park. The nickels dropped steadily on the meter and he grinned. He was building a perfect alibi. His bookings must be equal to those of any of the night drivers or he would not hold his job long. It was all very well to be working for the government but he also had to account to Harry Tone. And when the taxi owner checked over Smooth's trip card in the morning he would find that Smooth had put in a good night's work.

At eight thirty he drove to the Pennsylvania Railroad Station, invested a dime for a quick washup in the men's room, parked his cab in a side street off Ninth Avenue and strolled into the lobby of the theater where Dorothy Manning was appearing. An extra half dollar to the ticket clerk got him a seat in the B row and he settled himself comfortably to enjoy the show.

Dorothy was all he had imagined and more. She sang and danced and Smooth wriggled like a contented cat when she noticed him during the second act and wrinkled the tip of her nose at him. The music swelled and throbbed. Smooth forgot about narcotic rings, gamblers and gunmen. He settled down into his seat and watched Dorothy. When she sang of springtime and roses, Smooth built a home in the country. When she danced, he furnished it and decided to add a nursery. When she blew him a kiss during the finale he said to himself, "Dorothy Kyle—Dorothy Kyle—What a pretty name!" And when the curtain came down he shrugged, shifted his shoulder holster to a more comfortable position and remembered he was an agent in the Bureau of Narcotics. He cursed silently but wholeheartedly and decided it was a rotten job for a married man.

THERE WERE FOUR men standing near the stage door when he parked at the curb. And when Dorothy hurried from the alley they stepped silently in front of her. Smooth slid from the seat and walked quickly toward the group.

"Want a cab, lady?" he said and grinned.

"No, she don't," said one of the four.

Smooth recognized him as Lunger Trout, a pal of the Slug Conners who had shot too late the previous evening. The others with him were Young Grippo, Eddie Malloy and Fred Scalise—and all four were men who worked for Big Spanish, the racketeer boss of the West Side. They were quiet and serious. Slug had boasted of a date with Dorothy and had been picked up by the morgue wagon near the Fort Lee Ferry House. They wanted to know why—and they intended to make her tell them the answer.

She drew back against the brick wall of the theater and stared nervously from one to the other. Her lower lip was held tightly between her teeth, her hands were rigid at her sides and she was frightened. When she saw Smooth her eyes implored him to go away, and at the same time expressed hope that he would not.

"Don't you mugs ever learn?" said Smooth.

"Take it on the lam, lousy!" barked Lunger. "You're cluttering' up the air. Screw!"

"And what do I tell the boss?"

For just an instant none of the four spoke. They stiffened and looked at Smooth with new interest.

"Oh, the *boss*, eh?" said Lunger. "An' who's the *boss?*"

"Ask *him*," said Smooth and pointed to a slim shouldered youth talking to a group of musicians who had just come from the stage entrance. He was one of Rudd's men.

"Hey, Humpty," said Lunger. "C'm here!"

"What you want, Lunger?"

The runner was nervous and Smooth noticed that his eyes drifted quickly from one gangster to another and then brightened a little as they came to rest upon the taxi driver. He flicked a hand toward Smooth and grinned.

"Who's this guy?" asked Lunger. "Who's he work for?"

"How could I guess?" said Humpty. "What's up?"

"None of yer business," snapped Grippo. "We're askin' the questions. C'mon—give!"

"Well—if yer figurin' on takin' the lad fer a ride," said Humpty, and he drawled his words with evident pleasure, "I know a guy what might get sore. He's big, too—got plenty of weight."

"You mean Rudd?" said Lunger, and it was almost a whisper.

"I ain't sayin'," grinned Humpty.

Grippo backhanded the runner with a quick swing. Blood welled from between a pair of split lips and Humpty cursed—shrilly and steadily. He wiped his mouth, backed away from the group and started toward Broadway.

"Fer smart guys," he shrilled, "yer actin' pretty dumb. G'wan—burn him. I hope you do. I'd like to send a wreath to yer funerals."

LUNGER STEPPED CLOSE to Smooth and stared into

his eyes. Kyle did not move. One hand was toying with his necktie, the other was clamped firmly about Dorothy's right wrist. He exerted a slight pressure and drew her slightly behind him. He smiled and his gray eyes were as hard as those of Lunger.

"Satisfied?" he said.

"Not quite. It don't make sense. Rudd's too smart to make a play like that with one of Big Spanish's boys. There ain't no quarrel between 'em and I never knew Rudd to go fer a dame. Maybe you and her better come along and talk it over with Spanish, eh?"

Smooth's hand was no longer on his necktie. It had slipped beneath his coat and the eyes of the four gunmen were steady upon it. He backed toward the cab, keeping Dorothy behind him and watching the men closely.

"Sorry—we ain't goin' your way," he said. "Maybe some other night. And don't play stupid—I'm fast with this thing."

"All right, chump," said Grippo. "It's your play, this time. Take the dame and roll."

Lunger and Scalise stepped forward, their hands lifting a little and their shoulders hunched. But Grippo waved them aside with an angry curse and pointed to the cab.

"Get goin'!" he barked.

"With pleasure," laughed Smooth, and helped Dorothy into the cab. He was careful not to turn his back as he slid in behind the wheel and he used only one hand to put the car in motion. The other was still beneath his left armpit.

He streaked north and cut over to the waterfront. It was not until they had reached the lower section of Riverside Drive that he slowed the pace and twisted to smile at Dorothy.

"You were great," he said. "I never liked contraltos until I heard you. And the dancing—perfect!"

"Never mind all that, Mr. Kyle," she said. "I'm waiting for an explanation."

"The name is Peter," said Smooth. "You'll see it on the card—just in front of Kyle. But when people like me, they call me Smooth."

"Oh, Smooth—for Lord's sake be serious. What's all this about?"

"Don't you read the papers?"

"You mean—about Slug Conners being shot last night?"

"Right."

"Of course. I've been frightened ever since and I haven't the slightest idea of how it happened. And now—all this tonight—oh, what is it all about?"

"Nothing much."

"You've got to tell me," she insisted. "Those men thought you were carrying a gun. That little fellow who takes the bets on the horses said that you worked for Rudd. I've heard of him—Bet-a-Grand Rudd! And if you are one of his men, why are you driving a cab?"

"So many questions," laughed Smooth. "You'd make a fine lawyer."

"Yes, so many questions and you don't answer any. And another thing—when you talk to me you speak one way. When you were talking to those men you were—oh, like a hard boiled gangster or—"

"Your eyes are beautiful," said Smooth.

"Does that mean you won't tell me anything?"

"It means your eyes are beautiful. And as for all this excitement tonight—it won't happen again. I promise you that."

"But you haven't told me a thing. I might even stop at one of the hotel grills and have a drink with you—if you'd promise to talk."

SMOOTH GLANCED UP into the mirror and met her eyes. He twisted the wheel and crossed to West End Avenue but he did not answer until the cab stopped at her corner. If there was anything in the world that he really wanted to do, it was to talk with Dorothy somewhere other than from the front end of a taxi. And now she was offering him the opportunity.

Smooth liked things to break fast. But this was one time they were coming too quickly for him. Through his acquaintance with Rudd he had a lead that promised to put him on the inside track to the completion of his assignment. Under ordinary circumstances he would have been grinning and happy. But to follow this lead he must be at the corner of Bleecker and Sullivan Streets before two in the morning.

The assignment was important—part of his job as a Federal Agent. But Dorothy was important, too—very important. He had been slightly interested in her the previous evening, but when he saw her stand tight-lipped and silent before four of Big Spanish's toughest men, and follow his lead without a murmur—Smooth Kyle went overboard. Here was a girl worth twenty of any he had ever known. And a few hours' conversation above cocktail glasses would spell a perfect evening for Smooth. It was a tough break.

"Whatever made you think that a hackman could afford drinks in a hotel grill?" he asked.

"He might be able to—if he could afford an orchestra seat at a musical comedy when he should have been working."

"Oh, that was different," said Smooth, and realized that Dorothy was going to be a difficult little lady to lie to. "Sometime I'll tell you about it—in a hotel grill, if you like."

"That's a bet," she said, and stepped from the cab. She opened her purse to look for a bill but Smooth was drawing away before she found it. "Wait—how about the fare?"

"I'll take it out of the five you gave me last night," he answered, and winked.

5

CUT DOPE

HE HAD BEEN standing at the corner of Bleecker and Sullivan for ten minutes when the runner appeared. The man hesitated a moment, peered into the empty cab and looked at Smooth.

"Where's the big guy?" he asked.

"I'm picking up the junk for him," said Smooth, and handed the runner a bill. "Let's have it."

"Dis ain't regular. How do I know ye're on the up an'up?"

"Call him on the phone at Big Joe's place. I'll wait."

"Aw, I'll gamble," said the runner, and passed a paper package to Smooth. "But tell him Winkie says to be careful who he sends."

"Are you Winkie?"

"Yeah!"

"Okay, I'll tell him. Where can I reach you in case I need some of this for another customer?"

"Margello's Cafe—around the corner. Any time after twelve at night."

Smooth nodded and left him. He rolled up Hudson into Eighth and stopped near the monument in Columbus Circle. McNeary and another Federal man were waiting and stepped quickly into his cab. When they were spinning along the silent drive of the park, Smooth motioned for them to sit forward on the small drop seats and handed McNeary the paper of cocaine.

"I want this stuff cut* and cut plenty," he said.

"What's the idea?" asked McNeary.

"It's going to Bet-a-Grand Rudd and if it doesn't start things rolling, I miss my guess."

"This is a little out of order, Kyle," said McNeary. "Sure you're not making a mistake?"

"I hope not. But how about it—can you cut it now?"

"Henderson will take care of it," said McNeary, and turned to the man beside him. "Meet Kyle—a new man in this division."

The government chemist acknowledged the introduction with a nod and rubbed one finger lightly over the cocaine.

"Pull up for a moment," he said. "And tell me what sort of a job you want."

"Just use a little sugar—not too fine a job but not too raw. Can you do it now?"

Henderson grinned and drew a leather case from his pocket. Smooth watched him for a moment and then turned to McNeary.

"That killing near the ferry—read about it?" he asked.

"Who did it?"

"I did," said Smooth. "Sorry, but it was necessary."

"Include it in your report, said McNeary gruffly. "And

---

* Cocaine, like whisky, can be cut. It is seldom peddled in its pure state, but is mixed with powdered sugar to increase the bulk and the profit. As in the days of prohibition when a customer bought cut liquor, there is no legal redress.

watch out for these show girls—some of them are bad medicine for a man in your trade."

SMOOTH DID NOT ask McNeary for an explanation of that remark. It was obvious the District Chief had his own sources of information and little that his agents did escaped his knowledge. But Smooth noticed that McNeary asked no unnecessary questions nor demanded too many explanations. It was going to be nice, he thought, working with a man like this.

He accepted the paper of cocaine from Henderson, let both men out near a cab stand on Central Park West and headed toward Big Joe Silva's place. At the door, he paused to slip a bill to Mullans, the doorman. He told him to let Rudd know he was there and drew into place at the end of the hack line.

Lucky Carmine was chatting with a group of drivers and saluted gravely when Smooth stepped from his cab.

"The boy wonder," he laughed. "He finds money when there ain't any out. How much you got booked, Smooth?"

"Little over two pounds."

"What a guy! And I'll bet you're waitin' for a steady rider, now."

"Good guess—waiting for Rudd. And by the way, Lucky, what's Big Spanish doin' now that the booze racket is shot?"

"I wouldn't know," said Lucky. "Maybe puttin' out a little hop or workin' the protection racket. I understand he's backin' a few shows and has a piece of two night clubs. That's about all."

"But you wouldn't know," laughed Smooth. "Not much."

"I might know that you had a run-in with a few of his

boys," said Lucky with a thin smile. "Dangerous stuff, Smooth. Why don't you keep in the clear? Be smart."

"Where did you pick that up?"

"Oh, just bouncin' around. And let me tell you, pal—that bunch is mean. Plenty tough."

"Thanks for the tip," said Smooth. "I got let in on that by accident. Didn't know what was happening when Lunger and Grippo ganged up on me but I had to play it through."

"You ain't tellin' all you know, eh, Smooth?" said Lucky quietly.

"I've got nothing to hide."

"It's no hair off my chin," said Lucky. "Just thought I'd put you wise."

Mullans signalled just then and Smooth pulled around to the marquee. Rudd smiled, tipped the doorman and seated himself in the cab.

"Get it?" he asked.

Smooth passed him the paper and started toward the gambler's home. He cut across the park, driving slowly and careful lest he hit any bumps in the roadway.

A glance in the mirror confirmed his suspicions as to what Rudd was doing and as he turned down Madison Avenue he was not surprised to hear Rudd cursing.

"Who gave you this stuff?" snapped Rudd.

"Said his name was Winkie—same guy we met last night."

"It's cut! That little punk never did this job—hasn't the brains." He leaned forward and thrust the paper toward Smooth. "Put this in your pocket. I may want you to take it back and jam it down someone's throat. Now park this rig and come up with me."

THEY HAD STOPPED before a towering apartment building and Smooth followed the gambler across the lobby and
into the elevator. He knew that Rudd was a very wealthy
man but he was amazed at the display of luxury that met
his eye when they stepped from the elevator. A silent butler
in livery opened a door that led from the private hall into a
larger foyer. A Bessarabian carpet with a Georgian design
against a black background covered the floor; against one
wall stood a beautiful yew commode and above it hung a
walnut and gilt Georgian mirror.

Smooth's eyes opened wide as he walked between lace
paneled doors into a low ceilinged library. On the walls he
saw three famous paintings that would have paid a king's
ransom. Rudd hurried to a court cupboard standing solidly
at one end of the room and from it withdrew a decanter
and glasses.

"Help yourself to a drink, Smooth," he said. "I've gotta
make a call."

He snatched a phone from a near-by desk that Smooth
guessed to be a priceless Queen Anne, and twirled the dial
furiously.

"Grumbach?" he barked. "Is this Grumbach?—Oh, it is,
eh? What t'hell's the idea of givin' me cut stuff?"

Smooth sipped his drink quietly and made mental
note of the name. He was sure that Grumbach was a few
steps farther up the ladder than Winkie, the runner who
had sold him the deck of cocaine for Rudd. He might be
important, but then again he might only be another of the
many smaller intermediaries. But things were breaking fine
and Smooth hoped for the best.

"Don't give me an argument!" Rudd shouted into the

phone. "You two-bit punks are all alike. Sooner or later you try to put across a fast one—clip out a few extra bucks. But it don't go with me—see?" There was a pause while Rudd tapped irritably on the desk top, then: "Oh, I'm crazy, eh? Well, get this, smart guy—I know more about that racket of yours than you do. And you can tell your boss if he don't watch his step I'll bounce in and take it away from him!"

Smooth refilled his glass and drank silently to the gods of chance. He saw the color drain from Rudd's face and noticed that the first flush of temper had subsided into a cold rage.

He crossed his fingers for luck and waited.

"So I'm clowning, am I?" Rudd continued, and his voice had dropped to a whisper. "If you think so, you're crazy as hell. And you can tell Big Spanish I said so."

He dropped the phone and turned to face Smooth. The taxi driver was standing rigidly, glass poised before his lips and a slight smile playing about his mouth.

"What's so funny?" barked Rudd.

"Nothing much," said Smooth easily. He realized that Rudd was not quite normal, the cut drug had not fulfilled his needs and his nerves were jumpy. He was suspicious and looking for trouble. "Only, I was thinking what a chump that guy is to argue with a customer. In my trade the customer is *always* right. It saves a lot of trouble."

"Too bad those punks didn't spend some time on a cab."

"It might have saved them a lot of headaches," agreed Smooth. "But that isn't helping you any. Do you want me to scram out after some stuff or have you got any in the house?"

"I've got enough—wait here. Take another drink."

RUDD LEFT THE room and Smooth walked slowly along the rows of book shelves. As he examined the titles and bindings, he wondered how many of them had been opened since they had found their way into this library. He took a Shelley from the rack, saw that it was a rare first edition and opened it. To his surprise he found marginal notes in a hand that compared with writings that were scattered about the desk top.

Rudd smiled at the puzzled expression he found on Smooth's face when he again came into the library. He glanced over his shoulder at the book and winked.

"Do you like my friends?" he asked, and Smooth noticed that the sudden flurry of anger was gone.

"Very much," said Smooth.

"I've always found them sympathetic. Now this chap"— he thumbed through the book, pausing at times to read a line—"when my political acquaintances bore me or the gutters need washing. My friend Byron"—he touched another rare print—"when the ladies are unkind. Perhaps Fitzgerald when I begin to wonder about the future—good old Omar—"

He seated himself on the edge of the desk, swung one leg indolently and studied Smooth.

"You know them, too," he said suddenly. "I can tell by the expression in your face. How come, Smooth—what's the answer?"

"There isn't any," said Smooth. "I drive a hack to keep alive. There's two ex-lawyers in my garage and a former professor who once lectured on psychology.

"Sometimes I think there are more brains on the front end of the cabs than there are in the back seats."

"Sometimes I agree with you," laughed Rudd. "And I like you, Smooth. How'd you like to be my guest tonight? The evening is early—hardly three o'clock."

"The carriage awaits, m'Lord," said Smooth, and waved toward the door.

They marched to the elevator, walked arm in arm across the foyer and Rudd insisted upon holding the door while Smooth climbed in behind the wheel. The gambler had entirely forgotten his anger at finding the poorly cut cocaine. He was at peace with the world and an odd quirk had sent him out for a night's enjoyment with a taxi driver. He decided they would visit Big Joe's place and have a turn at the wheels—later they would find bigger and better things to do. Smooth saluted gravely and stepped on the starter.

The wheels had turned but once when a car swept around the corner ahead of them. Smooth caught a glimpse of the driver's face and started. Lunger was crouched over the wheel and beside him was Fred Scalise.

It needed no second thought to know that Young Grippo and Eddie Malloy were in the back of that car, and it was a fair guess that a Tommy gun was resting across their knees. **THERE WAS A** squeal of brakes and Lunger went into a sharp turn. Smooth stepped down hard on the gas and raced toward Hark Avenue.

"What's wrong?" said Rudd. He leaned forward, grasped Smooth's shoulder and shook it. "Where are you going?"

For answer, Smooth jerked his head in the direction of the other car. It had completed its turn and was streaking after them. Rudd leaped to the rear window and studied the faces of the men.

Smooth heard him cursing and a light click came to his ears—the safety had been thumbed back on an automatic.

"How'd you spot 'em?" barked Rudd. "Spit it out!"

"I don't make them," said Smooth from the corner of his mouth. His arms dragged at the wheel and he swung wide on a turn into Park Avenue. "The driver came down on the brake when he saw you and it looked like trouble. When they doubled after us, I figured I'd guessed right. Now you give me the answer."

"That's Big Spanish's mob—Lunger's at the wheel. Know him?"

"Yeah—a little. Want to gamble and stop for a talk?"

"Act your age! Those mugs are hot," said Rudd. He looked again from the rear window. "I make it now! Grumbach called Spanish and told him some cockeyed story. Spanish is jittery and figures to bump me—the louse!"

"Two and two make four," said Smooth. "And if that's our number—it's up."

"Any chance of shakin' 'em?"

"I'm doing my best, feller. I don't wanna die—even if I haven't got a first edition of Shelley."

6

A TIGHT SPOT

THERE WAS LITTLE doubt in Smooth's mind as to the reason for this visit by the four gunmen. Rudd had guessed a mile wide of the mark. Even though Grumbach had reported his conversation with the gambler to Big Spanish, Smooth knew that Spanish would not make a move like this. No, there was another reason, a more direct reason, and the name of it was Slug Conners.

Smooth was playing with dynamite now, and he knew it. The cocaine cutting had brought greater results than he had hoped for. It had been done merely to give him a lead that might take him further into the narcotic ring, but when it tied in with Big Spanish, hell started to pop. The various rackets were so closely interwoven that the slightest disruption in one was certain to set off a blaze in others. Smooth was riding the lightning and it was hot.

He twisted back through a side street and raced toward a park entrance. The gunmen's car was drawing closer and Smooth felt a tingling sensation twisting along his spine. He wondered if a burst of machine gun fire hurt very much. The cab leaped across Fifth Avenue, missed the front of a bus with a foot to spare and darted into the park. Behind them there was a scream of rubber biting against concrete, a crash of metal and shouts. Smooth dared not look back but his heart raced with hope.

"Crack-up?" he asked.

"They clipped the bus—not bad. It spun 'em a little but they're still comin'."

"Some fun!"

"What t' hell you doin' in the park?" rasped Rudd. "That was a dumb play, Smooth!"

"Yeah?" said Smooth and kicked at the brake. He spun the wheel, the car leaped from the roadway and crashed through a clump of bushes beside an outcropping of rock. Rudd was thrown heavily against the sidewall of the cab. His elbow splintered the door window and he slumped to the floor, unconscious.

"That helps!" grunted Smooth.

He leaped from the seat and scrambled back toward the roadway. The gunmen's car was hurtling up the drive toward him, dragging each last ounce of speed from the motor. Smooth aimed at the left front wheel, squeezed the trigger—and hoped.

There were five quick shots and the tire blew. The car swerved sharply to the left, hung for an instant on two wheels, then turned over. And even as he jammed fresh shells into the clip, Smooth realized that nothing looks quite so awkward as a car with its wheels in the air.

Grippo was crawling from a shattered window. His face was a red smear and a steady stream of oaths bubbled from his lips. He was flat on his chest, pushing with his feet and bracing himself on his elbows. There was a Tommy gun in one hand and he shoved it in the general direction of Smooth and pulled the trigger.

Smooth buried his chin in the soft earth and wished that he was far away. He expected a staccato stutter of explosions and a stream of lead. For an instant he did not move. Nothing happened and the instant seemed to spin into an eternity. Then he was up and running toward the overturned car.

The Tommy gun had been ruined in the smash. Grippo had dropped it and was tugging at a shoulder holster with one hand and wiping a smear of blood from his eyes with the other. He got the gun clear when Smooth was three yards distant and raised it. Smooth's hand went up.

"If you gotta have it, Grippo," he said, and squeezed, "here's a quick one."

GRIPPO'S HEAD SLAMMED against the road. From behind the limp body another gun went off. Smooth squatted, swung his gun toward a movement beneath the wreckage and kept it leaping in his hand until the clip was empty. He turned and sprinted toward the cab, yanked open the door and slipped onto the driver's seat.

Two cars had drawn to a stop not far from the wreck. The drivers sat staring and mute as though turned to stone by the sound of the gunfire. Smooth backed onto the roadway, skirted the overturned machine and fed gas to the motor. He kept his right foot tight against the floor boards, screaming around the sharp bend of the East Drive and finally cut over to Fifth Avenue.

Rudd was up now, holding his head tightly between the palms of his hands. He was dazed and mumbled vaguely for a moment about the fifth race at Belmont. Smooth rolled slowly down the Avenue, turned west at the Plaza and became one of thousands of cabs that hummed through the theatrical district. He stopped before Linky's Restaurant on Broadway, dusted the dirt from his clothes and walked around to open the door.

"Think any of your friends will be in here?" he asked and lowered the broken window.

"It's a piece of a dream, still," said Rudd. "Give it to me quick."

Smooth explained in a low voice all that had happened and Rudd stared at him in amazement. When he had finished they stepped into the restaurant and seated them-selves at a rear table. Rudd ordered rye for Smooth and milk for himself and fingered the menu silently for a time.

"I didn't know you packed a rod," he said finally.

"Sorry?" asked Smooth.

"Not any," laughed the gambler, and then became very serious. "Smooth—we're in a jam. It's just tough you were let in because of me, but there's no use weepin' about that now. Just sit quiet and let me do the talkin' and we'll see what's what."

He lifted a hand and beckoned to three men sitting at a near-by table. They had nodded when Rudd and Smooth entered the restaurant but had made no move to join them. Now they brought their drinks and seated themselves.

"This is Smooth," said Rudd by way of introduction, "and he's right—a good friend, see? Hoegy Bright, Yitz Cohen and Tout Ender"—he checked them off with a forefin-ger—"pals of mine."

There were no handshakes but Smooth lifted his glass and drank to them. Rudd leaned forward, tilted his glass of milk and made wet circles on the table top. He looked slowly from one face to the other and sipped the milk.

"Big Spanish sent four boys to gun me tonight," he said quietly. Three pairs of eyes opened slightly but nothing was said. "I don't quite make it but I'm swell at taking hints. You, Tout—scram uptown and see what they dragged out from under a crack-up in the park. We'll be here for half an hour. If you miss us, call my place. Get goin'."

Tout Ender reached for his hat and coat, nodded and left the restaurant. Rudd was thumbing through a small notebook, pausing at times to check off a name, and at length he left them and entered a phone booth. When he had gone, Cohen and Bright turned to Smooth and their eyes asked questions.

SMOOTH SMILED BUT said nothing and did not take his gaze from the door until Rudd had returned. Then he drew his trip card from his pocket and methodically set down a number of calls that covered the outlying district of Brooklyn.

"What's the gag?" asked Yitz Cohen. "Why the book-keepin'?"

"The cops will be lookin' for a cab like mine," said Smooth. "They'll be checking over all the rigs in New York—but me?—I'll be in Brooklyn. Get it?"

"Smart," said Rudd. "They named you right—Smooth."

"And where do we go from here?"

"Up to my place for a little chat."

Rudd handed a bill to the waiter and led the way from the restaurant. Cohen and Bright walked silently beside him and Smooth brought up the rear. They were about to step into the cab when Rudd stiffened and pointed to a man standing near the door.

"Bring him along," he ordered.

Smooth turned and his eyes widened. It was Joe Salters, and Joe was right hand man to Big Spanish. It was common knowledge along Broadway that Salters would step into Spanish's shoes when the big gangster went the way of all his kind. And Smooth was surprised to see him here, now that Spanish had practically declared open war on Bet-a-Grand Rudd.

A sudden thought stopped him. Suppose Spanish did not know? Grippo and the boys might not have been gunning for Rudd. In fact, the chances were all against it. Probably wanted to have a little talk with him, thought Smooth, and they brought along the artillery just in case. When Smooth had tried to get away from them their suspicions had been confirmed and they had given chase.

Smooth was walking on quicksand. He had started an open breach between two of the largest mobs in the city. If they got together things might be patched up—and Smooth would be found in the river, neatly bundled in a sack.

His hand was on his gun when he moved in on Salters.

"You're goin' places, Joe," he said.

Salters did not move. He was short, heavy shouldered and a little overweight around the hips. There was a noticeable bulge beneath his left armpit and his coat was drawn together by the bottom button only. His dark eyes measured Smooth, traveling slowly from his head to shoe tops. He leaned against the building wall and his lips opened thinly when he spoke.

"How come?" he said.

"This is a murder rap, Joe—and you're it."

"You a copper?"

Smooth grinned and drove an open hand against Salters' cheek. The gunman stiffened but made no move to draw a gun. Smooth knew that Rudd and his men were watching from the cab. They could not hear what was being said but if he had drawn on Salters with no provocation, their suspicions would have been instantly aroused. It had been quite legitimate for him to emphasize his command with a blow—they could understand that. And if Salters had gone for his gun they would not have blamed Smooth for shooting first. But the gunman had spoiled that play when he took the blow with no attempt at retaliation. It was Smooth's move now.

"Rudd wants to see you—c'mon, move!" he snapped.

Salters grinned and walked to the cab. The door swung open and he seated himself on a drop seat, his back to Hoegy Bright. He turned slightly to face Rudd.

" 'Lo, Rudd. Who's the tough punk in the driver's seat? You ought to teach him manners before he gets himself hurt."

RUDD DID NOT answer until the cab was off Broadway and streaking across to Madison Avenue. He studied Salters, holding his eyes steadily. Behind the wheel, Smooth kicked hard at the gas and raced for the gambler's apartment. If Joe Salters could come through with a logical explanation of the night's madness, this might prove to be Smooth's last call. He wanted to have a hand in the questioning. He must have! And he thundered along through the silent streets, sliding past cruising taxis with scant margin of safety and taking the turns on two wheels.

"The guy's a nut!" barked Salters. "Slow him down before he dumps us in a sewer."

"Relax," said Rudd. "He'll get us there in one piece. After that—it's up to you, Joe."

"What's it all about?"

"Suppose you guess."

"Me? I pass. There ain't no quarrel between us."

"No?" smiled Rudd. "Maybe Grippo was just bein' playful with that Tommy gun tonight. Maybe he didn't mean to be rough, eh?"

"This is news to me," said Salters. "When I left Spanish he told me you were sore about some cut junk—but he didn't say it was serious."

Smooth slid to a screaming stop before Rudd's apartment. He leaped from his seat and swung open the door.

"Unload, Joe," he said.

Salters watched him closely as he stepped from the cab. Yitz Cohen had taken Salters' gun and was standing quietly behind the gangster. Rudd walked quickly to the entrance and nodded for the rest to follow him.

It was a weird group that gathered about the Queen Anne desk in Rudd's library. The gambler seated himself and toyed with a few papers, much in the same manner as would a business executive about to open a conference. Salters dropped into an easy chair, lit a cigarette and tried to conceal his nervousness. But his hand trembled slightly as he held the match. Bright leaned against one wall, his narrow cheeks and dark eyes creating a curious likeness to that of a painting of Charles the First that hung in its heavy frame close to the gunman's head. Yitz Cohen was examining an armor, tapping the breastplate sharply with a fingernail and grinning.

"These babies knew their stuff," he said. "The original bullet proof vest—with extras."

Smooth stood so that he faced Salters, but was careful to keep his own face in the shadows. He alone knew that the man before him was not the only one on trial for his life. Cohen and Bright were amused. Rudd was skeptical but inquisitive. Salters was puzzled and frightened. Smooth kept his fingers crossed.

"Why did Spanish send Grippo after me?" asked Rudd suddenly.

"He didn't," said Salters. "There's something screwy about all this. Spanish didn't want no quarrel with you, Rudd. That's on the level!"

"Then why is he beating up Rudd's men?" asked Smooth.

"What do you mean?" snapped Salters.

"I saw Grippo take a smack at Humpty tonight—a little after showbreak. Why?"

"Why didn't you tell me this before?" asked Rudd and reached for the phone.

IT HAD BEEN a wild shot in the dark for Smooth and he regretted it instantly. He knew Rudd was dialing a number that would put him in touch with Humpty and he hoped the little runner would not go into too much detail as to the cause of Grippo's blow.

"It didn't seem important," he said. "But now it fits right in."

Rudd nodded and held his eyes squarely on Salters as he spoke into the phone.

"That you, Humpty?… Grippo hit you today?… He did, eh?… *Why?*"

Smooth's breath caught in his throat. The answer to that

question would take Salters off the spot and at the same time moved him onto it. A single word about Dorothy would change the entire course of questioning.

Salters' chair was close to the desk. He was hunched forward, arms sprawled before him and one hand was toying with a brass, two-edged paper knife. He lifted the hilt, flipped it upward and caught the point between thumb and forefinger. The hilt swung like an inverted pendulum— moving slowly on a line with Rudd's chest.

Smooth made his move. He jumped toward Salters, crashed into him with lowered shoulder and knocked the knife from his hand. It spun in a short arc, twisting and wobbling, and landed against Rudd's upthrown arm. The force of Smooth's rush carried him against the desk and swept the phone from Rudd's hands.

He was up in an instant and his gun was covering Salters, who was crouching on the floor, staring at Smooth in amazement.

"What the hell!" he barked.

"Hold it," said Smooth, and turned to Rudd. "This guy is a whiz with a shive. You'd have got it in the throat in a minute."

"It was close enough," smiled Rudd, and looked ruefully at the ripped cloth of his coat sleeve. "Thanks, Smooth— that's twice in one night. It's getting to be a habit with you, saving my skin."

"The guy is out of his head!" yelled Salters. "I wasn't makin' a play with that shive."

Rudd looked again at his torn coat sleeve and then nodded to Bright.

"Take him to the river," he said, "and show him all the pretty boats."

"No—no—you can't do that, Rudd!" howled Salters. "You've got me wrong—I ain't got anything against you! I wasn't goin' to do it. You can't—"

Rudd said nothing but gestured toward the door. Bright and Cohen prodded Salters along before them and Cohen saluted gravely as they went out.

7

KIDNAPED!

THE SOFT HUM of a distant buzzer announced someone at the door. Rudd was sitting silently behind the desk, his arms folded on the top and his head resting upon them. He looked up at the sound and waited, as though in expectation of an announcement from the butler.

"Answer it, Smooth," he said when the buzz was repeated. "Simpson must be napping. Guess I'm keeping too late hours for the old boy."

Smooth stepped through the foyer and opened the door a crack. Tout Ender, one of Rudd's men, grinned at him and flicked a thumb toward four men who were standing beside him in the hall.

" 'Lo, Smooth," he said. "Met some of the boys on their way up here. Did the boss send for the reserves?"

"Maybe," said Smooth. "You come in, but the others can wait till I get an okay from Rudd."

"Don't you ever take chances?" laughed Tout. "They're friends of ours—take my word for it."

"Sorry," said Smooth.

Tout grinned and stepped inside. The others smiled also but made no move to follow. Smooth closed the door, followed Tout into the library and waited.

"Chick Binder, Bert Lovette, Augie and Little Tommy are in the hall," said Tout. "Your new butler won't let 'em in without a pass."

"They're all right, Smooth," said Rudd. "I sent for 'em. But thanks for being careful—I like smart guys."

Smooth nodded and ushered the men into the library. They took chairs.

"Let's have it, Tout," he said. "How many?"

"Grippo is through—took one right between the eyes. Scalise caught a couple in the chest and checked out before the ambulance arrived. They took Lunger to Bellevue—after they unwrapped him from the steering post. He may brighten up, but the chances are rotten."

"We'll make them worse," said Rudd. "What else?"

"Eddie Malloy scrammed—got away clean."

"Are you sure?" snapped Smooth.

"Positive! The cops know there was another man in the car; a couple of suckers who saw the shootin' spilled the works. But Lunger wouldn't talk and the others couldn't. Malloy made it in the clear."

Smooth glanced at a tall clock that stood in a far corner of the room. It was four thirty—more than an hour after the shooting in the park. Malloy had certainly been in touch with Spanish by this time. What would be their first move?

Spanish would send for Salters, thought Smooth, and would learn that his lieutenant was missing. For a time there would be confusion—but only for a time. Someone would report that Salters had been seen getting into a cab with Rudd. Lunger might get a message through to his chief. And then active warfare would start in earnest. Spanish was not the sort of man to take it lying down. He would fight back—hard. And his first move must necessarily be to secure information. Why? What had started it? What was the reason for Rudd's sudden fury?

THERE WAS ONE person in the city who could give him the answer. Slug Conners, the first of the casualties, had wanted her to be his girl. She had been talking to him on the night of his death. And Smooth knew that Big Spanish would want to talk to Dorothy Manning!

"I'm going to scram," he said. "There's a little job I've got to take care of, tonight."

"What's the idea?" asked Rudd.

"I wanna have a little talk with Malloy. I've got a present for him."

"Act smart!" barked Rudd. "That ain't a job for one man. Spanish would burn you down before you got to first base."

"Did I make any mistakes, yet?"

"There's always a first—and a last."

"I know it," said Smooth. "But this is my lucky night. I'll try one more job while the luck holds and I'll call you in the morning. Fair enough?"

"It's your body, feller," said Rudd. "If you want to load it down with lead—that's up to you. I'm not sendin' you."

"It won't break your heart if I put it across, will it?"

"See you tomorrow, Smooth," laughed Rudd, and fingered a few bills from the desk drawer. "Here—this is carfare. Good night, feller."

Smooth accepted the money, grinned to the men in the room and left. He drove to the park, cut through one of the crossovers and hurried toward Dorothy's apartment.

It was one of the less pretentious buildings fronting

"You're first, Eddie,"
Smooth said quietly

on the side street off West End Avenue. Earlier in the evening a doorman would have questioned him and probably would have sent him around to the servants' entrance. Now, however, there was no one to ask questions but a sleepy elevator boy whom Smooth shook to wakefulness.

"Whatcha want?" he mumbled.

"Take me to Miss Manning's apartment—quick, monkey!"

"Aw, what's eatin' you? She ain't awake this hour of the mornin'."

SMOOTH HANDED HIM a bill and the questions stopped. They stepped into the elevator and at the fourth floor the boy pointed to a door half way down the hall.

"That's hers."

Smooth rang the bell. He waited and when there was no answer, he rang it again. He pounded softly on the metal panel and shook the knob. There was no answer.

"Anyone come up to see her tonight?" he asked.

"Not since I been on."

"How long is that?"

"Since one o'clock—why?"

"Did a couple of fellows come in a while ago and get off at the third floor—or the fifth?"

"Yeah—just a few minutes ago—maybe a half hour. They was tough lookin' birds and shut me up when I asked questions. Gee—is anything wrong?"

"Did you see them go out?"

"I—I— Cripes! That's right! I did see 'em! They must've walked down the stairs because I didn't ride 'em down. I saw 'em just as they went out the door—and there was a broad with 'em. She had her coat collar turned up—maybe it was Miss Manning, eh?"

"Maybe it was," said Smooth dully and stepped into the elevator.

"I guess I should've asked, but they were such hard lookin' eggs I didn't want to start no trouble. Yeah, maybe I should've asked."

"You're lucky, kid. It might have been your last question," said Smooth.

He hurried to his cab and started downtown. And for the first time he realized the enormity of the game he was playing. The death of a few gunmen meant little to Smooth. He had been raised in a hard school and the streets of New York had taught him how cheap was the life of a gangster. The years he had spent on a cab had seen the rise and fall of a half dozen mobs.

The early period of Prohibition, when the racket chiefs were fighting it out for control of the trade, had been bad ones. There had been killings on Broadway and on every other street in the city. Gangsters had shot it out in night clubs and in hotels. Smooth had more than once been forced to hurry some wild eyed gunman from the scene of a killing. It was part of the routine of hacking—part of the job of dragging a living from the streets. He was used to that and had little respect or fear for the mobsters.

But now they had Dorothy. That was different. It ceased to be a game of wits in which the loser got killed. It was a cruel, filthy business in which there was no quarter and anything went. It was rough-and-tumble with a vengeance. Smooth had a definite job—he was to provide evidence for the wiping out of a dope ring. But that would have to wait.

DAWN WAS SENDING its slanting rays of red gold through the silent streets of midtown Manhattan when Smooth drew to a stop before a Forty-sixth Street hotel. He walked across the lobby, lifted the house phone and announced himself. A few moments later he was seated facing the chief of the New York Division. McNeary was in bathrobe and slippers and his fingers drummed nervously on the edge of a small writing desk as he listened to Smooth. At times he drew deeply at his cigarette. And when Smooth had finished his story, he flipped the butt from an open window and smiled—grimly.

"In other words, Kyle," he said, "you've started hell popping in New York. That it?"

"Just about."

"Well—consider yourself officially reprimanded." He extended his hand which Smooth grasped. "And personally congratulated for a fine night's work. Washington might not approve—in fact, I am sure they wouldn't. Or let's say, rather, that they would not want to hear about it—officially. They never will—officially. But let me tell you, son, this town has been ripe for a going-over ever since Repeal and it's going to get one. We'll crack down on those birds so hard it'll leave 'em gasping for breath—and most of them will be seated in the electric chair while they're doing their gasping."

"But I can't go through with it," said Smooth. "Don't you understand? This girl—Dorothy Manning—she had nothing to do with it at all. She doesn't know what it's all about. I let her in without meaning to and now Big Spanish has grabbed her. God knows what sort of a deal she's getting. And if you think I'm going to chase a bunch of hopheads around the streets of this burg and let her dig out any way she can—you're all wrong."

"You mean you're quitting?"

"Call it that if you want."

"Would it make any difference if I gave you a different assignment—temporarily?"

"What t'hell do I care about assignments?" snapped Smooth. "I've put that kid on a spot. It's up to me to get her off it, and damn quick!"

"I suppose you know the Bureau of Narcotics is out to break up a dope ring headed by Big Spanish," said McNeary. "Right now, Spanish is wanted for questioning. As the Supervisor of this District, I'd like you to devote all your time to that angle of the case. Break it—and just between the two of us "—he lowered his voice—"I expect to hear that Spanish and some of his boys have been killed, er—resisting arrest, of course."

"You're a swell guy, Chief," said Smooth. "A swell guy!"

"Forget it! How can I help?"

"First, I'd like to have you pick up a few of Rudd's runners. There's one in particular—Humpty, they call him. You'll find him in the theater district. He takes bets from most of the pit orchestras and some of the hams. Grab him fast, before he spills what he knows to Rudd, and don't let him get to a mouthpiece. Take in a guy called Guesser McCann. He works around Lenox Avenue and a Hundred and Forty-second, generally in the barber shops. Then there's Spot Martin—he hustles up near the Circle; and Joe Plender, a smart lad who makes the rounds of the ticket brokers."

"We'll take 'em tomorrow," promised McNeary. "What's the reason for the roundup?"

"Rudd will figure it's Spanish doing it, and that's what I'm counting on. And then I want you to grab some of Spanish's men—for instance, Winkie and Grumbach. Get them quick, and a few more. Keep 'em a few days and by that time things will be going fine."

"It sounds like fireworks, Smooth," said McNeary. "But I like the idea. And now, what's your first move?"

Smooth had opened the door and was half way out of the room before he answered.

"Me? I'm going to have a talk with Spanish," he said, and slammed the door.

Within a half hour Smooth had cruised the entire theatrical district. At length he located Lucky Carmine's cab standing in front of a white tiled lunch room on West Forty-second Street. He parked his car, ordered coffee and seated himself beside the little hackman.

LUCKY WAS BUSILY checking off the calls on his trip card and figuring his night's take.

"Where you been, feller?" he asked. "You look as though you were rolling plenty shekels."

"I took a long rip to Brooklyn and played there till a while ago," said Smooth. "How about you?"

"Aw, I was playin' Joe's place across the board*—nothin' much. But it was a big night in the burg. Couple of knock-offs in the park."

"Yeah?" said Smooth. "Who got it?"

"Some of the boys that run with Big Spanish."

"They did, eh?" He looked at Lucky with evident surprise. "By the way—where does Spanish hang out now?"

"I wouldn't know," said Lucky. "Why?"

"Oh, just curious. You were sayin' he had a piece of a few night clubs. Which ones are they?"

Lucky went to the counter and came back with two more cups of coffee. He set them on the table, offered a cigarette to Smooth and flipped one into his own thin lipped mouth. He lit the butts, studied the flare of the match silently for a time and tossed it into the dregs of his emptied cup. Then he swung to face Smooth and hunched forward. When he spoke his voice was a whisper that carried less than a yard.

"I like you—see?" he lipped. "You and me always hit it off swell in the old days, or else I wouldn't be givin' you this steer. You wasn't in Brooklyn tonight—not any! You got jammed in a scrap with Rudd! Right?"

"If that's a guess you ought to hook up with a mind

---

* "Playing a place across the board," is a term borrowed from the slang of the race tracks. It means, to the hackman, to come back immediately to a certain place at the completion of a call, without doing any cruising.

reader—he could use you to call the tough ones," said Smooth. He twisted the cup and watched Lucky. And as he watched he knew that the little hackman was not guessing. Lucky knew plenty!

"I click, don't I?" said Lucky.

"So what?"

"So lay off Spanish! Him and Rudd are goin' to town—all the smart boys know that after tonight. And if a guy like you was to stick his snoot in, he might get it shot off."

"What's the argument about?"

"Your guess is as good as mine. A dame, maybe. Anything could start those two mobs shootin'."

Smooth raised his eyebrows at the word "dame." He showed a little surprise, but not too much. There was just a chance that Lucky might be a friend of Spanish.

"Don't kid me," he said. "Would two smart guys like them get hot over a dame?"

"I wouldn't know," smiled Lucky, using the phrase that had kept him out of trouble for years. "It's just a guess. But if you're smart as I figure you—keep out of it."

"Thanks, Lucky—I'll do that little thing. Maybe you could tell me the spots to duck."

"That sounds like another way of askin' where Spanish hangs out."

"Why not?" said Smooth. "If you know I got jammed with Rudd, so do other people—Spanish, for instance. And I ain't anxious to bump into him if he's hot."

"Fair enough," said Lucky. "Maybe I'm sendin' you into a piece of lead when I tell you this, but if I don't someone else will. Spanish runs the Trocado Club in Fiftieth Street.

There's usually a few of his boys there after show time and it's a good spot for you to keep away from."

"Much obliged for the tip," said Smooth. "That's one hack line I won't play."

Lucky smiled and winked in emphatic agreement. They walked from the restaurant, stopped at the curb to exchange a few words with two other drivers, and Smooth headed for his cab.

"See you tomorrow, Lucky," he said. "I'm callin' it a night."

"Be seein' ya, feller," said Lucky. "An' keep yer nose clean."

8

RESCUE

WHEN SMOOTH ROLLED up the garage ramp he noticed an unusual air of silence that was strange to the smoke filled building. The washers were busily engaged hosing down the incoming cars. A mechanic's helper was checking over the oil and water, and already a number of men on the day line were swinging their cars into place before the gas pumps.

Usually at this hour of the morning there would be a group of night drivers standing before the office talking over events of the evening. But today there was only one and he was nervously answering questions that were being fired at him by two men whom Smooth instantly recognized as detectives from the Homicide Squad.

The cigar in Harry Tone's mouth was revolving at a rapid rate. He started slightly when Smooth rolled his cab to the wash stand and took the meter reading. The detectives, apparently satisfied with the driver's story, dismissed him and turned to Smooth.

"Let's see yer card, driver," said the taller of the two.

He was an old timer in the department and Smooth recognized him as Bones Haggerty, a man who could be tough when the occasion arose. He glanced at the trip card, held his thumb over one of the noted calls and stared at Smooth.

"Where was you at three o'clock this morning?" the plain-clothes man asked.

"What does the card say?" Smooth replied.

"Never mind the card—I'm askin' you a question."

"Well—to be exact, I was makin' a turn off Bergen Street into Flatbush Avenue, and my front wheels were just hitting the car tracks."

"Smart, eh?" barked Haggerty. "Would ya like a rap in the teeth?"

"No, I ain't bein' smart, I'm givin' it to you straight. I happened to take a look at a clock just then and almost got hit by a trolley car—that's why I'm sure of the time."

"Don't I know you?" asked Haggerty suddenly.

"Maybe," said Smooth. "I always buy tickets for the police games."

Haggerty grunted and his partner laughed. Tone had left the office and was standing beside Smooth's cab, which was now on the wash stand. Smooth saw him nodding in reply to some question that had been asked by the washer and then his attention was distracted by another question from Haggerty.

"What were you doin' in the park at half past three?"

"Headin' for Harlem," said Smooth.

"I thought you were in Brooklyn all night," snapped Haggerty.

"I was—all *night*. But I took a call to Harlem at half past three this afternoon. Look at the card—you'll find it there."

"All right, you'll do," said Haggerty, and turned to Tone. "Any more of 'em?"

"He's the last," said Tone. "All the other cars are in."

The detectives left and the taxi owner said nothing until they had walked down the ramp, then he jerked a thumb towards Smooth's cab and grinned.

"Did you get that broken window in Brooklyn, too," he asked.

"Yeah," laughed Smooth. "I got that turnin' back into Bergen Street from Flatbush Avenue. I was lookin' at another clock and another trolley car—"

"Gimme yer bookings and get the hell out of here," said Tone. "Every copper in New York has been in tonight. They're drivin' me nuts. It's gettin' so that every time there's a killin' they try to hang it on a hackman."

SMOOTH NODDED, FOLDED his cap and stuck it in his back pocket. He picked up his black fedora that he had left in the taxi office, jerked it over his eyes and walked out into the street. He was tired. So tired that every joint in his body was yelling in protest.

He hailed a cab and sank wearily onto the cushions.

"Fiftieth and Seventh—on the corner," he said to the driver.

He leaned back, closed his eyes, and tried to figure his next move. It had been a tough break for him when Eddie Malloy crawled out of that crack-up in the park and escaped. Smooth knew the gunman had lost no time in getting to Spanish, and he wondered if Malloy had pinned the shooting on Rudd or whether the gunman had seen who actually did the job. There was no doubt in Smooth's mind but that he was on the spot even without this additional indictment. Malloy had heard him identify himself as one of Rudd's men when Dorothy was stopped at the theater. He would be sure to pass this information along to Spanish and the word would go out to pick up Smooth.

As for the girl, Smooth realized she was having a bad time of it. Unwittingly he had also identified her with Rudd. It had seemed smart at the time but now he cursed himself for a fool. Big Spanish would try to drag information from her that she did not have and could not give him. He would want to know about the killing of Slug Conners—if Rudd had ordered it, and why. He would also want to know if Rudd intended to crack into the narcotic racket. The girl's inability to answer these questions would certainly be misunderstood by Big Spanish and his men. They would naturally attribute it to an unwillingness to talk on her part and they would probably admire her—yes, even respect her before they killed her.

Smooth paid off the driver at the corner of Fiftieth Street and walked slowly down the block. The early morning traffic was bringing New York to life, although the sidewalks were still practically deserted. There was a taxi garage across the street from the Trocado Club and Smooth stood by the door and studied the three story building where Dorothy might even now be getting ready for her last ride.

He thought for a moment of calling McNeary and asking for help but decided against it. Even if a dozen men rushed the Trocado and made their way to the apartments above, they would find no one there when they arrived. There must be a dozen ways to get out of that joint, thought Smooth, and after a play like that he would be spotted as a Federal man. The word would pass quickly and he would have Rudd's men as well as those of Big Spanish gunning for him.

As he watched the door of the club, it opened and Eddie Malloy stepped quickly onto the sidewalk. Smooth stiffened. Here was a break. If he made it to order it could not have been better.

A cab was standing a few feet down the curb and the driver was writing the meter readings on his trip card. Smooth stepped quickly behind him.

"Sorry, pal," he said and clipped the driver behind the ear. The man staggered and Smooth followed it up with another looping right. The driver went down and Smooth slid into the seat.

Malloy was walking quickly towards Sixth Avenue and Smooth followed until he reached a spot where there were no pedestrians about. He pulled to a stop, climbed from the cab and slipped up behind the gunman. His gun was out and prodding Malloy in the ribs as he turned.

"You—"

"Shut up, heel!" snapped Smooth. "Take off your hat and get into that driver's seat or you'll get one in the belly sure as hell!"

MALLOY LOOKED ONCE into Smooth's eyes and did as he was told. Smooth stepped close to him, took a gun from under his left shoulder, grabbed Malloy's hat and got into the back of the cab. Wearing a Fedora, Malloy would have instantly attracted the attention of a policeman, but bareheaded he would be dismissed as one of the hundreds of taximen who disliked to wear uniform hats or caps.

"Get over to Fifth Avenue," said Smooth. "Drive slow and listen. If you try to pull a phony I'll burn the back of your head off."

Malloy nodded and drove slowly.

"Where is she?" said Smooth.

"Come again," said Malloy. "I don't get you."

Smooth hooked the sight of his automatic below Malloy's right ear. He jerked the gun up and back and tore away a piece of flesh. Malloy flinched and cursed.

"Spit it out," said Smooth. "Where is she?"

"Up with Spanish—over the Trocado."

"She all right?"

"Ah, she got slapped a few times. She's a close mouthed dame. But nothin' else happened to her—yet."

"Where were you headed?" asked Smooth.

"Me? I was goin' home."

"Sure you weren't goin' to pick up a car?"

Malloy's head drew down slightly between his shoulders and the car lurched as his foot trembled on the gas. Smooth noticed the man's hands were white on the wheel, and when he spoke again, Smooth's voice had dropped to a whisper.

"I guess it, eh?" he said. "You stinkin' rat—you were on your way to steal a rig and take her for a ride. Tomorrow the cops would have picked her up in a sack. That right?"

"You got me wrong, feller," said Malloy.

"No—I got you right—right where I want you. Now swing back to Eighth Avenue and stop in front of a drug store. C'mon—roll!"

The cab cut across town, moving quickly through the early morning traffic. Malloy's eyes drifted at times to the sidewalks and Smooth knew he was weighing his chances of a successful break. But New York was not yet awake. There were no crowds to offer a shield for Smooth's bullets.

Eighth Avenue stretched out before them as a deserted thoroughfare. Malloy drove.

"Pull over—by that drug store," said Smooth. "And listen close—damn close! We're goin' in and you're goin' to make a phone call. This rod of mine will be pointing square at the middle of your backbone. If you try a fast one, Malloy, I'll get you."

"I ain't no sucker," growled Malloy. "Don't tighten up on the gat. I'll play ball."

"You're damn right, you will," said Smooth and slipped the gun into his coat pocket. He stepped from the cab and motioned to Malloy. "Inside, punk—and straight to the phone booths."

They walked across the sidewalk and into the store. Malloy was careful to head directly toward the phones and he looked neither to left nor right. Smooth was just two paces behind him, his hands in his coat pockets and his eyes on the center of Malloy's back.

"Call Spanish," he said when they reached the phone. "Tell him you got a cab and you're heading toward the club now. And tell him to have the girl at the door when you get there. When you're talking, remember I'm prayin' for an excuse to give you the works."

MALLOY DIALED THE number and when an answering voice came over the wire, he started to close the booth door. The movement was instinctive and Smooth grinned slightly as he thrust his shoulder against it. He leaned forward and moved the receiver a short distance from Malloy's ear. Then he nodded.

"Eddie talkin'," said the gunman. "I gotta rig—a cab... Yeah, I know it ain't so good, but that's all there was...

I'll be in front of the club in three minutes… No… No, I don't wanna come up… Have her at the door when I come through… 'Bye!"

"Nice work, Malloy," said Smooth.

"You may get out of this alive if you play nice. Let's go."

"I got a grand to bet that *you* don't," said Malloy when he had seated himself behind the wheel.

"Too bad Rudd ain't here to take that bet. Now shut up and drive. And when you get to the club, don't get off the seat. Sit still and play dumb till they put the girl in—then roll."

Smooth could see a satisfied smile on Malloy's face when he glanced up into the mirror over the driver's seat. And he knew the gunman was thinking of the reception Smooth would get when the cab swung in before the Trocado. Smooth was also doing some heavy thinking and he did not look forward to the reception with any joy. But it was a gamble—and it seemed that his luck was in.

He crouched back in the corner of the seat as the cab crossed Seventh Avenue and he wished the manufacturers had been less generous with their window spaces. He seemed to be entirely surrounded by transparent walls of glass and as the car slowed to a stop at the club, he leveled his gun at Malloy's neck and looked up into the mirror. His eyes locked with the gunman's.

"You're first, Eddie," he said quietly. "Think of that before you do anything stupid!"

The door of the club opened slightly and a man stepped into the street. He glanced at Malloy, lifted his eyebrows in a silent question and winked when Malloy nodded. He opened the door wider and Dorothy stepped out beside him. Just behind her was another man.

Smooth drew back hard against the cushions. His eyes swung from the mirror in which Malloy's face was visible, to the tableau at the club entrance.

"Tell 'em to hurry," he whispered.

"Make it snappy," growled Malloy. "Get the dame in first."

Smooth's fingers tightened on the gun. That last remark had tipped Malloy's hand. With Dorothy standing in the line of fire, his gun would be useless. Spanish's men had no such scruples. It looked to Smooth as though this were going to be a one-sided game, with him on the receiving end. But there was just a chance that Spanish's men would not start a jam in front of the club—a very slim chance.

He caught a glimpse of Dorothy's face as she walked toward the cab. It was deathly white except for a vivid streak of red across her left cheek. Smooth noticed that her left eye was slightly puffed, and he hoped that one of the three men before him had delivered that blow. Then the door opened and she was stepping into the cab.

"Oh—you?" The cry was short—shrill with surprise. Her hands went to her mouth and she drew back.

"Get in!" cried Smooth. He reached forward, gripped her wrist, and yanked her toward him. Another downward twist sent her to the floor of the cab. "Stay there!" he snapped.

Malloy was out of the driver's seat and sprinting toward the door of the Trocado. The other two men were backing away from the cab, guns in their hands and expressions of bewilderment on their faces. Smooth jerked the door closed, opened the one on the far side and scrambled out into the roadway. He ducked around the rear of the cab and started toward the driver's seat.

"Get him, you fools!" shrilled Malloy. "Give it to him—quick! He's one of Rudd's mob!"

THERE WAS A split second's hesitation on the part of the two gunmen—not much, but enough to give Smooth the break he needed. His gun was in his hand, it was leveled at the stomach of the nearer of the two, and as they hesitated Smooth squeezed.

The shot was flat and sharp. It sounded like a thin board hitting against the surface of a puddle. The gunman went down, his arms locked across his stomach and his legs thrashed. His heels drummed the sidewalk and tangled in his partner's legs, tripping him. There were a few curses, three shots that sailed harmlessly into the air, and Smooth tried one more shot at the writhing mass.

Malloy had scooped up the gun that had whirled from the hand of the first man to go down. He was standing rigidly against the building wall, his right arm extended and his heels together. A splash of flame jumped from the gun barrel, and Smooth felt a giant hand smash against his shoulder. It spun him against the cab and his knees buckled.

His gun weighed a ton and his arm was a feathery thing with no substance or power to move. His left hand gripped the edge of the cab window and something burned across his thigh.

His eyes would not focus, building walls were racing past in a mad dance, the sidewalk was turning and tilting: He searched for Malloy in twisting shadows. Suddenly the dance stopped and he spotted the gunman. His arm was still held rigidly before him, his eyes were smiling over the sights. Smooth tried to lift his gun. His arm would not move. He glanced into the little round hole that was the muzzle of Malloy's gun—and wondered if his shoulder would stop hurting when he died.

He heard a shot—three more, closely bunched, and then another. He grinned. It hadn't hurt—not a bit. Dying wasn't so tough, after all. There had been five shots, and he hadn't felt one of them—only that damn burning in his shoulder and thigh had not stopped.

"Smooth—are you hurt?"

He shook his head and tried to clear it. That had sounded like Dorothy. He stared ahead and saw Malloy flat on his face and immobile. Smooth turned slightly. The cab door was open and Dorothy was crouching on the floor. In her hand was a gun—it looked like the one he had taken from Malloy.

Yes, thought Smooth, that was the same one. He had left it on the back seat. And she had used it—plenty!

"Close the door," said Smooth. "I'm all right, and we're goin' places." He lurched into the driver's seat and started the cab rolling.

A dozen cars had stopped at the corner when the shooting commenced. Now they formed a barrier that blocked the approach of a pair of radio patrol cars. Sirens were yowling and screaming, a police whistle shrilled, and to add to the general confusion the drivers of every car in the vicinity had clamped their hands down on the horn buttons. That section of midtown Manhattan was a raging madhouse.

And Smooth was in the middle. He jockeyed the cab around onto Sixth Avenue and raced south to Forty-sixth Street. It was an eastbound thoroughfare, but Smooth swung west, dodging a delivery truck and a street sprinkler. He fought the wheel with one hand and kept his foot on the gas. His thigh was burning and a steady, throbbing pain spread from his shoulder and sent hot fingers probing across his chest.

At the door of a hotel he kicked at the brake and stalled the motor. He lurched to the street, grabbed Dorothy's arm when she opened the door, and hurried her across the lobby.

"Where are we going?" she asked She was breathless and dazed by the crash and fury of the past few moments. "Smooth—tell me—where?"

"No time now," said Smooth. "Gamble with me—just for one more play. I'll explain—on the level!"

Two bell boys were standing near the desk and they hurried toward the disheveled pair. A siren screamed in the street, and the bell boys hesitated.

"What's the meaning of this?" cried the desk clerk. "Hey!—you can't come in here!"

SMOOTH IGNORED HIM and hurried Dorothy toward an elevator. He pushed her inside and nodded to the boy to close the door. There was an instant in which the boy glanced at Smooth's blood-soaked coat and at the bulging outline of a gun in Smooth's pocket, then the door was slammed shut.

"What floor?" he asked, and started the car upward.

"Eighth, sonny," said Smooth. "And thanks for being smart."

"Mister—I never argue with a guest. Watch yer step gettin' off."

Smooth limped along the corridor, an arm tightly linked through one of Dorothy's. He paused at the last suite and jabbed at the bell. There was a questioning growl from within, and the door swung back to reveal McNeary standing before them in pajamas and slippers, one hand on the door knob and a gun balanced lightly in the other.

"What t' hell is all this?" he barked. "Come in—you, too, miss."

He latched the door behind them, struggled into a bathrobe and pointed a finger at the stain on Smooth's coat. "How'd you get that?" he asked.

"T'hell with it," said Smooth. "This is Dorothy Manning—and, Chief, for the Lord's sake tell her who I am. The poor kid expects to get killed any minute."

"Hello, Miss Manning," said McNeary. "Pretty tough night, eh? Well, settle down and take it easy. It's all over now. I'm McNeary, of the Treasury Department—Bureau of Narcotics. Smooth is one of my men. Here"—he reached into the pocket of his coat that was draped over a chair back and withdrew a wallet; he opened it and showed his credentials to Dorothy—"that make you feel better?"

"Well—I—I've wanted to faint for an hour," she said. "I've been afraid to, but now I—I—"

She staggered slightly and tried to brace herself against a table. McNeary jumped forward and eased her into a chair. He hurried to the bathroom and returned with a glass of ice water. Some of this he sprinkled upon her face and the rest he forced between her lips. She nodded, smiled, and pointed to Smooth.

"Hell!" said McNeary. "This nurse business! Now what's the matter with you, Smooth?"

"Got one in the shoulder, Chief. They creased my—my leg, too. But that'll keep. You're goin' to have a million coppers bangin' on that door in about two minutes. They're after me for a double-header on Fiftieth Street—two of Spanish's men. And they want Dorothy for finishin' off Eddie Malloy. Think you can handle 'em?"

"Get in the other room, both of you," said McNeary. "Close the door and call Doc Barnes. He's one of us. You'll find his number in here."

He tossed a notebook to Smooth and helped Dorothy to her feet. As they stepped into the bedroom, a furious pounding sounded on the hall door.

McNeary cursed silently, motioned them to shut the door, and left them. Smooth pulled the spread across the bed and turned to Dorothy.

"Still feel like fainting?" he asked. "If you do, make yourself comfortable."

"Don't be a fool," she said. "Call the doctor, or you'll be the one to faint. No—I'll call him. You lie down."

Smooth tried a sickly grin and found that it wouldn't work. The room was spinning and Dorothy's face was drifting off into a white blur. He eased himself onto the bed, saw the ceiling go into a mad dance, and slid into darkness.

9

A NEW ALLY

HIS SHOULDER WAS bandaged when he awoke, and it was hurting like the very devil. He looked about and saw no one in the room. The shade was drawn, but an autumn sun was making a white splash against the linen. He tried to sit up, and a stab of pain tore through his leg. He cursed and lay back against the pillows.

"Hey!" he cried. "Where's everybody?"

The door opened and McNeary grinned at him. Behind the Chief, Smooth could see a glint of dark hair and a white forehead. He twisted to one side and saw Dorothy, smiling and coming toward him.

"Enjoy your nap?" she asked, and seated herself near the bed.

McNeary dragged a chair in from the other room and sat beside her.

"Pals, eh?" said Smooth. "What time is it?"

"A little after three," said McNeary. "Not that it makes any difference to you. You're not goin' anywhere."

"How about the cops? Did you get them straightened out?"

"Yes, I fixed that."

"That's good," said Smooth. "Information has a way of

leaking out at the station house, and if the word was passed that I was a Fed I'd be worse than useless. How about Dorothy—is she in the clear?"

"Oh, it's *Dorothy,* eh?" smiled McNeary.

Smooth smiled ruefully at the girl and attempted to thumb his nose at McNeary. When he found that his right arm wouldn't work he tried it with his left.

"I don't know," he said, and winked at Dorothy. "Is it?"

"I guess that's what it will have to be," she said. "You see—we're both working for the same firm now."

"What?"

"Take it easy," said McNeary, "or you'll be popping your eyes out. Miss Manning and I had a little talk while you were sleeping. I think I can fix things at Washington and hurry her appointment through."

"But I don't get it, Chief," said Smooth. "What does she want in an outfit like this? She had enough excitement last night to last her forever. Besides, she's got a swell job in the show business—one that pays more in a week than we get in a month."

"Suppose you tell him, Miss Manning," said McNeary.

"There's not much to it, Smooth," said Dorothy. "In the first place, the Chief is a fine salesman, and in the second place I was anxious to be sold. When a mob can start backing shows on Broadway, buy up hotels and run the night clubs, it's time something was done about it.

"The people in the profession are the ones to suffer most. I've had to put up with more insults and abuse in the past few years than I ever expected in a lifetime. And if I can add my little bit to change things, it's okay with me."

"You mean that?" asked Smooth.

"Sure I do," she said. "Do you think I'll make a good partner?"

Smooth grinned. He looked at McNeary and his smile widened. "We're goin' places now, Chief. Gimme that phone."

McNeary put the instrument on the bed and lit a cigarette. He passed it to Smooth and listened with a quizzical expression upon his face as the call was put through.

"Hello... Lemme talk to Mr. Rudd... This is Smooth..." He winked at McNeary, drew deeply at the cigarette and blew a cloud of smoke about the telephone. "This you, Rudd?...Oh, I'm all right... Picked up a slug in the shoulder, but nothing serious... Did you hear about the argument?... You did, eh?... The girl? Oh, she's a pal of mine. She's takin' care of me now... No, I don't need anything... "I'll be up tomorrow—limpin' a little—but still hittin' on all eight cylinders... 'By!"

HE HANDED THE telephone to McNeary and leaned back against the pillows. Once again he blew a satisfied stream of tobacco smoke toward the ceiling and winked at the Chief.

"And that makes little Smooth the fair-haired boy with the Rudd outfit," he said. "Now, Chief, where do we go from here?"

"It all depends," said McNeary. "Those two mobs are hot. Rudd is strong, and he's got a fine organization. But Big Spanish is no slouch. I can't quite figure him, Smooth. He was never long on brains, but for the past year or two he's been making some very clever moves. This business of moving in on the dope racket and using show business as a front is too wise for Spanish. There's a smarter man doing the thinking for that mob."

"Who, for instance?" said Smooth.

"I wish I knew. And it's our business to find out. The men who are putting out narcotics in New York must have a foreign connection. The Department has been working on that for months without any success. If this fight with Rudd's mob doesn't give us a lead I'll admit that I don't know just where to turn."

"How do I help?" asked Dorothy.

"Don't be impatient," said Smooth. "McNeary will probably have you driving a hack tomorrow."

The Chief laughed and patted Dorothy's hand.

"You might do a better job of it than Smooth," he said. "But, to be serious—if Rudd intends to cut in on Spanish's dope racket, he must know of some source of supply. That's where you fit in, Smooth. Do you think you can locate it?"

"Your guess is as good as mine, Chief," said Smooth.

"And my guess," said McNeary, "is that you can. Once we know that, we'll make short work of both outfits. Because it's the same old routine that the mobs used during Prohibition, They've got to derive an income that's steady. Bootlegging used to provide the bank roll—now it's dope."

"I don't quite understand," said Dorothy. "What do you mean by the 'same old routine'?"

"Simply this—organized crime is Big Business," McNeary said. "The pikers—that is to say, the individual holdup men and dozens of other varieties of small crooks—are not difficult to cope with. The municipal and State authorities can handle them very nicely. But when an organization is formed, that's different. They hire lawyers and political fixers; they make loans to judges and members of parole boards, and never demand payment in cash. The police make arrests and in an hour the criminals are out on the streets again. *That* costs money—big money."

"But I thought all that was done away with when Repeal went into effect," said Dorothy.

"So did a lot of other people," laughed McNeary. "But you can't legislate crime out of existence. When the booze racket went to pieces, the mobs turned to other sources of income. First it was wholesale bank robbery." He paused and winked at Smooth. "I think the G-men were supposed to have put a stop to that. And then it was kidnaping, not the usual type, but a systematic business of extortion amongst the gangsters with money. That was robbing Peter to pay Paul, and didn't get them anywhere."

"And now," said Smooth, "the mobs are peddling dope to finance all the lesser rackets. That's where the Bureau of Narcotics comes in. Simple, isn't it?"

"It's horrible," said Dorothy. "There ought to be some way of—of exterminating them—like rats."

"There is," said McNeary. "And as soon as your appointment is approved by the Treasury Department you'll be a member of this crew of exterminators. For that is really what we are."

"I—I don't exactly approve of the name," she laughed. "But it *does* seem to fit."

"Well, you've had your first lecture from the Chief," said Smooth. "Some of them are less instructive and more emphatic—especially when you've made a mistake. Now, what's your next move? Are you going to the theater tonight or have you quit?"

"We've settled all that," said McNeary. "Miss Manning will keep on with her work for a time. I'll detail a few men to the theater to keep an eye on her."

"Be sure they're *good* men, Chief," said Smooth quietly.

"They will be."

"And I suppose I stay on the hack, eh? Well, that means I've got to square myself with Harry Tone and take a few days off to heal up."

10

GILDA GARLAND

TWENTY-FOUR HOURS IN bed was the limit of Smooth's endurance. McNeary argued, threatened and cursed, but at length helped Smooth into his clothes, adjusted his necktie, and stepped back to look him over.

"You'll do," he said. "A little pale around the gills, but not much the worse for wear. Now, how about this?"

He pointed to a shoulder holster that was hooked over the back of a chair. Smooth slipped the gun from the leather, dropped it into his left coat pocket, reached for his hat, and tossed a salute to his Chief.

"There's times when I can almost forgive Kennedy for those workouts he gave me on the pistol range," he said. "That mick was the toughest instructor I ever ran up against. If he'd had his way he'd have made us rookies learn to shoot with our feet after he taught us to handle a gun with both hands."

"You learned to put one where it counts," said McNeary. "Stop weeping—it came in handy yesterday."

Smooth adjusted the sling around his right arm, walked to the elevator, and pushed the button. The same boy who had taken Smooth and Dorothy up the previous day answered the buzz. He glanced at the sling, winked, and closed the door.

There was a cab at the door, and Smooth directed the driver to a cigar store in Times Square. He sent him in after cigarettes, and when they rolled again he changed his mind a half dozen times as to their destination. Each change sent the cab doubling and twisting through traffic, and Smooth was convinced that no one could have trailed him when he at length paid off the driver a block from Rudd's apartment.

The gambler seated Smooth in an easy chair, poured him a drink, and demanded the story of the shooting in front of the Trocado Club.

"Nothin' much to it," said Smooth. "I promised to get Eddie Malloy, and I did."

"Who was the girl?" asked Rudd. "And where does she fit in?"

"She's a pal of mine. She's workin' in a show that Spanish is backing, and he's got a yen for her. I asked her to put the finger on him for me, and she didn't quite make the grade. But what t' hell—she gave me Malloy, and he's next best."

"So you were after Spanish, were you?" smiled Rudd. "You're a tough kid, Smooth. Plenty of guts. I checked over that song and dance you were giving me the night I met you, and it don't click. You been doin' something for the past few years, but I can't get a line on it."

SMOOTH RUBBED HIS cigarette out against the bottom of a silver ashtray on Rudd's desk. He slipped his hand into his coat pocket as though looking for another and fumbled with the butt of his gun. Bet-a-Grand Rudd was treading on delicate ground when he talked of the past few years. He might know something—and if he did, Smooth wanted the satisfaction of taking him along when the guns went off. His eyes locked with Rudd's.

"So what?" he snapped.

"Don't get hot, kid," laughed Rudd. "Your business is none of mine. If you been doin' a bit, that's your hard luck. I'm not interested. But if you play ball with me, you'll never do another."

"Are you a magician, or do you own the keys to the jails?"

"Neither. I'm a business man, and I take care of my employees. Just now, business is good and it's goin' to get better. How about it—do you sign up?"

"I'm in," said Smooth.

"Fine! Now let's get organized. In the first place, does Spanish know you?"

"Never met the guy. I've heard what he looks like—tall, big shoulders, and thin around the hips. Wears a dinky little mustache. That him?"

"Just about. How about his mob—they know what you look like?"

"That's a laugh," said Smooth. "The only ones in his outfit that ever got a squint at my pan are dead. Think it over—Grippo, Scalise, Lunger, and Malloy. Then there were two other punks with Malloy in front of the Trocado, and they're out. That makes it a full house, if you come through."

"What do you mean?"

"The last I heard, Lunger was in the hospital. Is he still there?"

"He's in the morgue."

"Fair enough," said Smooth. "The boys took Joe Salters

for a ride, I suppose, and that just about winds it up. If you ask me, Spanish is goin' to be short of men in a few days."

"What do you know about Slug Conners?" asked Rudd suddenly.

"Never heard of him."

"He was one of Spanish's mob. Someone gunned him near the Fort Lee ferry house. It wasn't any of my men. Who was it?"

"I pass," said Smooth. "Who?"

RUDD TOYED WITH the ashtray. He twisted it slowly along the desk top, drew patterns in the ashes with a burnt match, and studied them intently. Smooth noticed that his fingers were as delicate as those of a woman. The skin was white and soft, and through it showed a fine tracery of blue veins.

There was a deftness to the touch of the match that characterized the man. Smooth's eyes drifted upward to Rudd's face. The features were aquiline—a prominent and hooked nose, small ears, and eyes that seemed like bits of glass. At times they softened and became those of a dreamer. And at such times the man was as deadly as a cobra.

"I've tried to piece out the pattern, Smooth," he said. "There's only one answer—someone in Spanish's mob is trying to step up."

"Any idea who it is?"

"I wish I knew. Whoever it is, is the man who's been supplying the brains to that outfit. That greaseball Spanish is just a front. He's tough and he's a pretty good mobsman, but that lets him out. There isn't a dime's worth of brains in his skull."

"For a dumb guy, he's been doin' all right, so far," laughed Smooth.

"Yeah—but he's not the guy I'm after. I've got to get the brains, Smooth—the *brains*. Then I move in!"

"No use moving in if you can't give 'em what they want," said Smooth. He slipped a cigarette between his lips, lit it and allowed the smoke to drift about his face. "Where you goin' to get the junk—big chunks of it, I mean?"

He watched Rudd closely through eyes that were screened with smoke. For an instant he thought Rudd would curse him and tell him to mind his own business. Then there came a slow smile and a far-away, dreamy wink.

"One thing at a time, Smooth," said the gambler. "I'll cut you in on that deal—later. First, there's a little job for you."

Smooth smothered his disappointment with a yawn. He set his butt in the ashtray, downed a drink, and twirled the glass. One word from Rudd would have cleaned up the case. And Smooth had been close—so close that he felt like choking the word from Rudd's throat.

"What's the gag?" he asked when he was sure his voice was steady.

"Can you get along without that sling, or is the shoulder too bad?" asked Rudd.

Smooth untied the sling and lowered his arm gently to his side. At first, there was a twinge of pain that sickened him, but it left and he grinned at Rudd.

"It doesn't exactly tickle," he said. "But it'll do. What's the hurry?"

"If you could drive a hack," said Rudd, "I'd tell you to hit the line in front of the Trocado and see what the hackmen knew. They're a smart bunch. They keep their ears open and don't talk too much except to their own kind. You could hear things the man on the street would never get in a thousand years. But that's out for a while. Instead, I want you to take that dame of yours and buy a little wine there. Spend plenty—and learn something."

"I don't like to mix the kid in it," said Smooth. "She's in a tough spot now without lookin' for more headaches. Figure it out for yourself. She puts the finger on Malloy, and then you want to send her in to take one in the chest. Not so good!"

"You're right. That's out! But how about the show—is she quitting?"

"No," said Smooth. "That would look bad. Spanish might think that shootin' was an accident, but if she checked out of the show, he'd get wise in a minute. She stays in the show."

RUDD LIFTED THE phone and dialed a number. He nodded to the decanter in suggestion that Smooth help himself. Again his thin fingers guided the match through a series of intricate designs in the ashtray.

"That you, Gilda?" he said when a voice came over the wire. "Rudd speaking… Busy?… Fine! Come right up."

He pushed the instrument across the desk and drew a few bills from the drawer. He flipped them to Smooth and looked him over carefully.

"She's a nice-lookin' number, and she doesn't talk," he said. "She'll do what you tell her. Now stand up and walk across the room."

Smooth did as he was directed, turning and seating himself when Rudd ordered; and he grinned when the gambler nodded his approval.

"You're okay," said Rudd. "But that rod is too heavy—it drags your coat. Let's have it."

Smooth hesitated an instant. He knew Rudd was capable of playing a game with the finesse of an expert. Suppose the gambler knew him to be a Federal man? All this talk might be nothing more than an elaborate setup. That phone call might have been a signal to the mob—the notice that Smooth was ready for his last ride. And this careless request for his gun?

The wheel was about to spin, and Smooth held his last chip in his hand. It was time to quit or lay it on the line. He grinned, drew the gun from his pocket and slid it across the desk.

Rudd dropped the gun into the open drawer and from beside it drew another automatic. Smooth's teeth clicked shut. The chances were a million to one, now. One arm useless, no gun—and Rudd facing him with a load of death in his hand.

For a moment Smooth was sorry he had ever drifted from the taxi trade—the Bureau of Narcotics could have gotten along nicely without him.

"Better use this," said Rudd, and extended the gun. Smooth's fingers closed around the barrel and his chest swelled with new life at the feel of the metal. "A twenty-five is smaller," Rudd continued. "I always use 'em. They don't drag your clothes out of shape and they make a big enough dent when you hit the right spot."

"Thanks," said Smooth, and tried to draw back the slide to see if a shell was in the chamber.

He made a bad job of it, and Rudd threw it back and showed him a seated shell and full clip. He dropped the gun into Smooth's pocket and glanced at the door where the butler was standing.

"What is it, Simpson?" he asked.

"Miss Garland, sir."

"I'm expecting her," Rudd said, and turned to Smooth. "Like blondes?"

"At times," laughed Smooth.

He looked at the doorway and saw that Rudd might be conservative in his tastes in many things, but that women were not included in this category.

Gilda Garland had passed the blonde stage and entered the platinum. Her hair was a fluffy mass of silvery ringlets, and beneath it were features that might have been chiseled from white marble.

Her eyes were wide, blue, and strangely innocent. Her nose was straight and slightly flared with nostrils that dilated imperceptibly when she breathed. And Smooth noticed that her mouth would have been equally beautiful without the perfectly applied make-up. But it was also this mouth that gave the lie to the innocence of her eyes.

"Hello, Gilda, my dear," said Rudd. "I want you to meet Mr. Kyle—he'll be 'Smooth' to you."

GILDA EXTENDED A firm hand and her eyes did not miss a detail as they ranged over him. Smooth would have sworn she knew the caliber of the gun and the amount of money in his pocket.

"Is that a promise?" she asked.

"A name and a promise both, if you like," said Smooth.

"And where do we go, and when?" she laughed.

"Smooth and you are going to spend a little money at the Trocado tonight," said Rudd. "Your job, my dear, is to be charming—both to Smooth and anyone he may suggest during the evening. And for that you will probably add another stone to that ever-growing collection of diamonds you keep in the vault. Satisfactory?"

"Quite," she said. "You're a dear, Rudd. Sometimes I think I could even stand you as a husband. Is Smooth as nice as you?"

"Suppose you tell *me,* later in the evening," suggested Rudd. He turned to Smooth and his fingers drummed rapidly on the desk top. The light from a huge gem flashed myriad light reflections across the backs of his fingers. The drumming stopped, and he glanced at the stone. "Sometimes, Smooth," he continued, "I wonder at the beauty of women, and I compare them with the other gifts of nature. Gilda, for instance—scintillating, brilliant, flawless and invaluable—a perfect match for this stone."

"Thank you, Rudd," said Gilda. "I'll consider that a promise."

Smooth glanced at the ring and smiled. The stone was a trifle loose.

"Shall we go?" he said, and extended his left arm.

Rudd waved toward the door in a gesture of dismissal, and they walked to the elevator. Smooth was conscious of a deep, heady scent, rich but intangible, that suited Gilda to perfection. It was one he had never known, and he fixed it quite automatically in his mind.

In his trade he had been taught to remember and index things that might seem inconsequential at the time but which were apt to be invaluable later.

TIMES SQUARE WAS a shifting mass of solidly banked taxis when they rolled across town. It was the theater hour, and a long line of cabs fed toward the door of each showhouse. Men and women in every degree of dress and undress poured from the cabs and wiggled their way through the sidewalk throngs to the entrances. They made a colorful sight, one that had held a fascination for Smooth from the day he first became a part of New York's night life.

He glanced from the window of their cab and watched the flaring panorama of flashing electric signs that gave to this section of Manhattan its name—The Gay White Way. Reds, blues, opalescent greens, and glaring whites mingled and fluxed. A myriad of hues danced into the night sky, coloring it, giving it life and substance. They formed a man-made Aurora Borealis that spread a flaming canopy above the heart of New York, cloaking in beauty the follies of its side streets.

From all about there arose the whir and hum of speeding wheels. Horns blared and brakes screeched. There were muffled curses that sprang from the thin lips of drivers. Street cars rattled and clanked. Traffic officers ripped through all other sounds with shrill blasts of their whistles.

The steady tide that had rolled through east and westbound channels was suddenly stilled.

"No matter how you spell it," said Smooth, "it's a great town."

"The battle cry of the New Yorker," laughed Gilda. "Sure it's a great town, but where do we go from here? It's too early for the Trocado—the place will be a morgue until showbreak. I've had my dinner, and I don't think I could sit through the supper show in that place—so where?"

"There's a grand show at the Clinton. Dorothy Manning is the lead. Want to look it over?"

"Let's go. Manning is always good."

"You're telling *me?*" said Smooth before he realized the

words were out. He stopped at the ticket broker's and spent some of Rudd's money for two orchestra seats. He smiled at the thought and realized that even a Federal man might find some compensation in a tough assignment.

The curtain was up when they reached their seats, but Dorothy had not as yet made her entrance. Smooth helped Gilda to remove her wrap, draped it over the back of her seat, handed her a program, and promptly forgot that she had been born.

He was sure that Dorothy saw him during the second act. In fact, it seemed that her eyes had met his just before she missed a difficult step in her tap routine.

He waited for some little sign of recognition, but it did not come. He shifted slightly and dislodged the hand that Gilda had rested upon his shoulder and was rewarded by an innocent stare from her wide eyes.

"Do I annoy you?" she whispered.

"No—not at all," he lied. "It's this metronome in front of me. He's bobbing around as though he were sitting on ants."

"When did you learn to speak like that?" she asked. "A while ago you were giving me 'dese,' 'dose,' and 'dem.' How come?"

"Sssh!" laughed Smooth. "It's an act—I'm tryin' to be a gentleman."

GILDA SAID NOTHING, but throughout the remainder of the performance her attention was equally divided between the stage and her escort. There was an enigmatic smile twitching the corners of her mouth when he helped her into her wrap and offered his arm as they walked up the aisle. She watched him closely as he handed her into the cab and was still smiling when they reached the Trocado.

"What's the laugh?" asked Smooth.

"You," she said. "I've met quite a few of Rudd's friends and each one surprises me a little more."

Smooth's fingers tightened on her arm. They were walking behind the head waiter toward a table in the far corner of the club, and Smooth slowed his steps until there was no danger of their words being overheard.

"Beautiful," he said, "if you'd like to stay healthy—forget that name tonight. You don't know him, and neither do I, except by reputation. Now, are you as smart as he says you are—or are you going to ask questions?"

"The orchestra blares so," she said. "Darling, don't you think we could get a table nearer the wall—without any windows behind it?"

"We think alike," said Smooth, and touched the head waiter's arm with a folded bill. "That table over there—near the wall."

"Sorry, sir; that's reserved. But would the one beside it be quite all right?"

"It would."

"Thank you, sir," said the head waiter, and held Gilda's chair.

Smooth ordered, choosing the wines carefully and disregarding the price list. He asked the head waiter's advice at times and flattered the dignitary by accepting his suggestions. Gilda distributed her glances equally among the women seated at the surrounding tables and received frigid stares in return—but those from their escorts were warmer.

11

A HOT PROPOSITION

THE ORCHESTRA WHISPERED a weird tune. Couples drifted onto the dimly-lit floor and moved to the broken rhythm. Drums throbbed and the reeds sent pulsing insinuations through the shadows. The soft swish of leather against polished wood built up the slow *throb—throb—throb* of the strings and woodwinds. Gilda looked at Smooth and lifted her eyebrows slightly.

"I've watched you walk," she said, "and it's like a cat. All the way from the theater I've been anxious to get on the dance floor. Won't you ask me to dance?"

"Sorry," smiled Smooth. "My corns hurt. Another time, perhaps."

"Sure it isn't that shoulder of yours?"

"Is it so noticeable?" he asked.

"No—not to most people. But you see, Smooth, I'm beginning to like you. Maybe I'm studying you too closely."

"Maybe you are," he said. "Suppose you drift those gorgeous eyes of yours around the room and tell me who's who at the Trocado Club. Know anybody?"

"The joint is full of farmers. The three B's are on the loose here tonight."

"What do you mean?" he asked.

"Brooklyn, Bayonne and the Bronx—all dressed up and rarin' to go. The wise money will come in later."

"Oh, I get it. You're one of those Beautifuls who think that all the brains grow in New York, eh? Get smart, Gilda. They grow hicks a million to the acre in this town."

"Be quiet," she laughed. "You sound like a hackman."

"Maybe I am."

"Now I'll tell one," said Gilda.

She glanced past Smooth's shoulder to an adjoining table. Her eyes narrowed slightly and she searched through her bag for a cigarette. Smooth struck a match and held the flame toward her. She leaned closer and words drifted through the smoke although her lips did not move.

"To your right," she said. "A little fellow... thin... smart looking... he's looking you over."

Smooth nodded as he blew out the flame. He looked casually at the dance floor, studied the orchestra and turned slightly to let his eyes drift toward the adjoining table. It was the one at which he had asked to be seated but which the head waiter had told him was reserved.

Now there was a man, immaculately dressed in a snug-fitting dinner jacket, seated at the table, his arms folded upon the white cloth and his head turned toward the entrance. From Smooth's position his head was in profile, but when he turned Smooth knew him.

It was Lucky Carmine, the hackman. And coming toward him between the tables was another man—a man Smooth had never seen before, but there was no doubt in his mind as to who he was. Lucky Carmine's visitor was Big Spanish.

SMOOTH TURNED TO face Gilda. His left hand dropped

*"You'll take this too," said
Smooth as he hit her*

into his coat pocket. He slid his chair a few inches farther from the table.

"Got your runnin' shoes, Kid?"

"So soon?" she asked and smiled.

"That's Big Spanish over there," said Smooth quietly. "It looks as though the party is a washout."

"Doesn't he like you?"

"He doesn't know me, but he could work up a quick hate if I was pointed out to him."

"And who's going to do that?"

"That guy he's talking to—Lucky Carmine. He knows me, and when he tips his mitt there's goin' to be fireworks in this joint."

"Something tells me," said Gilda, "that I'm going to earn my diamond tonight. Why do you boys have to play so rough?"

Smooth laughed. The waiter was setting their meal before them and the head waiter was hovering about superintending the service and according Smooth all the attention that his generous tip deserved. The orchestra had finished its number and the dancers were making their way past the closely-spaced tables, some stopping to talk at times to acquaintances and pretending a general hilarity that no one actually felt. It was night club—typically night club—and Smooth realized it was a perfect setting for a killing. He waited until the usual formalities of service were completed and nodded toward the exit.

"It's been nice knowing you, Beautiful," he said. "Sorry we didn't have time to get better acquainted. But you can leave now. Tell Rudd that I said you earned your diamond. He may never know what I mean, but if he doesn't pay off he's welshed on his biggest gamble."

Gilda looked at him in amazement and her eyes asked a thousand questions that Smooth could not answer. He was entitled to one little laugh, he thought. Bet-a-Grand Rudd had been willing to spend a diamond to obtain information about his enemies. He had received more than full value, for now his greatest enemy, the one agent in the Bureau of Narcotics who held his confidence, was on the spot.

"Scram!" he said. "I'll stay put until you make your break."

Gilda lifted a glass of wine, sipped, and studied him across the rim. She held the glass away from her mouth and Smooth noticed that there was not a ripple on the surface of the liquor. There was admiration in his eyes when they met hers and he raised his own glass in a silent salute to courage. She lifted her fork and picked at the entree.

"I never run out, Smooth," she said. "And, besides, I like you. I think I told you that before."

"Don't be a sucker," he said. "I've got goose pimples

chasin' up and down my back. And I'm not keepin' that back turned toward those birds any longer. When I turn around, somethin' is goin' to happen. Be smart—scram!"

She shook her head slowly, put down her fork and opened the clasp of her bag. Smooth looked past her fingers and saw the glint of a gun barrel. There was a hardness in her smile now and her lips were thin.

"You may turn when ready, Gridley," she laughed. "The marines haven't landed, but I think we have the situation well in hand."

Smooth laughed too—and turned to face Lucky Carmine.

For a moment the little hackman's eyes locked with Smooth's. He grinned and lifted his hand carelessly.

"How ya, feller?" he said.

SMOOTH WINKED AND waited. He saw Lucky's lips move in whispered speech to Big Spanish. Spanish nodded pleasantly toward Smooth, patted Lucky upon the shoulder and walked to another table. Lucky pushed back his chair and came slowly toward Smooth.

"You're full of surprises, Smooth," he said. "Can I sit a minute?"

Smooth stood up and pointed to an empty chair beside Gilda.

"Glad to have you with us, Lucky," he said and turned to Gilda. "This is Mr. Carmine—we call him Lucky." Gilda favored Lucky with her most innocent stare, lifted an eyebrow and smiled. "Meet Miss Garland," continued Smooth. "I call her Beautiful—but you mustn't."

Lucky seated himself and Smooth ordered the waiter to bring an extra glass. When the wine was poured, the little hackman raised his glass to Gilda and wet his lips. He turned to Smooth, hunched forward slightly, and nodded his head in an almost imperceptible tilt toward the girl.

"What shall I say?" he asked.

The question in itself sounded like a polite attempt at conversation—the usual preliminary to a bit of table talk. But Smooth knew that Lucky had asked him quite plainly—"How about this girl? Does she know anything about you? Can I talk freely, or shall I stall?"

"Give—Lucky," said Smooth. "Gilda is the girl friend. My business is her business. What's on your mind?"

"And I don't understand much English," added Gilda.

"Smart girl," said Lucky. "But I should have known—a friend of Smooth's would have to be smart." He turned the stem of his glass between his fingers. "What' re you doin' here, Smooth?"

"Listenin' to bum music and drinkin' wine that's only so-so. Why?"

"It don't make sense. I told you this was a hot spot for you and two nights later I find you here. If I tipped my mitt to Spanish, you'd get a swell funeral."

"Did you?"

"Why should I? I got nothin' against you, feller."

"I'm glad of that," said Smooth, "Now, suppose I give it to you straight?"

"I'm listenin'."

"Why should I duck Spanish? I got jammed in a scrap with some of his boys when I was drivin' Rudd. It wasn't my quarrel—I didn't know what it was all about. From then on I was careful to keep my nose clean. Why should Spanish hold it against me? I don't want to shove a hack in this town and expect to find a bullet waitin' for me at the end of each call. So I figured to have a talk with Spanish tonight and see where I stand."

LUCKY'S GLASS WENT around and around. He watched the wine slip past the rim and flicked a tiny piece of cork aside with the tip of his little fingernail. He seemed to be weighing Smooth's words—probing for the thoughts behind them and thinking.

"That sounds fair enough," he said at length. "But maybe it would be better not to spring it on Spanish tonight. There was a jam in front of the club this mornin' and he's edgy."

Smooth noticed that Lucky's eyes had lifted from the wine as he spoke and that they were now drilling into his own. He tilted a cigarette into his mouth before he answered and fumbled for a match.

"I read about that," he said. "What's the low-down?"

"I wouldn't know. A dame, I think. Maybe it's this Manning girl that works in one of Spanish's shows. Rudd likes her."

Smooth caught the quick glance that Gilda flashed toward him. There was a world of knowing laughter hidden behind it and he set his heel firmly upon her instep and pushed down—hard. She caught his cheek lightly between her fingertips, drew his head toward her and kissed his ear. When he drew away, the prints of her nails were two tiny red crescents in his cheek.

"See what love does to a gal, Lucky?" she laughed.

Smooth searched for that instep again, but she had drawn both feet beneath her chair. He lit his cigarette.

"How about it, Lucky?" he asked. "Does that put me in the clear?"

"Just about," said Lucky. "But maybe you're wondering about me."

"You guessed it. For a guy that's playin' it legit, you're careless as hell with your dough. The cover charge in this joint must set you back a night's bookin'."

"Not me," said Lucky. "I get off light. And as long as that blonde of yours is chucking kisses around I'll let my hair down and wise you to a love affair. I go for the little hat check girl in a big way. Don't laugh when I tell you we're figurin' on gettin' married soon as I quit hackin'. She's a corn-fed kid—a country member, and we're goin' to run a farm in the sticks. You know—cows, ducks and all that. We've been savin' our dough, and it won't be long now."

"Congratulations, feller," said Smooth. "Glad to hear it."

"Yeah, it's on the level. I know Spanish a little—played the line in front of his club for a while. He gives me a break and knocks off the cover charge. Lets the kid sit with me, too, when it ain't too busy. She'll be over, after."

The music started and they watched the dancers for a moment. The floor was not overcrowded, and Smooth saw that Lucky was watching him with a slight frown of bewilderment. He caught the little hackman's eye and nodded toward Gilda.

"She's slow and dreamy on her feet," said Smooth. "Try over the floor—maybe you'll get a brass ring."

"Fallen arches?" asked Lucky. "You used to be quite a stepper, Smooth. Why don't you dance?"

"Gentlemen," said Gilda, "you're tearing me to pieces. If

you both insist upon dancing with me I won't know how to choose between you. You eggs!"

"That puts it up to you, Lucky," said Smooth, and stood to draw back Gilda's chair.

THE LITTLE HACKMAN led Gilda out onto the floor and Smooth waved carelessly to them as they went by. Lucky's story sounded legitimate enough, and Smooth knew that a night club owner often made a concession to a smart taxi driver. There had been a time when the owners of these night spots had paid as high as thirty per cent of the total amount of the bill to the hackman who had brought a party of chumps to spend money in his place. Some of the old-time clip joints had existed wholly through the trade that was brought to them by the night drivers.

Things were different now, but it was reasonable enough to suppose that Lucky still brought an occasional customer with money to spend at the Trocado. Spanish wasn't losing anything by his generosity. And as for the romance with the hat check girl—that was a natural. Smooth had known dozens of girls who worked in night clubs, both in the check rooms and in the floor shows. It seemed to be the accepted thing for these Broadwayites to sit and drink with millionaires and marry a hackman. It was the old story. They made fools of hundreds of men and went overboard for one.

Yes, Lucky Carmine was all right. He might be shading it a little when he bragged about being legitimate, and he might be close to Spanish, but his story checked. Smooth felt a great deal more comfortable when Lucky and Gilda returned to the table than he had when he first saw Carmine and Spanish together. There was nothing but a gunshot wound in his shoulder to connect him with any of the recent killings, and Smooth had no intention of letting that throw him.

He insisted that Lucky stay at their table for another drink, and poured it himself. Carmine watched the wine trickle into the glass. He put a cigarette between his lips, but made no move to light it. Smooth struck a match and held the flame across the table.

"That's funny," said Lucky. "I never knew you were left-handed. Can you imagine that"—he turned to Gilda—"I've known this bloke for years and never clicked that he was a southpaw."

"Oh, I knew it," said Gilda lightly. "He always uses his left hand to beat me with."

Smooth was sorry for the undertable play he had permitted himself. Gilda hadn't deserved the heel on her instep. She was a regular—a good fellow!

"Speaking of southpaws," said Lucky, "I got a great gag to show you. I read this in a story once and it always works—never knew it to fail."

"What is it?" said Gilda.

"Got any book matches?" asked Lucky. "You know—the ones in the cardboard folder."

SMOOTH FOUND A package that had probably been in his vest pocket for a week, and flipped them across the table. Carmine picked them up and held them for a moment without opening the cover.

"Now this is the gag—see?" he said. "There was a detective lookin' for a criminal. He wasn't one of them ordinary flatties that hangs out in the Forty-Seventh Street Station-house—this was a scientific bloke. He used psychology—"

"Who?" asked Gilda.

"He used his skull," continued Lucky. "Instead of puttin' the pressure on a stool and milkin' him for all he knew, this guy sat down and did it all with his brains. Well—he visited the scene of the crime and found a package of book matches like these"—he extended the matches—"lying beside the murdered guy."

"Who was murdered and why?" asked Gilda suddenly.

"Say," said Lucky, "do I tell this story—or don't I?"

"Not if I can stop you," laughed Gilda. "I've had to listen to it forty times—or maybe it was fifty."

"Where do you get these smart gals, Smooth?" protested Lucky.

"Go ahead with the story," laughed Smooth. "Ignore her completely."

"You'll do nothing of the kind," said Gilda. Her speech was light, but to Smooth it seemed to be strained. He glanced quickly at her and saw that her eyes were trying desperately to tell him something.

"Well," said Lucky. "The story goes that a guy was murdered and the matches was lyin' beside him. The detective picked them up—opened the cover and said, 'The mug that pulled this job was *left-handed.*'"

"Ahaaaa!" said Gilda. "Old Sherlock himself. Now I'll tell one. It seems that there was a traveling salesman—"

Smooth knew that a game was being played at the table. Gilda was trying to keep Lucky from finishing his story. His mind whirled back in review of all the tales he had heard concerning book matches. But he drew a blank.

"So how did he know?" demanded Lucky.

"I give up," said Smooth.

"Because"—and Lucky opened the cover of the match-es—"on account of the guy bein' left-handed the matches were torn out from left to right. Like these—"

He extended the matches, stared at them foolishly for a moment and grinned. Half the package was empty. And the matches had been torn out from right to left.

Gilda's lips were tight. She was toying with her bag, nervously opening and closing the clasp. Smooth stiffened. He realized all too well now the trap that Gilda had been trying to talk him out of. He saw quick suspicion on Lucky's face and noted the speed with which the hack-man's glance swept toward his right arm. He winked to Gilda and lifted the bottle of wine to refill her glass—using his right hand. The pain that tore through his shoulder set the dim lights of the night club spinning in a dizzy procession.

"That one bounced back and bit you, Lucky," he said. And his mouth was dry as he spoke. "I use both hands—like a wop eatin' spaghetti."

"You know," said Lucky, "that's the first time I ever missed out with that gag."

SMOOTH RESTED HIS right arm upon the table and waited for the pain to subside. His stomach was quivery and sick, and thin beads of perspiration gathered on his forehead. Gilda had launched into a rather risqué story to distract Lucky's attention, and Smooth silently applauded his partner's coolness. She had turned the full battery of her charm upon Carmine. Her voice was low, confidential and throaty. Her eyes were alight with flattery and promise. She played up to Lucky as though he were visiting royalty—

and the thin shouldered hackman wriggled comfortably and listened.

He was laughing at another of Gilda's stories when Smooth saw Big Spanish threading his way between the tables that separated them from the door. The huge gangster was bowing and nodding to various acquaintances and breaking a path through the crowd for a girl who followed him. They were heading towards Smooth's table, and he noticed a flare of anger in the girl's eyes as she caught sight of Lucky.

Carmine turned just then and saw her. He was on his feet in an instant, his lips parted in a thin smile and his hands outstretched.

"Theresa—I didn't think you'd get off so early," he said. He caught her hands, squeezed them and turned to Big Spanish. "Thanks for the break, feller. And I want you to meet a pal of mine—shake hands with Smooth Kyle; he hacks with me."

Big Spanish extended a wide paw and Smooth set his teeth. He lifted his injured arm, set his hand in that of Spanish and braced himself for the shock. Spanish squeezed. The night club reeled and spun. Smooth shuddered and tried a sickly smile.

"Glad to know you," he said, thinly. "Meet Miss Garland, and grab a chair."

Spanish bowed to Gilda and received one of those blue-eyed, baby stares. He grinned, lifted his hand automatically to his small mustache and twirled one end. Smooth saw him go overboard and counted the screaming pain in his shoulder as paid for.

Lucky was standing beside Theresa, one arm about her

waist and the other hand clasped in the crook of her elbow. Smooth caught the girl studying him and guessed that little got past those dark eyes.

She was one of the most beautiful girls he had ever seen, but it was a beauty far different from that of the usual Broadway standard. Her hair was blue-black and drawn tightly back from her forehead. Her eyes were brown with large black pupils that gathered the light from the dim table lamp and sent it flashing in reflected brilliance. And the wisdom of centuries was in those eyes—inherited knowledge that had been passed through generations of Italian ancestors from the time of the Borgias. Her coloring was just off the white—like old ivory that had been kept from the sun. She used no make-up except for a touch of scarlet on her full lips. Smooth knew that when she smiled her teeth would show in an even, white line. But she was not smiling now—instead, she acknowledged Lucky's hurried introductions with a direct stare that was naked as steel and equally hard.

Smooth called for more chairs, and insisted that it was his party. He waved aside the protests of both Spanish and Carmine, ordered more wine and told them to settle down for a large evening. Gilda was being nasty nice. The opposite personalities of the two women had needed no spur to set them at war and a battle of wits was under way. **BIG SPANISH LIFTED** his glass and toasted Gilda's blond loveliness. And it was with obvious reluctance that he turned his attention toward Smooth. He stared at him for a moment, tilted one eyebrow and leaned forward.

"It's funny I don't make you," he said. "If you been shovin' a hack with Lucky I must 'a' seen you before. How come we don't know each other?"

"I been away," said Smooth.

"Yeah? How long?"

"Long enough. But I think you opened a place in the Village just before I quit—The Candle Flame, or some name like that."

"Yeah," said Lucky. "Smooth's an oldtimer. He knows his way around. I was thinkin' you might want to talk to him."

Spanish nodded wisely and winked at Smooth.

"We might do business," he said.

"Okay with me," said Smooth. "But first I want to come clean. Lucky tells me you had a knock-off this mornin' and you might be a little hot. But I'll gamble. I'm the guy that was drivin' Rudd the other day in the park. He's no pal of mine, but I happened to be shovin' the rig when the storm broke. So—how do I stand?"

Smooth watched Spanish's face closely. This should have been dynamite to the gangster. Anything might happen—a stream of curses, a sudden fit or even a blazing gun. In any event the news should have given him a start. But he took it without a tremor. Not a muscle moved in his face, nor did he show any sign of surprise. Smooth was puzzled. It didn't make sense, unless— unless Spanish already knew about Smooth. Those whispered words from Lucky may have been the answer. And if so, why had Lucky lied?

"That was a fast play, feller," said Spanish. "It took guts, to sling that in my teeth—and I like you for it. You must be on the level or you'd never have tipped your mitt. Suppose we step out to the bar and have a little talk? The gals can take us apart while we're gone."

"Do you mind?" said Smooth to Gilda.

"Sure I mind," she answered. "But what good does that do? Go ahead—roll your hoop. Theresa and I will struggle along."

The men left the table and walked to a small bar that was curved in a horseshoe at the far end of the club. Spanish led them to a spot near the wall, hooked one elbow upon the polished surface and nodded to the bartender.

"Lansons—on the house," he said and turned to Smooth. "We'll drink and figure a deal. Can you stand to make a few spare bucks?"

"Why not?"

"Do you okay this guy, Lucky?"

"A hundred per cent," said the little hackman. "Me—I can't afford to gamble like he does. I'm a piker on account of the lungs. But any guy what can sling a champagne party after two night's hackin' must know his oats. We met for the first time in years just the other night. At the time he don't look like he's worth a pretzel. Now he's in the money—swell lookin' blonde and everything. That's what I call fast work."

SMOOTH SAW ADMIRATION in Spanish's eyes. But there was also a question, unspoken but definite. Lucky had given him a clean bill of health, but had been careful not to let his recommendation cover the past few years. Carmine wanted no quarrel with Spanish, and while he was ready to put in a good word, Smooth noticed that the hackman was careful with his words. If things went wrong, Spanish could not hold it against Carmine.

"What's your racket?" asked the gangster.

"Drivin' a hack," said Smooth evenly. "The tips are big when you get good customers."

"There's fifty thousand taxi drivers in this town and I never met one that wasn't havin' a tough time payin' his rent," laughed Spanish. "But you're different, eh?"

"Yeah—I'm different. So what?"

"Ever been to Mexico?"

"Tijuana and a few spots near the line. Why?"

"Wanna hook up with an outfit down there?"

Smooth helped himself to a drink. It was as though he had bought three cards to an ace and king, and filled a royal! Rudd had sent him for information and Big Spanish wanted to deal him into the organization! And what would McNeary think of this situation? Smooth could almost see those blue eyes twinkle and a thousand wrinkles gather around them as he heard about it.

He needed time to think and it was going to require some smooth stalling to keep Spanish dangling until he figured his next move. To sign up-with the outfit would put him in a position that might prove invaluable for Rudd. But would McNeary approve? It would take Smooth out of the New York area and drop him in some flea-bitten town over the border. True, it would also reveal the method Spanish used for getting his narcotics into the country, but that was only one angle of the case.

"What's the set-up?" he asked. "Booze or Chinamen?"

"Why worry?" asked Spanish. "The dough is there—plenty of it. It's a pushover—no chance of a pinch. Wadda ya say?"

"Will it keep for a few hours? I'd like to sit with it over a bottle of wine."

Spanish shrugged and looked toward the table where the girls were sitting.

"Suit yourself," he said.

THEY LEFT THE bar and took their places at the table. Gilda threw a questioning glance at Smooth and he nodded slightly toward Big Spanish. She set down her glass and smiled at the gangster.

"Broadway says you're quite a dancer," she said.

"Broadway don't know the half of it," he laughed and pushed back his chair. "I'm practically a sensation—with blondes."

When they left the table, Smooth drew his chair closer to Lucky and Theresa. He filled their glasses and spun a thin stream of tobacco smoke toward the dance floor.

"Spanish thinks he's what little blondes cry for," he said. "For a guy with a big organization he don't seem so smart to me."

"You can't guess 'em by their fronts," said Lucky.

"Sometimes you can," said Theresa and looked at Smooth. "You—you're smart. I've been talking to your girl friend and she doesn't know any more about you than I do. A man who can keep his women guessing must be clever."

"Maybe you're underrating Gilda," laughed Smooth.

"Don't fool yourself," she said. "She didn't say anything because she didn't *know* anything. Oh, she's smart enough to take Spanish for a waltz when you tip her a nod, but that lets her out."

"This baby don't miss a thing," laughed Lucky. "Sometimes I think she's got eyes in the back of her head."

"Maybe she can tell me if I ought to take up Spanish's proposition," suggested Smooth.

"That's one you'll have to ask Goo-Goo Eyes about when she comes in off the dance floor," said Theresa. "I have enough trouble callin' the shots for Lucky."

"All right, call this one. Spanish wants me to go to Mexico and he says there's money in it. If Lucky goes, I go—fair enough?"

"Don't be a sap!" she snapped. "Lucky ain't after any hot money. Cut your own throat if you want, but leave him out of it. He's savin' up to buy a farm."

"Yeah," laughed Lucky. "With cows and ducks. When these dames get set on a thing nothin' can change them—ain't it the truth?"

The music had stopped and Big Spanish was holding a chair for Gilda. A waiter hurried through the crowds leaving the dance floor, and when the gangster seated himself he leaned above Big Spanish's shoulder and whispered into his ear.

Spanish started. He brought the palm of his hand against the table top with a force that set the glasses jingling.

"T'hell you say!" he barked and turned quickly toward Lucky. "They got Winkie and Grumbach!"

12

A SMOOTH PLAY

SMOOTH WANTED TO smile. When he had asked McNeary to pick up those two dope peddlers he did not expect to be in on the play when the news of their disappearance was announced to Spanish. It was a peculiar twist of circumstances that put him in a position to see the result of his carefully planned move. He had figured that this would be the last straw—that Spanish would actively swing into action when he heard that two of his men were missing. There could be no doubt in the gangster's mind as to the reason. Winkie and Grumbach were the only men with whom Rudd had come in contact in his purchase of narcotics. And now they were gone—plucked from the streets by an unseen hand. Smooth stared indolently at the cloth, penciled a series of boxes upon it with the burnt head of a match, and listened.

"When did this happen?" asked Lucky.

"How the hell do I know?" said Spanish. "They're gone, ain't they? That's what counts—and I know who did it. I'm gonna—"

"*We're* going out to powder our noses," said Theresa suddenly. She got quickly to her feet and tapped Gilda upon the shoulder. "C'mon, baby—outside while the gentlemen talk."

Gilda stared at her coldly for a minute. She looked at Smooth and when he nodded in agreement she left the table and followed Theresa to the ladies' room. Smooth pushed back his chair and looked inquiringly at Spanish.

"Want me to scram too?" he asked.

"Stay where you are," snapped Spanish. "You ain't goin' to hear anything." He turned to Lucky and his lips were thin. "How about it?" he asked. "Do I send the boys over to rub out that louse with the hook nose?"

"I wouldn't know," said Lucky quietly. His eyes were on the diagrams that Smooth was drawing. "It would take a smarter guy than me to guess that one. Why don't you go out to the bar and think it over?"

Spanish grunted and kicked back his chair with such force that it toppled to the floor. He barged through the tables, shouldering his way past laughing couples with little regard for the damage he did to shirt fronts and evening gowns. When he had disappeared through a door that led off the bar Lucky grinned a twisted smile and tapped Smooth on the arm.

"That guy is screwy," he said. "Sometimes he chucks questions at me like I was a mind reader. I never answer because he wouldn't listen anyway."

"He certainly is hot tonight," said Smooth. "It's a wonder he don't get himself knocked off when he boils over that way. Why don't you go out and try to cool him off?"

"That might be a good idea," said Lucky, and stood up. "Tell Theresa I'll be right back. She's a smart kid, eh,

Smooth?—takin' Gilda away so she wouldn't learn something that might get her in trouble."

Smooth nodded in agreement, and when Lucky had
gone he wondered if there had been a lightly veiled threat
in the hackman's last remark. It might be that Carmine was
trying to tell him he had heard too much and that it was a
case of throw in with Spanish or else—

HE GLANCED QUICKLY about to see if anyone was watching him and then drew an envelope from his coat pocket.
He tore a scrap from the corner and penciled a warning
that he knew would put Rudd on his guard. It was a long
chance, but Smooth did not want a few of Big Spanish's
gunmen to upset his plans by killing Rudd. He folded the
note into a compact ball, squeezed it between the first
and second fingers of his right hand and looked up to see
Theresa and Gilda coming toward him.

"Where's Lucky?" said Theresa in alarm.

"Just stepped to the bar. He'll be right back, in fact here
he is comin' across the dance floor now."

Carmine was all smiles when he joined them and he
waved a careless hand toward the bar as though in dismissal
of Spanish.

"He's all right now. He cools off quick. Nothin's goin'
to happen."

"Why *should* anything happen?" asked Gilda.

"Keep your damn trap shut," said Smooth suddenly.
"You dizzy blondes are all alike—always askin' questions."

"What's eating you?" snapped Gilda. "Been drinking
too much wine?"

"If I have, it's my money that's buyin' it. And as long as
you started it, let me tell you something else—when you're

with me send those baby stares in my direction. You been flirtin' with every guy in the place while I sit here like a chump."

Lucky was grinning from ear to ear and he nudged Theresa carefully as though to make sure that she was appreciating the joke. Cynicism and bewilderment mingled in Theresa's face. She half turned towards Smooth in evident surprise and then watched to see what would be Gilda's reaction. The tall blonde jumped up in sudden anger. One hand was clenched upon the table and the knuckles were white.

"I don't have to take that from you," she flared. "I'm not your wife!"

"You'll take it and like it. And this, too," barked Smooth. He was on his feet also, and his left hand caught Gilda a stinging blow across the cheek.

She jerked a glass of wine from the table and emptied it in Smooth's eyes. He lifted his right hand as though to drive it against her mouth. She reached forward instinctively and grabbed the hand. The pain in his shoulder brought his teeth together with a snap, but he worked the folded note against Gilda's open palm and felt her fingers close about it. A single swift stare from those wide eyes told him that she understood and was following his lead. Theresa stepped between them and pushed Smooth toward his chair.

"Sit down, you fool," she said. "The first rule of this place is drink here and fight at home. You're acting like a couple of two-year-olds."

"Sure, Smooth," said Lucky. "Wait until you get in the back of a hack before you put on a panic."

"T'hell with her," said Smooth in disgust. "She's always startin' a jam some place."

"That goes double with me," said Gilda, and gathered her wrap from the back of the chair. "I'm washed up on this party. Good night!"

She looked Smooth over slowly from his dripping forehead to his shoes, turned and walked out of the night club.

"And that," said Lucky, "seems to take care of everything."

"Does it?" asked Theresa and turned a long steady stare upon Smooth.

FOR A MOMENT he was too satisfied with the success of the little act he had staged to think about Theresa. Gilda had come through like a major. There was no doubt in Smooth's mind as to what she would do next. He could almost see her stepping into a phone booth and passing the information along to Rudd. As she had heard nothing at the table, she could in no way be accused of warning the gambler. Thanks to Theresa, Gilda had a perfect alibi—one that would even satisfy the suspicious minds of Big Spanish's mob.

As for himself, there was nothing that Smooth could do but sit tight and play his hand out. In spite of Lucky's statement that Big Spanish did not intend any reprisals, Smooth was certain that a car full of killers was on the way to Rudd's apartment. He would have enjoyed seeing their reception, but he consoled himself with the thought that he was less apt to collect another bullet in the Trocado Club than he would be at Rudd's place. Yes, he could afford to miss this show—there would probably be bigger and better affairs in the future.

He helped himself to another glass of wine, and it was then that he noticed Theresa's dark eyes watching him. Lucky made no move to dance with the girl, and Smooth realized he was not to be left alone that evening. He attempted an apology to Theresa for his lack of manners, but she cut him short with a wise smile.

"You smart guys certainly can do stupid things when you're out with women," she said slowly.

It was a simple remark and could have referred to Smooth's boorish actions. But some subtle shading in the tone of her voice brought Smooth sharply to attention and made him wonder. Had Theresa seen him pass that note? And was she telling him? Again he searched his memory for any sign that would have clarified Lucky's standing with Spanish. They were close—there was no doubt about that. But Smooth was inclined to believe that the hack-man took no active part in the work of the Big Spanish mob, Theresa had not been acting when she turned thumbs down on Smooth's suggestion that both he and Lucky go to Mexico. There had been sharp conviction in her voice then. And suddenly he became aware of the fact that he was judging Theresa by the fluctuations in the tones of her speech.

He led the conversation back to hacking. Both he and Lucky told of their experiences driving taxis through the streets of Manhattan. Theresa was at ease now. She laughed with them and added interesting tales of the night clubs. At times she spoke of the farm they intended to buy, and at such times her voice was low, wistful and pleasant. When Smooth mentioned Rudd and speculated upon the wealth and power the gambler must have acquired there came a subtle difference in Theresa's answers.

Lucky was always at ease. He smiled, joked and teased Theresa unmercifully. When Smooth asked him a direct question he shrugged it aside or made a noncommittal answer.

There were but two other occupied tables when Big Spanish came through the door beside the bar and spoke to the head waiter. The orchestra had long since finished the last number and left. A tired-looking band boy sat at the piano, a constant cigarette drooping from one corner of his mouth and his shoulders curved in a bow. His fingers stopped their restless fluttering over the keys when Big Spanish nodded. He stood up, stretched, flicked the butt at a waiter who was clearing away a table cloth, and shuffled to the door. The two remaining parties settled their checks and lurched out into the night.

BIG SPANISH CROSSED the empty dance floor and seated himself opposite Smooth. He glanced at Gilda's chair and lifted his eyebrows, inquiringly.

"Where's the girl friend?"

"Aw, I had to slow her down," said Smooth. "She was burnin' up the joint. She went home."

"Oh, yeah?" said Spanish suspiciously. "Now ain't that funny. I send the boys out to give Rudd the works and he meets them half way and rubs out three of them. But your dame couldn't know anything about that—could she?"

"What's the gag?" demanded Smooth. "You tryin' to say she framed you?"

"What do you think?"

"I think you're wrong. She didn't know a thing—neither

did I. Gilda and me have been pals from 'way back. She's on the level, If your boys let Rudd slip one across, it ain't no fault of hers or mine either. Ask Lucky—I been sittin' with him all night."

"That's straight, Spanish," said Lucky. "You got no quarrel with Smooth or his girl. They're in the clear. Suppose you tell us what happened?"

"Suppose you *don't!*" said Theresa and her voice was sharp. "Your business ain't any of ours, Spanish. Keep it under your hat."

"Fair enough," said Spanish. "But I'll tell you this much—I'm sort of short-handed just now and I could use a few men. There's some of my boys in Mexico that want to see the Big Town again." He turned and tapped Smooth lightly on the arm. "I can use you—see? If you want to do me a little favor you might get a lot healthier than you are right now."

"In other words," said Smooth, "my chances of gettin' out of this joint tonight ain't so good, eh?"

"Not if you're gonna be stubborn."

"So—what else can I do? Deal me in."

"Smart guy," said Spanish. "You start at a hundred a week—clear. There's plenty more where that comes from if you're wise. The job I got for you is practically a vacation, and if you want to take Blondie along, so much the better."

"Why don't you leave her out of it?" snapped Theresa.

"Aw, be nice," laughed Lucky. "Smooth'll do better to take along a gal he knows. Suppose he gets foolin' around with some strange dame down there? Then what?"

"Take her along," said Spanish. "Be at the Newark airport tomorrow afternoon and grab the plane to the coast. There'll be two tickets waitin' for you—Mr. and Mrs. Kyle."

"That's my real tag, Spanish," said Smooth. "Why use it?"

"Because what you're goin' to do is on the up and up. I'm tellin' you, it's the softest job you ever had. Just listen close and stop askin' questions." He hunched forward across the table and emphasized his words by jabbing a heavy forefinger at the cloth as he spoke. "When you get to the coast, report to Ed Jordan at the Trayton Hotel in Los Angeles. He'll be expectin' you because I'll shoot him a wire tonight. And from then on, just do as he tells you—get it?"

"So I go away on the blind, eh?" said Smooth. "Can't you open up and give me a little info on the deal?"

"Take it or leave it, feller."

"It's goin' to be plenty hot in Mexico when Gilda starts chuckin' those blue eyes at the peasants. But you win!"

SMOOTH STOOD UP and beckoned to a waiter. He drew a few bills from his pocket and picked up the check. Spanish reached up and took it from his hand, tore it in half and dropped it on the floor.

"This party is on me, Smooth," he said and smiled. "Be a smart kid and there'll be plenty more of them when you get back."

Smooth shrugged and patted Lucky on the shoulder.

"So long, feller," he said. "Look out for the horse cars and bicycles." He caught Theresa's ear between thumb and forefinger and shook it lightly. "Keep a quart of milk on ice when you get that farm goin'," he laughed. "We'll split it together when I get back."

He started toward the door and Lucky lifted a glass

of wine from the table. He raised it toward Smooth and grinned.

"I'll be seein' ya," he said. "If you meet any nice bulls, ship 'em to Theresa. We'll stock up the farm."

When Smooth stepped into the street the first hint of morning was in the sky above the Sixth Avenue Elevated structure. He breathed deeply, walked to the subway entrance at Fiftieth Street and Broadway and went slowly down the steps. He rode north to Seventy-second Street, left the subway and hailed a passing taxi. He directed the driver into the park and glanced through the rear window to make sure that no car was following.

When they swung into Times Square he paid off the driver and hurried to the hotel where McNeary was stopping. The door of the Chief's room opened instantly to his knock and Smooth was surprised to find McNeary fully dressed.

"Don't you ever sleep?" he asked.

"Not when one of my men is playing with dynamite," smiled McNeary. "You've kept four other men awake, too. And they've had one sweet job keeping an eye on you."

"Thanks for the trouble, Chief. But I was sitting pretty all night. It's a long story and it's going to hand you an awful jolt. But before I start, how's Dorothy?"

McNeary stepped to the door of the adjoining room and opened it. Smooth glanced over his shoulder and grinned from ear to ear when he saw Dorothy sleeping in an easy chair.

"What's the idea?" he asked.

"She hasn't learned to take orders yet," said McNeary quietly. "I've told her to go home and go to bed at least a dozen times, but it's no use. She came here directly from the theater and spent the rest of the night wondering if you were going to get killed. It seems she likes you—but I'm damned if I know why."

"She's a grand kid."

"As nice as that blonde you were mauling in the theater?" asked Dorothy suddenly and lifted one eyelid to squint at Smooth.

"Oh, you *did* see me, eh?" laughed Smooth. "And why didn't you wriggle your nose or say hello?"

"You were so interested in that clinging vine beside you that I didn't think you'd be interested. Who is she?"

"She used to be Gilda Garland—but now she's Mrs. Peter Kyle."

"What?" said Dorothy and McNeary in unison.

SMOOTH ROARED WITH laughter at their astonished expressions and proceeded to outline the story of his night's experience. He told them of meeting Gilda at Rudd's place and his instructions to obtain information from Big Spanish for the gambler. When he told of the raiding expedition that Spanish had sent out in an effort to trap Rudd, McNeary's face was grim.

"That was a sweet little mess," said the Chief. "Three of Spaniard's men were killed and two of Rudd's, according to the police."

"Where did it happen?" asked Smooth.

"Not far from Rudd's place."

"The way things look now, it won't be long before those two mobs clean each other out."

"You ought to know better than that," grunted McNeary. "It doesn't work out that way. New men keep feeding into

the organizations as fast as the old are wiped out. No—
we'll never get rid of the mobs that way, although I admit
it helps."

"Saves a lot of expensive trials," said Smooth. "And a
parole board can't turn a killer loose from his coffin. Well,
now you're due for a little surprise—I'm goin' to Mexico."

Dorothy and the Chief listened attentively while
Smooth explained to them how he had come to sign up
with Big Spanish. When he said that he was to leave for
the coast later in the day with Gilda there was evident
displeasure in Dorothy's eyes.

"Why must she go with you?" she asked. "Don't you
expect to have enough trouble without taking along
another armful—and she's quite an armful, too."

"You noticed that, eh?" teased Smooth. "A girl with your
eyes ought to do well in the Bureau of Narcotics and you're
right about that 'armful of trouble' as you call her. She's
working for Rudd, and if I'm not mistaken he'll know every
move I make, even before the Chief does."

"It sounds like a fine night's work," said McNeary. "My
advice is that you catch that plane—go to the coast and
find out how Big Spanish is getting his supplies of narcotics into the country. Report to Martensen in Los Angeles;
he's supervisor of that district and he'll cooperate with you
in any way possible. I'll wire him before you leave and he'll
be expecting you. As for the details of the work, I'm afraid
that is pretty much up to you."

"How about Rudd? Who's going to handle him while
I'm gone?"

"Turn about is fair play," said Dorothy suddenly. "While

you're honeymooning at the coast why not let me keep an eye on Rudd?"

"That sounds all right," said Smooth, "but it wouldn't work out. Rudd's a cagey bird. He'd throw you for a loss in no time. He's smart, suave and vicious as the devil. If he got wise to you he'd rub you out like an extra period. Sorry—that's out!"

"Just when did you corner the supply of brains?" she smiled. "I'll guarantee that I have less trouble handling Rudd than you will with that platinum-topped partner of yours."

McNEARY LAUGHED UNTIL the tears rolled down his cheeks. He laid a friendly hand upon Dorothy's shoulder and shook her gently. When he spoke it seemed to Smooth that he was listening to a proud parent expounding the virtues of an only child.

"I'm afraid you're underrating this little lady, Smooth," he said kindly. "She and I have had some long talks and I'm willing to back her judgment any time. Now let's think this out and see where we stand. Just what does Rudd know about Dorothy?"

"He thinks she's my girl friend," said Smooth and grinned broadly.

"You see—he's not so *very* clever," said Dorothy.

"That's what you think. However, he wanted me to take you over to Spanish's place tonight."

"Oh, he did, eh?" she said. "But you preferred a blonde?"

"Naturally! Spanish thinks that Rudd goes for you—you know that. I had a tough job getting you out of there once and I'd be an awful sap to walk you into the place again."

"Probably you're right," she said. "Besides, I'm sure you had a much better time with Gilda."

"Stop it, both of you!" said McNeary. "I think Dorothy's idea is good. If Rudd imagines that she is fond of you and he trusts you—she is just the agent to put on this case. Why not have her meet Rudd? Ask him to keep an eye on her while you're away."

"It's a long shot, Chief," said Smooth. "And how about her appointment—did that come through from the Treasury Department?"

"I'll take care of all that. If Dorothy wants to go through with this, you help her. And that's an order."

"Are you *quite* satisfied, Mr. Kyle?" asked Dorothy.

"*Quite,* Miss Manning," said Smooth shortly. "If you will find your hat and gloves we'll get started. I've got to report to Rudd, and this is the only opportunity I'll have to introduce you."

Dorothy gathered her things together, smiled knowingly at McNeary and crossed to the door. The Chief patted Smooth upon the back and pushed him gently toward her.

"Good-by, kids," he said. "Lots of luck. And keep in touch with me, Smooth—report every day if you can."

13

OFF TO LOS ANGELES

SMOOTH ESCORTED DOROTHY to the elevator and jabbed petulantly at the button. He was not at all pleased with this sudden turn of affairs. It was all very well for him to take chances—that was his trade. And when McNeary ordered him to a dangerous assignment it was to be expected as part of the routine of a Treasury Agent. Of course, it was true that women had done some splendid work in the bureau. Smooth knew of cases that had been broken in record time through the efforts of these tireless and efficient operators. But to him, these women had only been names—cogs in a huge machine of which he too was an infinitesimal part. Dorothy was different—she was an entity, and a very particular part of his scheme of things.

He said little during their trip across town and ordered the driver of their cab to stop two blocks distant from Rudd's apartment. He turned up the front window of the car, glanced about to be sure that no loiterers were paying too much attention to the parked taxi, and proceeded to rehearse Dorothy in the most important part she had ever played.

It was only logical to suppose that Rudd would question her at some time in the near future as to her relationship with Smooth. He outlined a plausible story of their meeting and of the time that followed. There was a span of a few years left open, and about this Dorothy was to be reticent.

She could hint that Smooth may have been in jail, but of necessity she must be vague.

When he was satisfied that she was thoroughly conversant with the manufactured history he opened the cab door and was about to help her to the street.

"No, that won't do!" he said abruptly. "You wait here and I'll come for you in a little while."

"But I don't understand," she said. "Why can't I come along now?"

"I'm not sure myself. But I've got a hunch—oh, I can't just explain it—but stay put! I'll be back."

He closed the door and walked quickly to the elaborate building that Rudd made his home. He was admitted by Simpson, the butler, who had grown two droopy bags beneath his eyes during the course of his night's wakefulness.

"Ah, yes," said Simpson. "Mr. Rudd's been waiting up for you."

Smooth found Rudd seated behind the Queen Anne desk in the library. He was immaculate as ever and showed little signs of weariness. His waxlike fingers were drumming their incessant tattoo on the polished surface of the desk, and his eyes, when they met Smooth's, were beady and bright.

"I was a little worried about you," he said. "As a matter of fact I was about to send some of the boys over to help you get out of the Trocado."

"Thanks," said Smooth. "I generally manage to dig out

of the tough spots. I hear you gave Spanish's mob a warm reception when they came visiting."

"They never did finish their visit, thanks to you. That was a nice piece of work, Smooth, and I won't forget it," Rudd said.

"It wasn't so hard. Gilda deserves more credit than I do—she's an ace."

"She told me about that little act you put on at the club. And in spite of your cave-man tactics she seems to think you're just right." He pointed to the decanter. "Want a drink?"

Smooth poured himself a glass of rye and was about to raise it to his lips when he became aware of a subtle odor. For a moment it remained an elusive fragrance that refused to place itself in any definite category. It was strong, heady and fresh in his mind. Realization brought a smile to his lips. Gilda Garland! That was it! She must have been in this room within the past few moments.

THAT HUNCH OF his had been right. In all probability Gilda was still in the apartment, and it would have been folly to bring Dorothy Manning along with him. There was no doubt in Smooth's mind as to Gilda's cleverness. Dorothy might be a match for her, but Smooth was glad he had prevented a meeting. Things were tough enough without it.

"I'm glad Gilda likes me," he said. "Where is she now?"

"Interested, eh?"

"Why not? A man should be interested in his own wife."

"Well of all the—"

Smooth turned quickly at the words. Gilda was standing in the doorway, hands on her hips and a cigarette drooping from the corner of her mouth. She was eying him with an expression of indignant amusement.

"Hello, Beautiful," he said. "Where did you come from?"

"Never mind that," she snapped. "What's all this guff about me being your wife?"

"Oh, don't take it seriously—it's a gag. Big Spanish wants me to go to the coast today and take you with me as my wife."

"Spit it out, Smooth!" said Rudd. "What's it all about?"

"Nothin' much to it. Spanish has been losing a lot of men here in New York. He's calling the boys in from the sticks and hired me to take the place of one of his oldtimers. I'm to report to a guy by the name of Ed Jordan in L.A. and take orders from him. Spanish says the job is legit, but I gotta hunch I'll be hustling junk across the line."

Rudd stared thoughtfully at the desk top. His fingers drummed lightly and his lips were thin. At length he nodded wisely and pointed a parchment-like finger at Gilda. "It looks as though you're going to earn another diamond, my dear," he said. "I can understand why Spanish wants you to go with Smooth. You're the front—you make him a respectable married man. And it's clever—damn clever!"

"Well, I like that!" she said. "You wave a finger—and I'm Mrs. Kyle, eh?"

"Oh, don't get kittenish," said Smooth. "I don't like this any more than you do, but it's business—see? We won't have to stay more than a few days. In that time, if you use your wits as hard as I expect to use mine, we'll have the lowdown on Spanish's supply. After that a word to the Feds and the chump is out of business."

"Quick thinking, Smooth," said Rudd. "When do you leave?"

"On the afternoon plane."

Rudd glanced at his watch and then to the window where the morning sun was making an intricate light pattern on the drapes. There was satisfaction in the look he directed at Gilda.

"Go home and get packed, my dear," he said. "Meet Smooth at the airport in time to catch that plane. I promise you won't regret it."

"I'm inclined to believe I'll enjoy it," she said, and lifted an ironic eyebrow at Smooth as she left the room.

WHEN SHE HAD gone, Smooth leaned across the desk as though he were about to impart a confidence.

"I'll play this through for you, Rudd," he said, "but I want you to do me a favor. My girl friend is plenty sore about me dancing off with a blonde. And, to make things worse, Spanish would give his right eye to get rid of her for keeps! I'm not any too happy about going to the coast and leaving her here without someone to take care of her, so I'm asking you to do that little thing for me."

"Why not?" said Rudd pleasantly. "If she's the little girl who put Eddie Malloy on the spot for me, I owe her a great deal. Of course I'll keep an eye on her—where is she?"

"Waiting for me in a hack downstairs. I didn't want her to bump into Gilda and I was afraid that dame might still be hanging around here."

"Smart boy," laughed Rudd. "Go and get her."

Smooth left the apartment and hurried along the street to the waiting taxi. He paid off the driver and extended his arm to Dorothy. Madison Avenue was awakening from its night's sleep and preparing for the business of the day. Busses rolled swiftly past them, an occasional truck rumbled from one of the side streets and clattered across the car tracks, and as Smooth and Dorothy turned in beneath the marquee of the apartment a group of children romped noisily past on their way to school.

Rudd came from behind his desk when they entered the library and crossed the room with both hands outstretched to Dorothy. He lifted hers, held them and looked steadily into her eyes and Smooth was again conscious of the magnetic personality this gambler could exert when he chose. The man was suavity in itself—a cultured gentleman whose charm was irresistible.

"So this is Miss Manning?" said Rudd. "Smooth hardly did you justice in his description. You're beautiful, my dear—beautiful! And it's going to be a positive pleasure to be associated with you. I might even hope that Smooth will be forced to stay away more than the few days he expects."

His tone was light, flattering, and Smooth saw that Dorothy was wholly unprepared to meet a man of this caliber. Big Spanish and his mob were the direct opposites of this smiling gambler and they were the type she had expected. But Dorothy was an actress—it simply meant playing a different role, and she was quick to accept her cue.

"I'll miss Smooth," she said, and when she spoke Smooth wished that she were not acting. "And I'm depending upon you to take his place."

"I can promise you," said Smooth, "that he'll be good company. And I 'll feel a whole lot better knowing that he's going to keep an eye on you while I'm gone. I'd like to sit and talk for a while until you two become better acquainted, but I've got to get my things together so I can grab that plane. If you don't mind, I'll run along."

He extended his left hand to Rudd, and the gambler caught it in both of his and shook it warmly. He winked to Dorothy and started for the door, but stopped when he heard her utter a startled exclamation.

"What's the matter?" he asked.

"Smooth! You're not going to kiss me before you go?"

He grinned. Dorothy was proving herself to be the perfect actress. In fact she was doing a better job than he was. Again he realized that an agent in the Bureau of Narcotics was entitled to any breaks that might come his way in the performance of his duty. This was a break—and he made the most of it.

He stepped beside her, held her closely to him with one arm and kissed her emphatically—not once, but three times. Her eyes were wide as she lifted her mouth, and Smooth thought he detected a trace of laughter within them. He withdrew his arm from about her waist and looked at her steadily for a moment.

To his surprise, she pulled his head down and kissed him again, then walked hurriedly to a window and stood staring down into the street.

GILDA WAS PACING nervously about the waiting room when Smooth arrived at the Newark airport. He stood near the door and watched her for a moment, and he decided he might enjoy this trip to the coast even more than he expected. She was smartly dressed in a tight-fitting gray tailored suit. Her platinum curls were crisp and fresh beneath a snug gray fedora. Smooth noticed her eyes were a trifle tired, but there was a springiness in her walk that made him wonder where she had summoned up such energy after a sleepless night.

When she caught sight of him she gave a little gesture of impatience and waved for him to hurry. He glanced at the clock and saw it was within a few moments of starting time and his bags had not yet been weighed in.

"Got the tickets?" he asked.

"Of course I have," she answered. "I've been here a half hour and I suppose you've been catching up on your sleep. You men are all alike—you need nurses. C'mon, let's get started."

She handed him the tickets and he picked up his bags when they had been okayed by the weigher. As they walked to the plane, the blast from the propellers whipped Gilda's skirt madly about her ankles. Smooth saw his fellow passengers grinning approvingly from the windows and realized he would not be called upon to provide all of the entertainment on the cross-country hop.

The plane rolled down field, swung and strained against the brakes as the pilot tested the motors. There was a smooth run past the airport buildings and they lifted easily from the ground. Smooth looked out of the window and saw a flutter of handkerchiefs from the people at the airport. He heard the man in the seat behind him calling goodbyes that could not possibly carry to his friends below. As the ship roared off into the afternoon sky he wondered if Dorothy Manning had only been acting when she gave him that last kiss.

He settled in his chair and decided to sleep through the first leg of the journey. A dig in the ribs settled that.

"Now what?" he asked, and turned to face Gilda, who was leaning from her chair across the aisle.

"Darling," she purred, "do you *have* to behave like a husband? After all—we've been married such a short time I should think you might show a little interest in your bride. Tell me where we're going to live—and why. And do you suppose Miss Manning will miss you?"

"Angel," he answered thinly, "how would you like to go to hell?"

"Oh, come on, Smooth—be a sport! This little joyride may wind up in a coroner's office. We're both in a tough spot, and I, for one, don't see why we have to make it tougher by fighting our way to California. Be nice! Smile for your bride—and see if you can dig up a piece of chewing gum."

Smooth handed her a package, twisted around in his chair and nodded.

"You win," he said. "But remember this—we're both working for Rudd. This isn't a joyride and we've got a fast job of work to put across. I don't know what we're going to bump into when we hit L.A., and I don't care much. I'm depending upon you to play smart and use those blue eyes of yours to get me any information that I can't. As for the bride stuff—nuts! You're poison, Beautiful—a guy in my racket can't afford to fall for a dame like you. And, believe me, Gorgeous, I don't intend to!"

Gilda laughed and twisted the gum wrapper into a tight wad, then flipped it into Smooth's face.

"Flatterer!" she whispered. "You're too good-looking to stay in circulation—watch what little Gilda can do when she makes up her mind. And now we've settled that, go on back to sleep. I'll look over the peasants in this crate and see if I can find one who'll keep a girl from being bored to death."

At Kansas City, when the plane drifted down from the night sky, Smooth saw that Gilda had dropped off to sleep. He hurried to the telegraph office and sent a wire to McNeary confirming his departure, and in it he asked the Chief to keep Dorothy out of trouble, if possible. There was time for a quick cup of coffee and then the huge air-liner was up and sliding along the dark airways again.

14

NEW SET-UP

MORNING SHOWED SMOOTH and Gilda the Painted Desert stretched out in a changing mass of greens and reds below the silver wings of the plane. The sky was cloudless—a metallic blue wall that ringed a horizon made dim by distance. It seemed to Smooth that he was a thing apart from the earth—a bodyless, intangible spirit that viewed the world from the vantage of the heavens. There was no sense of height or movement. The dull drone of the motors was lost in its own regularity and he leaned back comfortably.

The air was bumpy above the twisting spirals of rock that grew from tiny foothills into the giant peaks of the Rockies. The slight motion of the ship woke Gilda from her nap and she stared about in alarm. Smooth put a reassuring hand upon her arm and pointed to the warning light in the front of the compartment that flashed on before a landing.

"Fasten your strap. Beautiful," he said. "We'll be sliding into California in a few minutes."

The sharp slopes of the San Gabriel Mountains flowed past and they drifted down into a valley of deep green vegetation. The plane banked sharply and circled. The ground swooped up to meet them and they rolled to a stop before the Glendale airport.

Smooth gathered up their luggage and stood for a moment in indecision at the door leading to the parking station.

"What's the delay?" asked Gilda. "Were you expecting a brass band?"

"Not quite. But I don't like the idea of playing it blind out here. We're supposed to report to a guy by the name of Ed Jordan at the Trayton and take orders from him. All right—we'll do it. But first I want to have a talk with some boys I know. We might need friends in this village if things get too hot and I want to know where I stand."

"Who are they? In the racket?"

"Yeah—smart lads. They own a joint in town and they'll be glad to do me a favor if I need one. Suppose you grab a cab and take our things to the Trayton. Check into a suite—Spanish is footing the bill—and catch up on your rest for a few hours."

"Sounds good to me, Handsome," she laughed. "But don't let any movie scouts grab you off while my back is turned."

"Same to you," he said, and nodded to a taxi driver.

Her eyes were thoughtful when she looked from the cab window and she caught his hand in a tight grip.

"Watch your step, Smooth," she said. "You're too nice a guy to get bumped off—and I'm not clowning when I say I like you."

He pinched her cheek and hailed another cab. When Gilda's taxi had started toward Los Angeles, he gave his driver the address of an office building on Figueroa Street.

The car raced south from Glendale and Smooth's eyes picked out the various landmarks that were associated with his training period in the Bureau of Narcotics. He was not as familiar with this territory as with the Times Square neighborhood, but as he came into the business district the layout of the city unfolded as a map before his eyes.

He paid off the driver, strolled into the building and waited to see if he was being followed. Five minutes later he was on his way by cab to another building on Fifth Street. He opened a glass-topped door on the second floor and winked to a young man sitting at a desk beyond a wooden railing.

" 'Lo, Tom," he said. "How's the old Native Son gettin' along?"

"Smooth! How'ya, feller!" Tom extended his hand and lifted his eyebrows in surprise when Smooth grasped it with his left. "Bum wing?"

"A light one," said Smooth. "Is Martensen in?"

"Waiting for you—go on in and report."

SMOOTH STEPPED INTO an inner office and reported to the District Supervisor. Martensen had not been in command of this section when Smooth was serving his apprenticeship, but he was well known to Smooth by reputation. It had been through the efforts of this slightly built, soft-eyed man that the Honolulu opium syndicate had been broken up. It was a typical Treasury Department job and had been handled with the same speed and dispatch that many other cases with less newspaper publicity had received.

When Smooth had finished his report, Martensen

Smooth dove forward as Gilda fired

picked a code telegram from his desk and waved it toward the hackman.

"McNeary thinks well of you," he said. "That's as good a recommendation as any man needs. Suppose you follow through on this case in your own way. Keep in touch with me and if you need help, ask for it. Don't try to break it alone—it can't be done."

"Thank you, sir," said Smooth. "I'll holler when I need a hand. Just now, I think I'd better report to this man, Jordan."

"Don't be too anxious," laughed Martensen. "Play along with them for a while and let's not have any loose ends left over when the crash comes."

Smooth nodded and left the office. He walked a few blocks from the building and found a cab parked at a street corner.

"Trayton Hotel," he said to the driver. "Step on it!"

The taxi driver looked him over slowly, threw the flag

and proceeded to take his time. Smooth grinned and realized that he, too, had done the same thing in New York on many occasions. These "hurry-up" riders were old stuff to the hackmen. They yelled for speed and expected the driver to pass traffic lights and ignore the speed laws, and at the end of the trip they presented him with a big dime. If a motorcycle cop happened to pass out a ticket during the ride, they slumped back against the rear cushions and muttered about it being a "damned outrage," but Smooth had never known one to offer a few dollars toward the payment of the fine.

And now he was asking for speed, like any other hick. He shrugged and slumped down in the seat. They rolled out of the business section and spun along the smooth surface of Wilshire Boulevard. When they arrived at the Trayton, Smooth inquired for the number of Mr. Kyle's suite and went up.

GILDA HAD APPROPRIATED the most pleasant room for herself and was in negligee, busily unpacking her bags. She blew him a kiss and went on with her work, pointing to the door that led into the adjoining room.

"That's your cage, Monkey," she said.

"Fine. Any word from Jordan?"

"Not yet. Why not wait until tomorrow before you call him? He may want us to start working today—and, mister, I'm *tired!*"

"I'll handle him."

"How'd you make out with your pals? Any luck?"

"The best. Tell you all about it later. Lock the door, if it will make you happy—and take a nap."

"Don't be an umpchay!" she said and threw a slipper at him.

He closed the door behind him and tossed his bags into a closet, not bothering to unpack them. There was an easy chair near the phone and Smooth stretched out in it for a few moments, dragging at a cigarette and staring at the ceiling. At length he called Jordan and asked him to drop in to see him.

A few minutes later there was a knock on the door and Smooth drew a deep breath and set his teeth.

"Come in!" he called.

Ed Jordan was somewhat on the same type as Big Spanish. He was tall and heavily muscled. His coat was snug across the shoulders and his hands looked like huge hams that dangled from the ends of the sleeves. He tossed a careless salute to Smooth and seated himself on the bed, swung his legs up from the floor and stretched them out before him. For a moment he said nothing and both men studied each other without taking the trouble to disguise the fact.

Smooth decided that Jordan was about of the same mental caliber as Spanish, and again he wondered how men of this type could conduct a business that spread from coast to coast and netted them a fortune. Jordan was undoubtedly possessed of a certain amount of cunning but it was evident he was no mental giant. His heavy jaw and close set eyes might be signs of a ruthless determination that swept everything along before it, but Smooth knew this man would have blundered into a mistake had it not been for some guiding hand at his shoulder.

McNeary was right in suspecting an unknown leader as the man who controlled Big Spanish and his mob. There must be more brains calling the shots than Smooth had seen as yet. There was a chance that Jordan was not the top man here at the coast—he also might be taking orders and passing them along to Smooth. But if the head outfit was working out of Los Angeles, Smooth was determined to locate him before he bounced back to New York.

"Do I pass?" he asked at length.

"You're okay with me, Kyle. Spanish says you're goin' to take over Luke Taylor's job in Tijuana, and give Luke a crack at the bright lights again. That mug has been squawkin' about the Big Town ever since he hit the west coast. Whatta sap! Me—I go for this burg in a big way. Anything they got in New York, we got double out here—includin' dames."

"You can keep 'em," said Smooth. "What's the lay?"

"Take your time, you'll get it. And it's a pushover, pal! Nothin' to do but run a joint on the other side of the line and be respectable. Not bad, eh?"

"Where does the wife fit?"

"She just acts respectable, too. When do I meet her?"

"Tomorrow. Both of us are due for a little sleep after that cross country romp. Suppose you look me up in the morning."

"That's good with me unless you wanna bounce around with me tonight and look over the town. The liquor's good and there's some swell spots in Hollywood that might open your eyes."

"Thanks, but count me out. See you in the morning."

Jordan shrugged his shoulders as though Smooth were missing a golden opportunity, swung his legs down from the bed and slouched across the room.

"I'll see you at ten," he said, and left.

SMOOTH AND GILDA had finished a late breakfast and were arguing as to whether or not there was time for her to get a manicure when Jordan barged into them. She favored him with one of her most charming baby stares and when Jordan beamed like an idiot, Smooth dropped him one notch lower in his estimation. There was a car waiting for them and soon Smooth noticed they were heading along the waterfront toward San Diego.

"What happens?" he asked.

"This is your car," said Jordan. "And the chump out front is the family chauffeur. We're on our way to your house and when you see it, feller, you'll be glad you made the trip."

"How lovely," said Gilda sarcastically. "Now suppose you stop all this mystery hokum and open up. All I've been getting for the last two days is, 'Eenie, meenie, minie, moe—first do this—then do that—and then see what happens.' I'm sick of it!"

"It's simple as hell," laughed Jordan. "Luke Taylor owns a house in San Diego and he owns a souvenir store over the line in Tijuana. He drives to work in the mornin' and drives back home at night. Smooth gets the house—buys it—gets a bill of sale, mortgage and everything. He does the same with Luke's store. The car goes with it and so do the servants. Simple?"

"It don't make sense," said Smooth. "Why?"

"For a guy in our racket you're askin' too many questions. You're gettin' paid big money to do a soft job. Why not take it and stop lookin' for trouble?"

"It sounds like the old run-around to me," said Gilda. "We go scampering back and forth across the border twice a day—for what? Are we running stuff over the line? And if we are—what happens when the Customs boys crack down on us?"

Jordan laughed and dug an elbow into Smooth's ribs. He seemed to consider Gilda's outburst a great joke and expected Smooth to share it with him. When he had wiped the tears from his eyes, he turned to her patiently, as though explaining an obvious fact to a child.

"There ain't no catch, Mrs. Kyle," he said. "You don't need a passport on the Mexican line and after you make the trip a few times the Customs guards toss you a big smile on the way through. Hundreds of people in the States own stores in Mexico and they commute—see? Just like the Bronx express. Over the line in the mornin' and back at night. At first the guards look you over careful, but not for long. Then they check back on you and see if you're legit. When they find that everything is on the up an' up—that lets you out."

"And when do they catch us with the stuff?" asked Smooth.

"They don't! You don't ever carry any stuff—you're just a blind. They never do get wise to the way the stuff is comin' over."

"It sounds fishy to me," said Gilda. "But if Smooth wants to go through with it—that's settled."

"Good girl," said Jordan. "You won't be sorry."

"You're damn right, she won't," said Smooth. "Where's this house you were talking about?"

"We'll come to it in a minute. It's near Balboa Park—a swell layout with a two-car garage. And if you get lonesome for Broadway you can walk to it from the house."

"Sez you!" snapped Gilda.

"Sure! There's a swell Broadway in San Diego—not quite like the home town, but plenty of lights."

"You can have it," she said.

THE CAR STOPPED before a walk that led up to a one family house set well back from the street. The chauffeur opened the door and picked up their luggage. Jordan lurched along the walk, chatting with Gilda and promising that she would enjoy her stay in San Diego. He sounded to Smooth like a real estate salesman trying to sell lots in a dying sub-division and again Smooth wondered when he would come in contact with the man who really handled things for Spanish in California.

Luke Taylor proved to be a typical Broadway smart guy. He cursed the climate, the date palms and the sunshine. His bags were packed and standing near the door when Jordan led Gilda and Smooth into the living room. He waved to a decanter of whisky, told them to help themselves, looked Gilda over with an approving eye and hurried to a taxi that had drawn up at the curb.

"Pleasant fellow," said Gilda. "Are the cops after him? Or does he always do a 'shuffle off to Buffalo' when visitors arrive?"

"Don't mind him," laughed Jordan. "He's one of those New Yorkers that bums up the roads gettin' to the Big Town and then stands on the corner of Fiftieth and Broadway, squawking his head off when he arrives."

Gilda examined the house with the curiosity natural to her sex, selected the brightest bedroom as her own and found fault with the closet space and just about everything else she saw. Smooth turned his things over to a Japanese servant and poured drinks for Jordan and himself.

"When do we go to Tijuana?" he asked.

"Whenever you're ready. There's a clerk handling the store now and he'll stay on with you. The sale is being recorded and in a few days you'll get the papers. I'll take care of the Mexican red tape—I'm used to it. All you got to do is play boss, and keep out of trouble."

"All right, let's go," said Smooth. He walked to the door leading off into the dining room, listened for a moment to Gilda telling the cook how to prepare a salad, grinned and cupped his hands to his mouth. "Hey, Beautiful! Stop tryin' to fool the public and get out of that kitchen. We're goin' to Mexico—want to come along?"

She left the kitchen, stuck the tip of her tongue between her teeth and pouted at Smooth. They were getting into the car when Jordan suddenly gripped their arms and stopped them.

"Almost forgot," he said. "Either of you got a gun on you?"

"Do I look dumb?" said Smooth. "Of course I'm packin' a rod."

"Leave it home. You can't take it across the line. The Mexicans don't trust a gringo with a gun. And if you did get it across, the Customs guards on this side would take it away when you came back. Sorry—no dice on the rod."

Smooth nodded in understanding and started back toward the house. He had gone but a few steps when Gilda dropped a small automatic into his pocket.

"Check that, too," she said.

Jordan looked at her with more respect. He was still expounding upon the beauties of California when they rolled up to the wire gate that blocked the street leading over the border.

HE CALLED THE Mexican Customs men by name, introduced both Gilda and Smooth in Spanish that was fifty percent sign language and said that these were his *amigos—muy bien amigos!*

"It's a pleasure to know you," said one Mexican in perfect English, and bowed from the hips.

Jordan continued for a few minutes in his miserable Spanish, not in the least affected by the subtle hint of the Mexican guard. He explained that Señor Kyle and the *señora* were the new owners of a store in Tijuana—that he, acting as agent, had handled the business. The guard smiled tolerantly and saluted as the car rolled along the road and swung into a street lined with saloons and souvenir stores.

At the corner of an intersecting side street, the driver stopped and Jordan pointed out to them their new place of business. It differed not one trifle from the many others in the neighborhood. There were shelves full of postcards, potted cactus, painted shells, and all the interminable variety of knick-knacks that tourists buy cheerfully and cart back to their friends—and the friends in turn dump into an empty corner of the attic.

A row of the inevitable slot machines flanked the door and a smiling Mexican youngster not more than sixteen years of age was in charge of the cash register. His teeth flashed a welcoming grin to Jordan; he bowed low before Gilda and again to Smooth. It was a "playsure" to serve them, he insisted—although since "thees meeserable reepeel law," tourists did not spend quite so freely as in those good days of "Proheebeesion. *Nos es verdad?*"

Jordan said he was a good boy and could be trusted to conduct the affairs of the souvenir business. He led them out into the sunbaked yard that extended from the rear of the store and showed them a two car garage built of 'dobe and sheet iron. There was a high board fence fronting the side street and a solid looking gate that let into the garage runway. Smooth noticed a heavy padlock caught between two staples in the inner side and he also saw that another lock held the garage doors securely fastened.

"Why all the heavy hardware?" he asked, pointing to the locks.

"Oh, them—" said Jordan. "Well, we had a little trouble with the kids—nothing serious, but they were stealing Black's tools out of the garage."

"Black—who's he?"

"Your chauffeur—the chump sitting out in the car. He's a nut on motors—always tinkerin' with 'em. He's a pal of Spanish's and we gave him this job to keep him happy. He'll drive you here in the morning and amuse himself all day playin' with the car, and then he'll drive you home at night. Don't pay any attention to him—he expects to invent a new motor or somethin'."

"So we've got a nut in the family!" said Gilda. "Well, of all the screwy outfits I ever hooked up with! Your souvenir joint looks like a run-down Jap concession at Coney Island. The location is swell—for raisin' pigs, and I'm hot and tired and thirsty and—"

"And you're goin' to take it and like it," finished Smooth.

"Don't kid yourself—Handsome," she snapped. "You're the one who takes it—I leave it! You can peddle these desert pin cushions to the rubes—I stay in San Diego. This is my first and last appearance in Tijuana!"

"I think you'll change your mind about that," said Jordan. "I've been holdin' an ace up my sleeve—a surprise for you."

"Sure it isn't a cockroach?"

"Positive!" laughed Jordan. "We'll have Black drive us to Agua Caliente for lunch, and, Sister, that joint will open your eyes."

"The name is *Mrs. Kyle!*" snapped Smooth.

"No offense, Smooth. I can see you're one of them touchy guys, but you'll soften up down here in the sun."

He laughed again and Smooth measured his chin, deciding it was a great place to drop a looping right-hand swing. He promised himself this one bit of enjoyment when the break came and led Gilda back through the store and into the street. Jordan handed them into the rear of the car, nodded to Black and they started off in a smother of dust.

15

AGUA CALIENTE

WITHIN A FEW moments they had left the dirty streets of Tijuana and were rolling along a smooth road that led into a valley between a series of low foothills. A bright patch of green foliage was set like an emerald in the little valley and from the center of it rose the graceful lines of a Spanish bell tower. The car turned left and swung into a wide, curving driveway that was lined with a riot of bloom.

"Here we are," said Jordan, pointing to a series of low-roofed buildings that edged the driveway.

"Agua Caliente—that's Mex for hot water, and when you get a look at the casino and hear the chips clickin' you'll get the idea."

"When do we eat?" demanded Gilda. "The scenery is swell, but it doesn't help that dent in my stomach."

Jordan led them into a shaded patio where a fountain leaped and splashed among the palms. Birds swooped in beneath the striped awnings and darted for crumbs that fell from tables spaced evenly about a low balcony. There was a distant sound of throbbing strings and the soft notes of a Mexican love song. A breeze swayed the banked flowers into a changing pattern of beauty that edged the stone floor beneath them.

A waiter led them to a table near the fountain, handed them gayly colored menus and waited for their order. Jordan ran his thumb down the wine list and ordered champagne.

"It's swell for breakfast," he said. "Starts you off right."

"Yeah," said Gilda, "but this is lunch."

"Stop weepin' for a few minutes and look around," said Smooth. "This place is a chunk of heaven and you sit there barking at each other. Be nice, Gilda—do you understand?"

The lid of his right eye drooped slightly as he spoke and he looked first at the champagne that was set in a cooler and then slowly at Jordan. Gilda opened her eyes wide, reached across the table and patted his chin and turned a flattering smile upon Jordan.

Smooth noticed throughout the luncheon, Gilda was careful to see that Jordan's glass was always full. She played up to him, laughed with him and ignored Smooth completely.

And when the dishes had been cleared away and a Mexican troubadour stood beside the table and fingered his guitar, she kicked Smooth lightly in the ankle and nodded toward the archway leading from the patio.

"You serious drinkers can sit and watch the fountain," he said, and pushed back his chair. "I'm going to look around and see what this place has to offer."

"Nothin' mush doin' till night," said Jordan above the rim of his glass. "Lotsa pretty flowers 'n' things—go ahead, look 'em over. Me 'n' Mish Kyle's gonna drink."

"You're only half right," said Smooth softly, and patted Gilda's hand. "See you later."

He strolled through the palm lined walks, stopped at the

parking station and noticed the car was gone, looked in at the race track and at length located the swimming pool. For the next few hours he sat beneath the shade of a giant palm, stared at the blue water and wished that his shoulder had healed enough to permit him to swim.

THE SUN HAD dropped behind the hills when he wandered into the patio in search of Gilda and Jordan. The place was empty and a waiter directed him to the dining room. At a secluded table in a corner of the huge room he saw Jordan weaving unsteadily in his chair and even above the music of the orchestra Smooth could hear his jarring laugh. Gilda was smiling and seemed to be living for the sole purpose of listening to this petty gangster's ravings. Smooth pitied her, but seated himself at a table across the room and enjoyed his supper in peace.

He was toying with his coffee when a small, firm hand caught the lobe of his ear and pinched it. He looked up and into the furious eyes of Gilda.

"If you think I'm going to sit with that chump any longer, you're crazy," she snapped. "Look at him—dead to the world."

Smooth stood up, offered her his arm and walked out into the night. He found a seat near a splashing brook and led her to it.

"Nice work, partner," he said. "What did you learn?"

"Ugh! He gave me the creeps—the swine! He's done nothing but brag about what a big shot he is and he suggested that I get rid of you and marry a *real* man. Nice, eh?"

"Don't let it throw you. Remember, Rudd pays plenty

for anything he wants. Right now he wants information. Did you get any?"

"I don't know how much it's worth, but I managed to get this from his ravings," she said. "He's leaving San Diego tomorrow on a trip that will take him a few weeks. First he stops at Douglas, Arizona—then at El Paso and Del Rio, and then to Laredo and Brownsville. Does that help any?"

"*Help?*" exclaimed Smooth. "Beautiful—that's perfect! Listen and learn— Douglas is just over the line from Agua Prieta in Mexico. El Paso is a trolley ride from Juarez—a tourist spot that gets a better play than Tijuana. There's a little town called Eagle Pass near Del Rio that's over the line from Piedras Negras. Laredo in the States hooks up with Nuevo Laredo in Mexico and you can damn near jump from Brownsville to Matamoros over the border. A perfect set of contacts—do you get it?"

Smooth had been tapping off each town with a forefinger that dug into Gilda's arm. She grasped his hand and held it for a moment and her eyes were wise as they looked into his.

"When did you learn all that geography, Smooth?" she asked. "It's funny that a New York hackman should be able to rattle off the border towns that way. How come?"

"Aw, I was always good at that stuff," he said quickly. "Practically the teacher's pet when it came to geography—a sort of a hobby."

"Yeah? Where's Council Bluffs?"

"Eh? What's the gag?"

"I learned a little geography, too—playin' one night stands in show business. I'm just seein' how good you are.

Where's Frankfort and Paducah, or maybe you can guess Jefferson City for me?"

Smooth tilted her chin and smiled at the seriousness in her eyes. She had tripped him and she knew it. He realized that he would have to offer a satisfactory explanation or a wire would pass those doubts along to Rudd in the morning. Gilda had been living on her wits too long to be fooled by a flimsy pretense at anger on his part. He thought fast.

"They had a law called Prohibition a few years ago," he said patiently. "You may have heard me say I know a few boys here on the west coast. Well—I met them when I was juggling rye and alky across the line at a few of those spots. Satisfied?"

"About halfway," she smiled. She leaned forward and kissed him on the lips. "There—that takes care of the other half."

The perfume of her hair sent Smooth's brains into a spin. The stars were tiny points in a jet sky, the palms rustled wistfully in the evening breeze, from the distance came the notes of a drowsy waltz—and Dorothy was three thousand miles away. He tilted Gilda's chin and kissed her.

"Feel yourself slipping?" she teased.

That tore it. Smooth stood up, held out his arm and drew her from the bench.

"C'mon," he said. "Let's bankrupt the casino while Jordan sobers up."

SMOOTH HAD WON three hundred dollars at black-jack and Gilda had promptly lost it back to the roulette wheel when Jordan staggered into the casino and hailed them. He seemed to have forgotten his ardent wooing of Gilda and looked at her as though she were a perfect stranger. He followed Smooth's play for a few moments and suggested that they get back over the line before the border closed.

They found Black seated at the wheel of the car outside the casino and in an hour they reached their home in San Diego. Jordan waved a cheerful good night, promised to see them in a week or two and instructed Black to drive him to Los Angeles.

"I think we can wrap this job up in two days," said Smooth when they were seated in the living room, "I'll check over the car tomorrow and see where they hide the junk and then we'll be ready to scram."

"Jordan said we weren't carrying any stuff," said Gilda. "He must know you're smart enough to find it—even if the Customs guards can't. After all, there's only the usual places to hide it—under the seat or some such spot."

"It's not quite so easy as that. We used to jack alky over the line in a lot of funny places. In the rubber—sometimes in flat tanks that fitted along the inside of the body—inner tanks in the gas tank—oh, a dozen places. There could be a thousand spots in that car big enough to hide a can of cocaine, and with us chasin' back and forth across the line every day—wow! What a supply!"

"Well, Angel—that's up to you. I handled Jordan for you, but I'm no mechanic. And now how's about another little kiss?"

"Don't make this job any tougher than it is, Beautiful. When we get back to New York I'll take you up on that—but just now you're dynamite. Be seein' you in the morning—'night."

THE JAPANESE SERVANT awakened Smooth when he drew the blinds and set out a light suit and shoes. He offered to shave his new master, but Smooth declined with thanks and stroked his own throat with the razor. Gilda came into the breakfast nook in a flowery negligee and kissed Smooth good morning before he realized what was going to happen.

"Did it ever occur to you that my wardrobe consists of two suit cases of clothes—and that's all?" she asked. "If you don't want a bill for some new rags, I'd advise you to gallop through this job in a hurry."

"Ixnay—don't crack wise," said Smooth, nodding to the maid who was serving them. "Sometimes you say the dumbest things—and do the nicest. Be patient, Beautiful—it won't be long."

Black was waiting for them at the door and seemed rather surprised when Gilda accompanied Smooth. He said nothing but drove them quickly to the border, paused while the Mexican guards looked into the car and nodded, then drew up before the store.

He went through the shop, out into the back yard and unlocked the padlocks on the garage and gate. Smooth heard the car roll along the driveway and then heard the garage doors close.

"That bird must be a lizard," he whispered to Gilda. "He sure likes plenty of heat when he closes those doors on a day like this."

"I hope he fries," she said. "He's got a face like a spoonful of alum. His nose looks as though it had tried to stop a freight car and if he could wave those ears of his, he could fly. Every time he stares at me I get the jitters. Ugh! He's slimy."

"He's not exactly a double for Clark Gable," laughed

Smooth. "But I don't think he's as tough as he looks. They seldom are. Just another mug making his few bucks a week supplying hop to Spanish. And by the way"—he lifted a stuffed gila monster and handed it to Gilda—"here's a fellow with a name like yours. Play around with him for a while and get acquainted. We can't do anything until our pal in the garage has a visitor."

"You mean until he gets a delivery of cocaine?"

"Yes."

"Maybe they deliver at night."

"Good for you, Gilda. That's one that got past me. The stuff is probably in the garage now and friend Black is hiding the body. We'll look it over at lunch."

A few tourists wandered into the store during the next few hours and Gilda amused herself trying to make sales. The Mexican clerk listened in open mouthed wonder to her description of the articles she showed to the tourists and his eyes popped when she asked for and got a price ten times in excess of the right one from a long whiskered Lothario.

Promptly at twelve Black parked the car before the door and touched the horn button. Smooth winked to Gilda, patted her lightly on the back and helped her into the car.

"Any other good spots to eat lunch, Black?" he asked.

"Yes, sir. A very nice restaurant a few miles south along the waterfront. Shall we go there?"

"Good idea."

THEY FOLLOWED A smooth surfaced road between the hills and soon were rolling past the opalescent blue of the Pacific. Smooth noticed there were stretches of country where not a house was visible in any direction. Few cars passed them and he nudged Gilda lightly in the ribs when they swung through a valley where a side road led off into the hills. He noted the landmarks on either side and saw that Gilda was doing likewise.

Less than five miles ahead, Black swung into a gravel drive and drew up before the doors of a rambling hotel. The dining room faced the ocean and a waiter led them to a table near a huge window overlooking the water.

"We've got to get rid of Black while I have a look at that car," said Smooth when he had given the luncheon order. "Any ideas?"

"Do I have to do all the thinking? Why not send him to the corner for the morning papers?"

"Helpful, aren't you? Maybe I could get him to lend me the rig while he finished another bottle of beer."

"Not a chance, Smooth. That egg wouldn't let go of the ignition keys if they were red hot and burning a hole in his hand. You've got to do better than that."

They toyed with their food, both thinking desperately for some plan by which they could lose Black. They had reached the dessert and had discarded a dozen unsatisfactory ideas when Smooth suddenly put down his fork and pushed back his chair.

"C'mon," he said. "This is too good to wait. Act a little drunky and when the car gets rollin' holler for your bag. Leave it on the chair now and push the chair under the table so the waiter won't hand it to you and spoil the play."

"By-bye bag," said Gilda, hastily grabbing her compact and date book. "No fear of Alfonso handing that back. He looks like Villa with his mustache shaved off."

SHE SLIPPED THE bag onto her chair and walked toward

the door, tilting unsteadily upon her heels and favoring Smooth with a silly grin when he paid the check. Black was seated stolidly at the wheel looking as though his lunch had not agreed with him. Smooth lurched as he opened the door for Gilda to get in and they both giggled foolishly.

"Home, James!" he said, and dropped back against the cushions.

He caught a glimpse of Black's face in the mirror above the driver's seat. The chauffeur's lips were parted slightly in a cross between a grin and a sneer. Smooth waited until the car had started to turn out of the driveway and then tapped Gilda's hand.

"Wait!" she cried. "Stop—stop immediat—immej—aw! Stop *now*, dammit! I've left my bag in that joint."

The car stopped and the driver turned in his seat to look inquiringly at her.

"Hop in and get it, Black!" said Smooth. "Make it snappy—before the waiter sinks it."

For an instant it appeared that Black would snap off the ignition and take the keys with him. Smooth yelled for more speed and the chauffeur slid out the side door and ran into the restaurant. He was hardly through the door when Smooth scrambled in behind the wheel, kicked at the clutch, dropped the car into second speed and headed down the driveway. It bucked and coughed. Smooth slipped the clutch, cursed silently and fed it more gas.

"If that guy's a mechanic," he barked, "then I'm an aviator. This crate runs like a cement mixer."

"Words won't help it, Handsome," said Gilda and twisted to look through the rear window. "Step on the gas, feller—Dracula is standing in front of that restaurant and he looks as though he had a mouthful of bumble bees."

They raced along the macadam until they came to the intersecting road that led off into the hills. Smooth swung right, eased off on the gas and crept along through two inches of dust. A brown cloud rolled up behind them and seemed to hang poised in the air indefinitely. If Black were able to commandeer another car that dust cloud would serve as a perfect marker. But Smooth was unfamiliar with the Mexican roads and had no alternative. He jogged along for a distance of two miles and when he saw there was no likelihood of finding a shelter in which to park the car he pulled to a stop and cut the motor.

"Keep your eye on the back road," he said. "I'll give this crate a quick going over. Tip me off when Black is coming and we can both pull a drunk act on him. It may get by."

"And if it doesn't?"

"We'll worry about that later."

He yanked out the front seat and rummaged through the tool kit. When he found a long shafted ice-pick, he grinned and showed it to Gilda.

"Black must have run with the wops," he said. "This thing makes a swell shive."

"Fine for a sore throat," laughed Gilda. "Get busy before he comes bouncing along with the mate to it."

16

THE CACHE

SMOOTH PRODDED THE cushions with the pick, twisting and probing at the corners. Next he started upon the upholstery and went thoroughly over each square inch of the interior of the car. The search was fruitless and Gilda stood in the dusty roadway, grinning at his efforts and turning at times to glance down the road. Smooth dropped to his knees in the dust, examined the underside of the fenders and squirmed beneath the car. He prodded and jabbed, cursed and spat dust from his mouth, but to no avail.

"Looks like a sell-out," he grunted. He got slowly to his feet, brushed the dirt from his clothes and stared at the car. "Only one spot left now—under the hood."

"Don't tell *me* about it—start looking!"

"Gimme a break," he grinned. "You know the gag about the fellow who thought he'd lost his bank roll. He looked through every pocket except one and then stopped looking."

"I'll play straight, man," she said, and got into the car. "Why?"

"He was afraid that if it wasn't there, he'd drop dead. And that's the spot I'm in now."

"Handsome, I could laugh at that in New York, but here it sounds very unfunny. Get busy—look!"

Smooth lifted the hood and bent above the motor. He searched through every possible nook and corner and at length slammed down the hood in disgust.

"I'm sunk!" he snapped. "It looks as though Jordan was on the level about us not carrying the junk. It's not in this crate and I'd bet a grand on it."

"It must be! Don't stand there and tell me I've been romping all over Mexico just for the fun of it. How about the tires?"

"No dice," said Smooth. "I got a quick look at the wheels when we started out for lunch. The tires haven't been off the rims in weeks—I'm positive. And that means we draw a blank."

"You draw a slug in the chest!" said a voice from behind the car.

Smooth turned and saw Black staring at him over the sights of a heavy automatic. The chauffeur was standing near the rear right fender and a few hundred yards behind him Smooth saw a rickety coupé parked at the roadside. Black's eyes were darting from Smooth to Gilda as though he were trying to make up his mind who was to be the first. The gun was rock steady and Smooth realized the man was a killer.

"Where did you come from, baby dear?" laughed Gilda. She was seated in the rear of the car, looking at Black through the open window.

"Shut up!" he barked. "A smart pair of punks, eh? Didn't know enough to keep your snoots out of trouble. Well, you ain't the first that tried to learn too much."

"Take it easy," stalled Smooth. "You win! But you can't hate us for wantin' to know the set-up. If we're jackin' stuff over the line, we're facin' a Federal rap. That means plenty years in stir—and, mister, I want to know what I'm up against."

"You find out—right now!" growled Black and leveled the gun barrel.

Smooth saw the tiny muscles in Black's jaw tighten. He saw the man brace himself and he knew that his number was up. This man was a killer and he enjoyed his work. Those telltale signs—a tightening of the jaw a slight crouch, wide eyes and a sharp intake of breath—Smooth had never known them to fail. He tilted forward on his toes to take the blast and hoped he might drive the ice pick into a soft spot before the lights went out. Gilda was a swell kid—too beautiful to die. And if he didn't make the grade with the pick, she was next!

"Start blastin'—rat!" he said, and leaped forward.

THE SHARP BARK of an automatic cracked across the hills, doubling and echoing in the distance. Once—twice—then two more shots that seemed to blend into one. Smooth jerked the pick toward Black's throat and drove forward, stiff-armed.

His hand slid past into empty air. Black's knees buckled and he jerked sideways as though a baseball bat had landed against the side of his head. He was down—sprawled flat on his face.

Smooth was carried past him by the force of his jab. He twisted and fought to regain his balance. He looked at the car window and saw Gilda pointing a tiny blue automatic at the silent form of the chauffeur. A wisp of smoke curled upward.

"Turn him over!" she snapped. "He may need another!"

"He's through," said Smooth after one hasty glance. "You rang the bell that time, Beautiful. Nice peggin'—but how come that gun? Don't you know you can't take a rod into Mexico?"

"So they told me. But I notice Black was hard of hearing, too. Besides, those guards look too nice to pat a lady on the chest. C'mon, Handsome—let's go places before the peasants start asking questions."

Smooth climbed in behind the wheel. He swung the car about and headed for the main road. It was slow going through the dust, but when he turned into the macadam highway he stepped down on the gas and sat back, waiting for speed.

He saw the pointer of the speedometer rise through a quarter arc and stop at fifty. His foot was hard against the floor boards and the road was level, but the car refused to do any better.

"Whatta junk heap!" he grunted. "Fifty on the level and about ten up a hill. And that guy was supposed to be a mechanic!"

"Talk nice to the motor," said Gilda. "Croon to it, or something. Maybe it's sick. Or maybe we dropped a few cylinders on one of the turns."

Smooth slammed down on the brakes. The car slid to a screaming stop and he vaulted from the seat. He jerked up the cover of the tool box, grabbed a wrench and stepped forward. A wave of heat drifted up from the motor as he threw back the hood and he waited for it to dissipate.

"What the—" gasped Gilda. "Are you nuts?"

"I was," he laughed. "But you fixed that. Whatta gal!"

"It must be the heat. Don't tell me I have another lunatic on my hands. What gives?"

"You called it, Beautiful. That crack about the cylinders—I must have been napping. Now just watch what little Smooth has to show you."

He fitted the wrench to a spark plug and twisted it out of the motor head. The hot metal seared his fingers, but he was laughing when he hurried back to the tool box and located a long piece of flexible wire. With this, he probed into the cylinder, twisting and turning the wire until he located the piston head.

"Get into the front seat, Gilda," he said. "Tap the starter with your toe—not hard—just a touch."

She stared at him as though wondering if the heat and the excitement had affected his mind. But his easy grin assured her and with a doubtful shake of her head she did as he asked.

SMOOTH PRESSED DOWN on the wire as the motor jerked and he cursed silently when he felt the piston slide down into the cylinders.

"No luck!" he snapped. "Stay where you are a minute!"

"This is a hell of a time to tune a motor, Handsome," said Gilda. "If you want to play mechanic, why not wait until we're back in San Diego?"

"Don't rush me, just sit pretty and watch me pull a rabbit out of this hat—I hope."

He set the wrench on another plug and spun it clear. Again he inserted the wire and felt for the piston top. He nodded and Gilda tapped the starter button again.

The motor jerked, but the wire did not move. He nodded again. Gilda held her foot on the starter until the motor had made a few revolutions. Still there was no movement in the cylinder.

"I'm right!" shouted Smooth. "I called the turn, Beautiful!"

"You're screwy as a dodo," she snapped. "But if you'll put that two-bit motor together again and get out of here, I promise not to feed you to the squirrels."

"Listen and learn," he laughed. "This cylinder is blanked off. There's no piston in it and the bottom is sealed off. There's a lid covering the top of it and I'll bet the walls are lined with asbestos. Does that mean anything to you?"

"Not a thing. It sounds like the answer to a cross-word puzzle."

"Nothing to it. This crate is a twelve cylinder job. My guess is that six of the cylinders are blanks—nice round little cells in the motor block. And in each of these we're going to find a can of hop. When Black pulled into the garage at Tijuana, he yanked off the motor head, packed the dead cylinders with junk and bolted the head on again. In San Diego he unloads them—and there you are!"

"Yeah, here we are. And half of us is just about due for a nervous breakdown. Congratulations, mister—now let's scram!"

Smooth twisted the spark plugs back into place, hooked up the ignition wires and dropped the hood. He was whistling happily when he sent the car humming along toward the border and seemed to have forgotten those few bad moments with Black on the back road.

THERE WAS A cursory examination by the United States

Smooth saw that he was trapped

Customs inspectors when they crossed the line, and Smooth headed along the waterfront that led up the coast.

"Now what?" asked Gilda.

"Los Angeles—in a hurry. I'm going to park you in a hotel for a while and we'll grab a plane back to New York tomorrow."

"Isn't that too, too divine?" said Gilda sarcastically. "I arrive in California with two suitcases full of clothes and a yen to see the Golden West. Two days later I'm on my way to New York minus the clothes and with nothing to show for my trip but two extra freckles on my nose."

"Don't forget the diamond, Beautiful," laughed Smooth. "When Rudd hears what we have to tell him, he'll want to give you the Junker or the Kohinoor, at least. Don't you realize that this puts Spanish out of business?"

"I don't get it. How?"

"Take it easy. You'll find out."

HE SWUNG IN from the waterfront at Long Beach and

threaded his way through the afternoon traffic of Los Angeles. Gilda said nothing when he stopped at a hotel and helped her from the car. And there was a cynical smile upon her face when he left her seated in the lobby and stepped into the manager's office.

Smooth explained his disheveled appearance to the manager, showed credentials that established his identity as an agent of the Bureau of Narcotics, and asked for a small suite. Within five minutes he and Gilda were escorted to a pleasant apartment on the eighth floor and Smooth put through a long distance call to New York.

"How come?" asked Gilda. "We look like a couple of gypsies, no baggage, you've got half of Mexico smeared on your nose, and we get the best in the house. Are you a magician, Smooth?"

"The manager and I used to play marbles together," he said. "Stop asking questions and I'll let you listen in on an interesting talk." The phone bell rang and he nodded toward the instrument. "That ought to be Rudd."

He lit a cigarette, motioned Gilda to sit beside him and held the receiver away from his ear that she might hear both ends of the conversation.

"Smooth talking—that you Rudd?"

"Yes—what's up?"

"We've got the goods on the delivery system—enough for a dozen pinches. I'm sorry to have to crack down so soon, but we had a little accident that forced our hand."

Gilda smiled and kissed Smooth lightly on the ear. He shook his head and winked, and his lips formed the words, "Shut up!"

"Nice work," said Rudd. "Think you can pass it along to the Feds without getting into trouble?"

"Easy! I'll tell 'em I got moved into the job without knowing what was on the fire—and that's on the level. I'll make a deal. They get the information and I scram. Right with you?"

"Yes. How about this end?"

"They'll take care of that. You sit quiet for a few days until the storm blows over. We're coming back on tomorrow's plane."

"Fine, partner. I'll be seeing you."

There was a click and Smooth grinned at the silent receiver.

"He doesn't waste many words, eh, Gilda?"

"He called you partner—and that's something," she said. "Smooth, if you play your cards right, you'll be in the big money soon. Rudd can make you a millionaire in six months if he wants to. That means yachts, servants, cars— all the things that money can buy. And with a bankroll, you'll be forgetting all about little me."

"It's going to be hard to forget the look on Black's face just before you shot me out of that jam. No, Gilda—I won't forget you—even if this bubble pops in a way you don't expect."

"I wish I'd known you longer," she said slowly. "At times I think I have you right—then there's a change and I feel thousands of miles away from you. You're different—sort of, oh—mysterious is the only word I can think of. When I expect you to make love to me, you laugh. And when—"

"When you expect me to laugh, I make love, eh?"

"No—damn it! That's just the trouble. You don't!"

"Just playing hard to get," he laughed and pinched her ear. "Make yourself comfortable while I get some of the mud off me. I'm going to make a social call on the cops."

"Please be careful, Smooth. The California jails are not so good, I've heard. And these cops out here play marbles for keeps—they actually think gangsters belong in jail."

"They're foolish," he said, and headed for the bathroom. "They'll never get rich that way."

17

SAN DIEGO COUP

IT WAS AFTER office hours when Smooth entered the building that housed the district office of the Bureau of Narcotics, but Martensen was still seated at his desk. He pointed to a chair near him, pushed aside a pile of papers that had held his attention and leaned back to hear Smooth's report.

He tapped lightly with a pencil tip against the desk top as Smooth quickly sketched out his activities and he smiled his approval when he heard how the hiding place in the motor had been located.

"Where's the car now?" he asked.

"At the hotel garage. The hotel manager detailed two house detectives to watch it."

"I'm sorry Black had to be killed," said Martensen. "That means we've got to move fast. I'll have men cover the border towns immediately. Let's see... Douglas, El Paso, Eagle Pass, Laredo and Brownsville... a nice set of contacts. It's fairly certain the gang operates the same way at all these points, and there must be cars that collect the supply at each town. Well, we'll take care of that!"

"What about the house in San Diego?" asked Smooth. "How do you want to handle it?"

"I'll send some men there with you. Put the car in the garage and see if the stuff is picked up. Those contact points cover a spread of about fifteen hundred miles along the border, and they may be shipping the stuff along every day or two." He reached for the phone and barked a number, then turned back to Smooth. "Make a list of as many of Spanish's mob as you know of. I'll get a call through to McNeary and have him pick them up. We'll get in touch with the Mexican authorities—they're expecting a call from me—and they'll crack down on the outfit that's working over the line."

"Looks like a busy night," said Smooth, and started to write as Martensen gave low-voiced orders over the wire.

One after another he listed the men he could recall as having been in the employ of Spanish. For a moment he thought of putting Lucky Carmine on the list, but dismissed the idea with a smile. Lucky was close to Spanish, probably a very good friend. But that was all there was to it. Lucky was too busy dragging nickels and dimes from the streets of the Big Town to get mixed up in a deal like this.

Smooth remembered the quick look of displeasure that had come to Theresa's eyes when he had suggested that Lucky go to the coast with him. No, thought Smooth, that girl was too clever to let Lucky jeopardize his freedom for the sake of a few quick dollars. Both she and Lucky were looking forward to the time when they could leave Broadway behind them and buy that farm in the country that seemed to have become an obsession with them.

Smooth made no mention of either Lucky or Theresa, but he made a mental note to visit them at some time in the future and tell them of the trade at which he was working. They'd probably laugh and maybe that antagonistic gleam would leave Theresa's eyes.

"Guess this is all," he said, and passed the list to Martensen. "McNeary will know where to pick them up and when you grab this bunch out here, you'll be able to make the case airtight. These punks will talk—they'll yell their heads off, looking for a light term."

"They better," said Martensen grimly. "Now get out of here. You've given me a job of work that will keep me up all night. You'll find three men at the garage, waiting for you—Tom Graley, Fred Gold and Joe Keit—you may remember them."

"Sure I do. Worked with them a few years ago and they're a swell gang."

"Graley and Gold will follow the car that picks up that stuff. You and Keit take care of the house servants. Get going!"

SMOOTH BORROWED A gun and left the office. He stopped at a phone booth, called Gilda and told her to get a good night's sleep and to expect him in the morning. She asked a few questions, but he convinced her he was not in trouble.

Joe Keit was standing near the car in the garage and shook hands with Smooth with a firmness that set his shoulder jumping. He pointed to Graley and Gold seated in a roadster at the curb and they nodded and winked.

"Let's roll," said Smooth, and swung the car out into the street. "San Diego is a hundred and thirty miles away and we've got to be there when the collector arrives."

"And I hope this is the night," added Keit.

During the trip along the coast Smooth explained the set-up. When they stopped for gas, Keit got into the roadster and relayed the story to Gold and Graley. Then they rolled along the smooth highway leading into San Diego and reached the house near the park shortly before midnight. The roadster stopped a few hundred yards from the house and Keit followed Smooth down the walk while the others waited outside.

"Keep your fingers crossed," said Smooth. "If we're late, Martensen is going to swear we stopped for a drink on the way. And when I get east, McNeary will scalp me."

"What happens first?"

"Anything," laughed Smooth, and rang the bell.

The Jap opened the door, stared fixedly at Smooth and seemed about to close it again when he saw Keit standing beside him.

"Where Missa Black?" he asked.

"Burning," said Smooth, and jabbed his gun in the Jap's stomach. "You wanna burn, too?"

"Hiiii! Me very nice person. No shoot, kindly!"

"Shut up and get inside!" ordered Smooth. He jerked his gun toward the Jap and Keit lifted an automatic from the man's shoulder holster. "Very nice person, eh?"

"You police?" squealed the Jap. "Me know very little. Can say nothing—very sorry."

"Police!" grunted Smooth. "Don't kid yourself. Take him down the cellar and shoot him, Keit."

"Why not?" said Keit quietly, and shrugged. "C'mon, Yellow Boy!"

"You not police?" cackled the Jap. "Oh! That very much different. You tough persons, eh? No shoot—me talk!"

"The wisdom of the Orient," laughed Smooth. "Okay, feller—when does the pickup car arrive?"

"Very quick, now. Maybe two, three minutes. Come every three day."

"Whatta break! How about the cook and the maid—they here?"

"Sleep home—get here early in morning. Me very much alone, yes, sir!"

"Get out and drive that car into the garage," ordered Smooth. "When the other car gets here, tell 'em Black is sick and couldn't get any more for them this trip. Hurry!" He turned to Keit and motioned toward the door. "Keep an eye on him and if those birds' get here within five minutes let me know. I'll be in the garage."

He hurried out of the back door and sprinted to the garage. A heavy padlock held the doors closed and he was forced to wait until the Jap drove up with the car. One of the keys opened the lock and while the car was rolled into place, he made a hasty survey of the small building.

"Know where the junk is?" he asked.

"Very sorry—never come in here. Missa Black say, 'Keep outta here or get shoot in belly.' I keep out!"

A SET OF steel lockers near a work bench opened to another of the keys on Black's ring. Smooth found a number of uniforms and two pairs of shoes in one. Behind the clothing was a fully loaded Tommy gun that he appropriated thankfully. On the floor of the other locker was a square metal box in which Smooth found what he was after. He glanced hurriedly at the cans of narcotics, closed and locked the box and shut the locker door.

"Remember, feller," he said, and prodded the Jap lightly

with the Tommy gun. "I'll be watching you from the house. When your visitors arrive, give 'em the keys and tell 'em to take the stuff that's in the box. And this baby is gonna make you *awfully* sorry if you get too smart."

"Me very dumb—most very dumb person."

"Glad to hear it," said Smooth, and crossed the yard to the rear entrance of the house.

He found a window in the kitchen that gave him a perfect view of the interior of the garage and settled down comfortably with the gun across his knees. Less than a quarter hour had passed when he heard the squeal of rubber in the street and two men walked quickly across the yard. Both were dressed in dark clothing and both carried suitcases. When the light from the garage illuminated their features Smooth recognized one as a man wanted in New York for bank robbery.

He noticed the hands of both go to their pockets when they saw the Jap and he heard the house boy quickly explaining Black's absence. There was a low-voiced argument and the sound of metal against concrete. Smooth knew the narcotics were being transferred to the suitcases and that the Jap's story had gone across. When the garage light went out, Smooth slipped the barrel of the Tommy gun across the window sill and waited.

The two men with bags walked quickly along the driveway, but he paid no attention to them. He wanted that Jap but he suddenly realized if the Jap made a break, a burst from the gun would warn the gangsters that something was wrong. He knew Joe Keit was in the alley, watching the men. And Joe would burn them down if things went wrong. But that was not the schedule laid out by

Martensen and Smooth knew better than to upset the plans of the chief.

He hurried quietly from the back door and ran to the garage. There was no moon and the yard was a patch of darkness out of which rose the darker walls of the garage. The doors were open and as Smooth reached them a silent form crept past the corner of the building and headed for the adjoining yard.

Smooth was after him in an instant. A thorn hedge surrounded the property, but the Jap seemed to melt through it. Smooth tried to follow through the narrow opening and felt a dozen prickly barbs sink into his legs and arms. He cursed the hedge and the man who had planted it, wrenched free and swung the barrel of the gun at the man ahead of him. He missed, sprinted across the yard after the flying Jap and swung again.

This time the steel of the gun barrel whacked against bone and the Jap went down. The chase had been soundless and Smooth thanked the little brown man for keeping his thoughts to himself in his attempted break. A single shout would have warned the gangsters but it would also have ended the Jap's career in a burst of lead.

SMOOTH LIFTED HIM, swung him across his shoulder and carried him into the house. A few moments later Keit joined him and grinned at the unconscious Jap.

"Very nice person got tough, eh?" he said.

"Very nice person wanted to go places," said Smooth. "How about the others? Did you get the car number and a description?"

"Yeah. Shall I pass it along to Martensen in case Gold and Graley lose them?"

"Yes, do that. I'll bet he's got a half dozen men scattered around San Diego waiting to go."

Smooth tied the Jap securely to a chair while Keit put through the call. When he had finished, he went to Gilda's room and packed her clothes. He was starting to put his own away when Keit called him and handed him the phone.

"Martensen wants you," he said.

"Hello, chief," said Smooth into the instrument. "What's up?"

"McNeary says your joy ride is over. He wants you back East. Keit will stay there and take care of things—I'll send a man out to help him. You catch the plane tomorrow—I mean *today*—it's morning now."

"Nice guy, McNeary," laughed Smooth. "Never a dull moment when you're working for him. Okay—tell the slavedriver I'm on my way."

He hung up, thumbed his nose at Keit and finished his packing.

18

NEW YORK AGAIN

GILDA WAS HAVING breakfast in her room when Smooth arrived at the Trayton. She looked in surprise at the bell boy who stood behind him with both arms full of suitcases. But she asked no questions and when Smooth tipped the boy and dismissed him, she refilled her coffee cup and handed It to him.

"Here—drink this," she said. "You look like an accident going somewhere to happen. Sit down and rest your frame while I order you some breakfast."

Smooth swallowed the coffee and stretched out on the lounge. Gilda was a peach. She knew just the right things to do and when not to talk. He watched her as she gave the breakfast order over the phone and he realized how much she had done for him on this trip west. There had not been a time when he needed her that she had not come through. He wondered what twisted circumstances had placed her in a position where Rudd could call upon her and expect her to do as he asked without question. Was it merely greed—the desire for money and all the things it could buy?

Smooth studied her through half closed lids. Her hair had been hastily brushed and at times a soft curl drifted across her cheek. Even at this hour of the morning her eyes were bright and alive and he noticed that although she had not yet applied her make-up her skin was smooth and clear. He had come to look for and enjoy the faintly mocking smile that accompanied her words—the slight lift of her head when she was pleased at anything he might have said—the pouting lips and twitched nose that meant she was displeased. They had both laughed when he called it "making snoots at him" and she had promised to reserve it for his benefit alone.

When she caught him watching her she crossed the room and seated herself beside him on the lounge. She loosened the knot in his tie, rearranged a pillow behind his head and tweaked his nose.

"Penny for your thoughts," she said.

"They're worth more, but I'll sell out cheap," he answered, and caught both her hands in one of his. "I was wondering how you ever got into the racket—and why you stay. Want to tell me?"

FOR AN INSTANT her eyes hardened. She stared at him silently; a long, questioning look full of the wisdom of woman. Then she smiled and laid her cheek against his for a moment, brushing her hair across his eyes.

"Are you really interested, Smooth—or just—just curious?"

"I'd like to know—but save it if you'd rather."

"I want to tell you," she said. "I want you to like me, so I'll give myself the best of it. Even at that I'm hard—hard as hell. I don't trust men, Smooth—any of 'em—even you. So far you're the most regular fellow I've come across, but I'm still waiting for that sock in the chin that always seems to come sooner or later. I won't like you any the less when it arrives—I'll be expecting it and I'll make allowances for the fact that you're only a man."

"This doesn't sound like the Gilda I know," said Smooth.

"It's the real Gilda. The small town kid that won a beauty contest and was given a part in a Broadway production. What a kicking around I got! The belle of Main Street trying to outsmart Broadway. Have a laugh, Smooth. Inside of a month I went overboard for a cloak and suiter with more money than I had dreamed was in circulation. It was the same old merry-go-round—dinners, diamonds and dancing. Then the well known hokum about a home of my own.

"Sure, I went for it. What kid wouldn't? And it was one hell of a jolt to find there just wasn't going to be any wedding because there was already a Mrs. Cloak and Suiter and a flock of little Cloak and Suiters somewhere in West-chester. In fact, that was the first jolt. The second came when I put up a squawk and found that his best pal was backing the show I was in. And I was out of work. Old stuff, eh?"

"Old to a New York hackman," said Smooth. "But sort of new and raw to that kid from the small town. Sometime let me meet that guy—I could work up an easy hate for him."

"You're a bit late, pal," smiled Gilda. "I found a man to do that little thing for me. His name was Rudd—still is for that matter. He caught me on the rebound when I was frothing at the mouth and howling for evens. He broke the former boy friend, as a favor to me. Then he did a few more favors and like a sap I still thought a 'thank you' covered everything. I learned, though, when he needed a good looking blonde to steer a few saps into one of his gambling joints, I was the blonde.

"When he closed his place and started to make book I was still useful, but I will say for Rudd that he always pays off. He grins when I fall for a new number, but he digs up a job for me when the inevitable kick arrives. Some of the jobs are messy—like this one—but a gal has to live."

"I've heard of gals working," said Smooth quietly.

"Don't give me that! Not when they get used to nice clothes and champagne, and have nothing to offer but looks. And don't tell me I'm going to wind up behind the eight ball—I know it!"

THE WAITER ARRIVED with Smooth's breakfast and Gilda told him to place the table near the lounge. When he started to open the eggs she tipped him and waved him out of the room. She drew up a chair, poured more coffee and seemed to enjoy playing housewife. Smooth tore into the breakfast with all the enjoyment of a man who had missed his previous meal and said little until Gilda passed him a lit cigarette.

"Want to hear all about the tip-off?" he asked, wisely making no reference to Gilda's story. Smooth also knew when to keep his mouth shut about certain things.

"I was wondering when you would get around to that," she said. "But first, when do we go east?"

"There's a 3:30 plane out of Glendale this afternoon that gets into Newark at 9:45 in the morning. That's us, Beautiful."

She threw a roll at him and swung her suitcases up onto the bed. When she opened the lids and saw the manner in which Smooth had packed them, she started after another roll, but he lifted his hands in protest.

"Nix! It was a scramble," he laughed. "And I'm not so hot at packing, anyway."

"What a mess!" she said, and emptied them on the bed. "I'll repack and you talk. Give me the best parts and tell me the rest on the plane. Then you can catch up with a little sleep while I see what the beauty parlors have to offer in this town."

Smooth had arranged a plausible story to cover his night's activities and he rolled it off with the ease of a hackman telling of a five-dollar call. At times Gilda interrupted him with a pertinent question and Smooth was never quite certain that his yarn was getting across. When he finished, he dropped his butt into a coffee cup, yawned and headed for the adjoining room.

"Quite a night, eh?" he asked.

"Grand!" she said. "This little pleasure trip has added ten years to my life. The land of sunshine and flowers—nuts! I'll take New York—you don't have to drive halfway across a desert to get shot at there. The boys are more considerate of your feelings—they pick a nice dark alley."

THE AFTERNOON PLANE swept Smooth and Gilda up into a cloudless sky and winged them across the mountain peaks. Desert and plains fell away behind them as the silver ship droned on across the continent. They banked and circled into Albuquerque and then on to Kansas City; a few moments at Chicago and a light breakfast in the clouds. The air was crisp and cool when they landed at the Newark airport and Gilda stood for a moment on the runway breathing deeply, her face turned toward the morning sun.

"New York in October," she said. It's the top!"

"You sound as though you'd been with Byrd to the Antarctic," laughed Smooth. "Five days ago you were standing here singing 'California Here I Come'—now you're acting like an immigrant."

"I feel as though I'd been gone a year. Look!" she said, and pointed to the tower of the Empire State Building, dim in the distance. "They cheer about their mountains at the coast, but they didn't build 'em. That pile of rocks over there—we *built* that!"

"Yeah! *We!* Ironworkers from Pennsylvania, stone setters from Brooklyn, carpenters from Indiana, painters from Colorado and—oh, hell! We're a great gang of New Yorkers, all right. I hear they located a fellow working on Broadway who'd been born in the Big Town and they shipped him up to the Museum."

"Listen to Mr. Broadway!" she laughed. "Soon as he gets a whiff of home he starts weeping. Now suppose you sling those bags in a cab and tell me where we go from here."

"Home, Beautiful—at least, that's where you're going. Meet me at Rudd's place tonight and collect that stone you earned. I'll give you a build-up that should be worth twenty karats."

"And how about you?"

"Oh, I'll scout around and see what's happening, grab a shave and a meal and see you this evening."

When the taxi swung down the midtown ramp of the West Side viaduct and turned east, Smooth directed the driver to stop at Eighth Avenue and Fiftieth Street. He lifted his bags from the cab, turned and held his hand out to Gilda.

"I'll be seein' you."

"Don't be so distant," she answered. She caught his hand and drew him toward her, tilted his chin and kissed him. "After all, the plane tickets read—Mr. & Mrs. Kyle."

"I wonder if Spanish realized what an expensive trip that was going to be?"

"When the word gets out that you framed him, it's liable to be expensive for you, too," she warned.

He closed the door and watched as the cab swept out into the crosstown traffic. He crossed the avenue, stepped into a taxi parked at the corner and told the driver to go north. At a drug store he called McNeary, told him he would see him later in the day and then went on to his hotel.

A FEW HOURS' sleep and the luxury of a shower and shave helped to dispel the accumulated weariness of the past few days. When Smooth rapped at the door of McNeary's suite he looked little the worse for wear and was even able to accept the Chief's hardy handshake without wincing.

"Come in and sit down," said McNeary. "Make yourself comfortable because you're goin' to get hell."

"I expected that, but will it wait until I ask a question?"

"Oh, she's all right! I told her you were going to be here this evening and I expect to see her any minute. She's a good girl, Smooth—has the makings of a fine operator. Thanks to her I think we'll get enough on Rudd to send him away for a long stretch."

"That's swell! Now I feel better and I'm ready for that bawling out. What's wrong?"

Smooth seated himself, hooked the toe of his shoe beneath the seat of a near-by chair and drew it towards him. He folded his legs across it, lit a cigarette and faced the Chief. McNeary was pacing nervously about the room, both hands deep in his hip pockets and his lower lip clenched tightly between his teeth. It seemed to Smooth that the Chief had aged years in the past few days. His eyes were deep in their sockets, bloodshot and restless. His movements were quick and irritable. And when he spoke there was a rasp in his voice.

"Martensen has done some splendid work along the border," he said. "I was talking to him this morning on the phone and he seems to have clicked all along the line. El Paso was the main drop.* They trailed that car out of San Diego and picked the men up at a hotel in El Paso. The mob was using the same racket all across the border— dummy cylinders—and they grabbed five cars. Martensen tells me they've got twenty-five men and six women and he thinks they've cleaned up that part of the ring."

"Great!" said Smooth. "Where's the kick?"

"There is none so far as the west coast divisions are concerned. But you certainly put us in a tough spot here in the East. I wasn't quite ready to crack down on Big Spanish, but I *had* to take him. That list you forwarded through Martensen helped and I had a few names to add to it. But you may remember that Big Spanish had been watching me. As a matter of fact, the day you reported for work here in New York, Vince Cartwright was keeping an eye on me. Still it was difficult and slow work dodging them. I was

---

* A drop is a central point where supplies of illicit liquor or narcotics are deposited for trans-shipment.

building a nice case. But I wasn't quite ready, and when the break came I think we missed a few."

"And that means," added Smooth, "that New York isn't going to be a healthy spot for me. Spanish will pass the word along that I crossed him and the boys'll be wearing out plenty of shoe leather looking for little Smooth."

"I know it," snapped McNeary. "Your chances in this town are about a hundred to one and I intend to detail two men to work with you until this case is cleaned up."

"Nursemaids, eh?" grinned Smooth. "Nothing doin'!"

The phone rang and McNeary jerked the receiver from the hook.

"Yes?" he barked. "Oh! Come up, I'm expecting you."

HE TURNED TO Smooth and nodded. And it seemed that some of the tension was gone from his voice when he spoke again.

"Guess we'll have to postpone that bawling out. That was Dorothy."

"Lord love her!" laughed Smooth. "Always getting me out of a jam. But before she gets here, suppose I tell you why we had to move so quickly."

"Martensen said there was a killing, but he had so many other things to tell me I couldn't get all the details. What happened?"

"A fellow by the name of Black was fronting as the chauffeur in San Diego. He was a tough customer—a killer. He happened to catch up with me when I was looking for the junk and would have spread me all over Mexico if Gilda hadn't—"

There was a light tap on the door and Smooth left his story unfinished. He crossed the room, opened the door and stood silently admiring the girl in the hall. Dorothy extended both hands, took his and held them, and her eyes seemed to catch fire as she looked at him.

"Smooth! You old fraud! You've had us worried to death. What on earth were you doing at the coast?"

"He's about half finished telling me," said McNeary. "Sit down, Dorothy, and listen to the rest of it." He turned to Smooth and nodded. "All right—what happened when Black held a gun on you in Mexico?"

"That'll keep, Chief," said Smooth uneasily. "Give me a chance to say hello to our new agent. Let's see—beautiful eyes, soft brown hair, lovely teeth—"

"Save that until later," said McNeary. "I want to hear about this trip."

"Yes, Smooth," added Dorothy. "Did Gilda vamp you?"

"Gilda is a grand kid," said Smooth seriously. "When Black had me dead to rights she cracked down on him and rang the bell. She's a regular all the way and if it hadn't been for her I'd never have put it across out there."

"Don't get romantic, Smooth," warned McNeary. "Gilda Garland is one of Rudd's mob. She may have helped you out of a tough spot when she thought you were working for him, but if she knew you were a Fed she'd turn that gun on you just as quickly."

"I doubt it, Chief. Gilda isn't that sort."

"Of course not," said Dorothy. "Nobody understands her—is that it, Smooth?"

"Oh, all right! She's a crook and a killer and she runs with a mob—*but*, I'd be a number in a Mexican cemetery if she wasn't handy with a gun."

McNeary winked knowingly to Dorothy and it seemed

to Smooth that her answering smile was slightly forced. He was human enough to enjoy this slight touch of jealousy and to be greatly flattered by it. He realized that McNeary had been wise in forcing the issue by making him tell the story before Dorothy. The Chief had just one concern and that was a smooth working organization. Half truths and mysteries were sure to cause friction and McNeary meant to keep his division in good shape.

"So Black's death forced your hand, eh?" said McNeary. "Well, I suppose it couldn't be helped, but it left us with a few loose ends. We've rounded up most of the distributors, but I know we haven't located the brains of the outfit. These men we've picked up are the usual mobsters—just run of the mill stuff. The real head of the organization is still laughing at us."

"How do you figure that?" asked Smooth.

"Easily! When we grabbed Big Spanish and started an investigation of his holdings we found they were all operated by corporations with dummy members. We traced down the officers and found them to be clerks and minor employees in each enterprise. We knew Spanish was backing the show that Dorothy works in, but when he was picked up we couldn't prove it."

"In other words, we only got the small timers," said Smooth. "But we did break up the distributing system and they have no source of supply. That helps a little."

McNEARY SHOOK HIS head in disgust and kicked fretfully a table leg. He walked to a window and stared thoughtfully at the street below. Smooth grinned at Dorothy like a school boy who has been reprimanded by the teacher and she stuck her tongue out at him by way of reply.

Without realizing it, Smooth found himself comparing her to Gilda. Both had a delightful sense of humor but there was no suggestion of that worldly hardness about Dorothy that characterized Gilda. Although Dorothy had been in show business for years, she had not acquired the cold veneer that Broadway usually spreads about its people. There was a certain naivete—a pleasing simplicity that set her apart from other girls Smooth had known, and it puzzled him.

By a peculiar quirk in the scheme of things, both girls had killed a man to save Smooth's life. It had shocked Dorothy—left her with a memory that would trouble her for years. To Gilda, it had been part of the day's work, part of the job she was being paid to do. Smooth remembered her words at the time—"Turn him over—he may need another!" It made him stiffen a trifle to recall them. Yes, Gilda was hard—hard and cold as ice.

McNeary broke him from his reverie with a sharp-voiced question.

"When do you see Rudd?"

"Later this evening," Smooth answered. "Any particular line you want me to follow?"

"Yes. Use him to locate the rest of Spanish's mob. It's a cinch that Big Spanish will blame this pinch on Rudd. And if the brains of the Spanish outfit are still running loose, it's only a question of time before they crack down. Rudd must realize that and he'll want to mop up—clean out the whole gang." McNeary laughed, a nervous, strained laugh that told of sleepless nights. "We'll be glad to cooperate with him!"

"What has Rudd told you, Dorothy?" asked Smooth.

"I think he likes me—more than he would want you to know. Of course he's been the perfect gentleman, but, oh!—I don't know how to explain it—it's just something a woman senses."

"I'll be damned!" said Smooth. "I hadn't expected that."

"Why not?" barked McNeary. "It's the oldest racket in the world. Rudd's a shrewd operator. He knows the human equation—he's probably used it all through his gambling career. He dangled Gilda before your eyes, knowing that no matter how smart a man may be he's always stupid enough to say the wrong things to an interesting woman. It's a twenty to one shot that right at this minute she's telling him all the little confidences you passed along to her. For instance—how you asked her what started her in the racket, and suggested that she quit and be a good little girl." He stopped his pacing and stood squarely before Smooth, staring down at him. "Do I call the turn?"

SMOOTH GRINNED RATHER foolishly. All the many things he had heard of McNeary's shrewdness came back to him. This man had an uncanny way of knowing the workings of other people's minds. He was known as a soulless machine—a man-hunter. His life was a series of battles against narcotic rings and in these fights, he used every trick at the command of his well trained mind. In dealing with criminals he was as pitiless and mechanical as a microscope. He considered it his duty to exterminate them and he did it.

He considered his agents as parts of a machine. He had no sympathy with a man who allowed his personal feelings to weaken the structure of that machine. And more than one agent had been curtly dismissed from the service for allowing, as McNeary put it—"his heart to interfere with his mind."

"I don't think I've made any mistakes," said Smooth at length. "Gilda thinks I'm up to my neck in the racket."

"Let her keep on thinking that way," snapped McNeary. He turned to Dorothy and laid his hand upon her shoulder. "As for you—*be a woman!* Be smart! Rudd is an old hand at this game. He'll play up to you, and because he thinks you're interested in Smooth, he'll play Gilda against you. Even though he trusts both of you, it will be to his advantage to break up this combination. The result would be that he'll have both of you watching the other and reporting to him."

"I think I can take care of my part of the job," said Dorothy, and she turned her eyes slowly toward Smooth. "And I don't think you have to worry about my partner. I only caught a glimpse of Gilda at the theater, but she seems old enough to be a mother to him."

"Meeow!" said Smooth.

"That'll be all of that!" barked McNeary. "Dorothy—tell Smooth what Rudd has been saying."

"He took me to Joe Silva's place the other night. It's a magnificent penthouse on Central Park West and I've never seen such an elaborate gambling layout before in my life. Rudd has a piece of it and now they're using it as a distribution center for narcotics. Only the wealthy trade, naturally."

"Nice work," said Smooth. "But have you any idea how he gets his supplies?"

"No—none at all. But I understand he's using quite a few of his men to break in on Spanish's old territory. You know the ones I mean—the men who used to work with him taking bets on the horses. Tout Ender handles them and keeps them supplied."

"Have you met anybody by the name of Yitz Cohen or Hoegy Bright?"

"No. Rudd talked to Cohen last night over the phone—said something about a full moon, but I couldn't get much of it."

"He did?" shouted Smooth, and jumped to his feet. "That's all I want to know. It checks with what I've been thinking." He turned to McNeary and grinned. "I know where I'm heading now, Chief. We'll wrap Rudd up in a hurry."

"Yeah," said McNeary, and for the first time there was a trace of a smile on his face. "I get it. They're working the old gag again. All right, Smooth—it's up to you."

Smooth nodded and walked to the door. He paused for a moment to grasp Dorothy by the elbow and shake it lightly.

"Will I see you at Rudd's place after the show?" he asked.

"Yes, about midnight."

"Great! Tell Rudd we had lunch together—he'll expect it. And—look out for the big bad gambler."

"Get out, you clown!" she laughed and closed the door.

19

TWO WOMEN

IT WAS AFTER ten o'clock when Smooth was admitted to Rudd's apartment by Simpson, the butler. He found the gambler seated behind his desk in the library and with him was Yitz Cohen. Both men grinned when Smooth entered and Cohen crossed the room to shake his hand.

"Nice work, feller!" he said. "Whatta cleanup you started! They're gonna have to build new jails to hold all the customers when the Feds get finished with Big Spanish's mob. Pretty goin'!"

"Yes, Smooth," added Rudd. "It was the smoothest piece of work I've seen in a long while. But then—Smooth is the name, eh?"

"Toss the bouquets to Gilda," said Smooth. "She's a wonder. The way she took Jordan over the hurdles was a work of art. All I had to do was sit back and coast along. Then when the break came, I tipped the Feds. Yeah, it was fast, but don't forget, Rudd, when we play with the Treasury Department, we're playing with dynamite."

"I've been thinking of that," said Rudd. "They may keep an eye on you for a while. Want to scram out of the country for a rest? You sure earned one."

Smooth walked to the window and stared off into space

as though in thought. He had spoken about the Federals because a man with the shrewdness that Rudd possessed would certainly have thought of that angle. It was only natural to suppose the Federal agents would watch a man who had been working for Big Spanish, even though he had tipped them off to a fine catch.

Smooth tried to clear his mind of the idea that he was working for the Bureau of Narcotics. How would he act if he were in reality a gangster in the employ of Rudd? Would he take that vacation? No—that wasn't the answer. The Feds wouldn't be fooled by the temporary disappearance. In fact, they'd immediately start a search for him, thinking that some member of Spanish's mob had acted in reprisal.

"That won't do," he said aloud. "They'd wonder where I was gettin' the dough to pay expenses. The smart move for me is to go back on a hack. It'll be a swell front and I might come in handy for you."

"Good headwork," agreed Rudd. "Better watch your step for a while, though. The Feds missed out on some of Spanish's men and you're plenty hot with those boys."

Smooth had been waiting for this. He tried to make his next question casual. He had to! Here was the information that McNeary was waiting for.

"Who'd they miss?"

"I wish I knew," snapped Rudd.

"Yeah, so do I!" barked Cohen. "They got two of my boys last night out in Brooklyn. Good men, too! Walked 'em up an alley and gave 'em the works."

SMOOTH LEFT THE window and swung one leg across the corner of Rudd's desk. He watched the gambler's slim white hands tapping out their ceaseless tattoo on the polished wood. If this man had been unable to spot the head of the Spanish mob, what chance had he? Rudd's parchment-like fingers were constantly on the pulse of the underworld. They extended in every direction through the maze of streets and alleys that was New York. The hop-heads who were now dependent upon him for their supply of narcotics would be only too eager to pass along any information they might have. It seemed incredible that a group could operate in this city unknown to him. But Smooth knew that Rudd was puzzled, and suspicious. There had appeared to be a trace of fear in his voice when he said, "I wish I knew." And Cohen was worried, too.

"Well," said Smooth, "it looks as though I'll need a rabbit's foot under the driver's seat of my hack. But what else can I do?"

"I've got one other spot for you," said Rudd slowly. "It's not a soft job, but it would keep you from getting a slug in your chest. And the Feds would never find you, either."

"Where's that?"

"Working with Hoegy Bright on the boats. You could ride the *Roulette*—she's a nice little cruiser that operates along the coast. South America, Mexico and New York— well, not exactly New York, but she stops off the Jersey coast. Get it?"

Smooth grinned and nodded. He had been right in his guess and when Dorothy had told him of Rudd's telephone conversation about the moonlight she had prepared him for this. Rudd was using the same tactics that the booze rings had employed during Prohibition. In fact, there was still a fleet of liquor carriers operating off the Jersey coast and sending in untaxed liquor.

"Sounds like old times," said Smooth. "I worked the boats for Vannie Higgins years ago and it was no picnic. If that's the way you're bringing in the stuff, it didn't take you long to get organized."

"It never does when you've got money to spend," said Rudd. "The *Roulette* brings a shipment up from the south and contacts me by radio. Hoegy Bright runs the small boats for me and I've got two beauties. They can chase circles around anything the Feds have in the water. Like to join him?"

"No, thanks!" smiled Smooth. "One cruise with the off-shore fleet was enough for me. I'll take a chance on the hack. If you want me to contact the shore boats, I'll do that—but nix on the winter sailing, it's hard on the ears."

Both Rudd and Cohen grinned broadly. It was obvious that Hoegy Bright had done his share of complaining and when Smooth proved he was an old timer, they raised him another peg in their estimations. The Jersey coast was a tough spot in the fall and winter months. The boats put out in heavy fogs and driving storms. Clear, moonlit nights were shunned by these blockade runners as too dangerous, and the worse the weather the better for their trade. It was a cold, wet, miserable business with all the chances against the men. The Federals had a nasty way of shooting first and then asking questions and more than one group of rum-runners had been chalked up as missing when their bullet-riddled boat had drifted ashore.

RUDD FINALLY AGREED that Smooth would fit into the outfit as a taxi driver, but again warned him of the chances of stopping a bullet. They talked for the better part of an hour and Smooth gave them the highlights of his trip to the coast. He noticed that Rudd's eyes were studying him closely when told of Gilda's part in the venture and he wondered what thoughts were taking shape behind those bright, jet-like beads.

The conversation broke off sharply when Simpson announced Gilda. Yitz Cohen patted Smooth lightly on the shoulder and said that he must run along. He tossed a light salute to Rudd, smiled to Gilda and left after promising to meet Smooth the following night.

Rudd did not leave his place behind the desk, but watched silently as Gilda crossed the room and stood beside Smooth. There was a slight lift to his upper lip when she caught Smooth lightly by the chin, tilted it and kissed him.

"Careful, Gilda," Rudd warned mockingly. "I'm expecting Miss Manning along in a few minutes. She might not enjoy that."

"Really?" said Gilda lightly. "I had no idea she was interested." She leaned against Smooth's shoulder and smiled at him. "You seem to be quite a man with the ladies, Handsome."

"Be nice, Gilda," said Smooth. "Park yourself in a chair and give me a break. If you behave, I'll tell Rudd what a swell job you did at the coast. It ought to add a few more karats to that stone he promised you."

"Oh, yes," said Rudd, and lifed a flat leather box from a desk drawer. He opened the lid and withdrew a folded tissue paper that he spread before him. A dozen beautiful stones were grouped in the center, each sending out a flashing brilliance. "Take your pick, Gilda—you've earned it. As for you, Smooth"—he tossed a package of bills across the desk—"here's your cut. Satisfied?"

"Plenty," said Smooth, and watched Gilda.

She was bending above the stones, touching them lightly with a forefinger, spreading them and judging of their worth. Smooth saw her at her worst, then. The diamonds seemed to have touched a spark that grew to a flame of avarice. Her eyes were wide and cold—cold as the gems that sent frosty sparkles about her fingers. Her lips were thin and hard against her teeth, and above the crackle of the paper Smooth heard the quick throb of her breath.

Rudd reached again into the drawer and brought out a small round glass with a curved eyepiece fitted to it. He set it beside the stones.

"They're all blue-white and perfect, Gilda," he said. "Try them under the loop—don't trust me."

"I never did trust you, my dear," snapped Gilda, and adjusted the loop to her eye. "There was no flaw in the job we did for you, and I don't want one in the payment. Here"—she moved one stone aside with her finger—"this is the best. Thank you, darling."

She tore off a strip of the tissue, wrapped the diamond and dropped it into her purse. She turned and looked at Smooth and smiled cynically at the expression in his eyes.

"Thinking of Black spread out on the road in Mexico, Handsome?" she asked lightly. "Well, so am I—and I'll take my pound of flesh, thank you!"

"Maybe I am," said Smooth. "Maybe I'm thinking it might have been me. Thanks, Beautiful."

HE FOLDED THE money, put it in his pocket and poured drinks for both Gilda and himself from the decanter. Rudd replaced the stones in their leather case, set them back in the drawer and closed it. He nodded slightly when Simpson appeared in the doorway and leaned back in his chair as though to enjoy a tight situation.

"Hello, everybody," said a voice from the doorway.

Smooth turned quickly to see Dorothy crossing the room. She smiled to Rudd and hooked a possessive arm through one of Smooth's. Gilda had seated herself in a comfortable chair near the bookcase and Smooth saw her eyes travel swiftly from Dorothy's maroon felt hat, down past her velour coat of the same color—saw them pause in grudging approval at gray kit-fox trimmings and again at Dorothy's small suede shoes. It was a single sweeping glance that missed not the slightest detail and when he turned to introduce Dorothy he noticed that she was silently cataloguing Gilda's ensemble.

He drew a deep breath, crossed his fingers for luck and wondered why women had to complicate an assignment that was plenty tough without them.

"Gilda," he said, "I want you to know Dorothy Manning—she's a grand girl." He turned and smiled at Dorothy. "I've told you about Gilda Garland—she's the girl who flew to the coast with me."

Dorothy favored Gilda with a stare that Smooth knew was the same she used in the third act when she was supposed to discover a hair in her soup. Gilda saw the raise and bet an extra blue chip by rising from her chair and holding out both hands to Dorothy.

"Hello, darling," she cooed. "I hope Smooth didn't tell you *all* about our trip."

"Only the high spots," said Dorothy evenly. "And they

took up most of the afternoon. He's probably saving the rest for our honeymoon. He's adorable in his weaker moments, isn't he?"

"Hey! Stop taking me apart," said Smooth quickly, and swung to face Rudd. "Let's get out of here while I'm in one piece—we'll hit a few night clubs or something."

"Why not?" said Rudd evenly. "We'll stop in at Silva's place and try the tables. Although, if I were you, Smooth—I wouldn't risk too much money. Lucky at love, you know—"

20

HIGH LIFE

SMOOTH WAS THE first to step out of the cab when it pulled up before the marquee of the apartment on Central Park West that housed Big Joe Silva's gambling establishment. Mullans, the doorman, was standing stiffly at attention, waiting to help Dorothy and Gilda. He started slightly when he caught sight of Smooth paying off the driver, but covered his astonishment by a murmured, "'Evening, Mr. Rudd," to the gambler. Rudd smiled and offered an arm to each of the girls, escorted them to the doorway and stood waiting. Smooth nudged a friendly elbow against Mullans' ribs and winked at him.

"How's tricks, Mullans?" he asked.

"Fine. Mr. Kyle—fine!"

"Mister your eye! I'll be back on a hack tomorrow night and you'll be callin' me Smooth again."

"Sure, you travel too fast for me," said Mullans. "I've missed you the last few evenings and I was askin' Lucky about ya."

"Yeah? Is he around tonight?"

"There he is, down at the corner—see him?"

Smooth glanced along the building fronts and saw a group of drivers standing near the first cab. A little to one side and leaning against the front fender of the taxi was Lucky Carmine. He lifted a hand above his head and made a gesture that meant "High Hat."

"Lucky thinks I'm putting on the ritz," Smooth said to Mullans. "He's trying to tell me I've gone high hat. Tell him if he's around in a few hours I'll give him a good call."

He hurried to join Rudd and the girls, and noticed that Gilda had stepped back on the sidewalk and was staring at Lucky. She said nothing until they were in the elevator on the way up to the penthouse, although Smooth caught her looking at him in surprise.

"What's wrong?" he asked.

"Wasn't that the little fellow we met at Spanish's place?" she said quietly.

"Sure. What of it?"

"Plenty, if he runs with that mob."

The elevator drew to a stop and they stepped out of the car into a small hallway that topped the shaft. A huge pair of bronze doors opened onto a short flight of stairs that led down to a garden. Tiled walks curved in graceful patterns about clumps of shrubbery and to one side a miniature waterfall splashed and rippled over a series of rock terraces in which were concealed dozens of vari-colored lights. It was as though some dream-like forest glade had been transplanted to the roof of this New York apartment. The crisp breeze of the October night rustled the branches of the evergreens and set them to whispering, and through them could be seen the lights of the penthouse set far back on the roof.

"What's the trouble, Gilda?" asked Rudd. "See some-body you don't like?"

"Oh, Gilda's got the fidgets," said Smooth. "One of the hackmen on the corner has a girl friend who works in the Trocado—Spanish's joint. We met him there and Gilda is afraid he may be looking for me with a hunk of lead."

"She might be right. If he's one of Spanish's men, I'll send a few boys down to get rid of him. What's his name?"

"Oh, Lucky's all right. It'd be a shame to bump him off just because he happened to know Spanish. He's a nice little fellow and he's not mixed up with that mob." Smooth turned to Gilda as though for confirmation of his words. "Don't you remember how Theresa acted up when I offered to take Lucky to the coast with us? Why, she almost had a fit—even wants him to quit the hack racket and become a farmer. No—I'm not worried about Lucky."

"Suit yourself," said Rudd.

BIG JOE SILVA was at the door of the penthouse to welcome them. Rudd introduced Smooth and said, "He's just in from the coast." Silva nodded wisely and Smooth noticed that he was sizing him up. Silva was immaculate in evening clothes that fitted him to perfection. Tall, rather thin, with black hair that was graying at the temples—he was a picture of the debonair New Yorker, catering to the cream of Manhattan's spenders.

"Did you bring your luck with you?" he asked. "If you did it's apt to be a bad night for the house."

Smooth smiled but said nothing. He followed Rudd and the girls through a large foyer and into a spacious room that was already well crowded. A hardwood bar curved in a semicircle across the length of one wall. Three white-coated attendants were busy mixing drinks and serving scattered groups of men and women seated at tall stools before the bar.

Ice jingled crisply in the shakers, women laughed and a hum of conversation filled the room, while through it sounded the sharp click of falling chips and the whir of balls spun against the rim of the roulette wheels by croupiers. Horseshoe shaped tables, elbow-high and covered with green felt, were set in a line against another wall. Behind each a soft voiced dealer flipped an endless stream of cards to the blackjack players. Long oval tables with banked sides occupied prominent positions in the center of the floor and about them grave-faced men and laughing women watched the white dice win or lose for them.

Rudd handed each of the girls a stack of gold chips that he had purchased from one of the dealers and led them to stools at a roulette table.

"There you are, kids," he said lightly. "Play anything but your age—that's never a lucky number." He slipped a hand beneath Smooth's arm and led him to the bar. "What do you think of the place?" he asked.

"Quite a spread," said Smooth. "Silva's take must run into the thousands every night."

"We don't do half bad. Silva is working with me now and if we don't take the suckers one way, we get them another. Sometimes I wonder where these dumb bunnies get the money that we take away from them—the chumps!"

Smooth ordered a drink and watched the bartender mix it. He realized that Rudd was opening up—taking him into his confidence far more than he had expected. It was unusual for this tight-lipped gambler to tell his employees more than was absolutely necessary. But since the trip to the coast, Rudd had been very communicative. It was obvious he trusted Smooth and intended he should have a major part in his enterprises.

"I can see that Silva won't have any trouble putting out the junk to the carriage trade in this place," said Smooth. "The word will go around to all the high-hat snow birds* in town and they'll come here for their hop. It should bring plenty of play for the tables, too. But how about the little fellows—the mugs with only a couple of bucks to spend for cut snow? Where do they get it?"

"Tout Ender handles that trade, I want you to meet him tomorrow and bounce around town with him for a while, then I've got another job for you in the evening."

"Sounds as though I'm gonna be a busy guy," said Smooth.

"You are. I like you, Smooth—like the way you work— you're fast and do as you're told without a lot of guff. This racket is big business—damn big, and I need a man like you to help me handle it. You're on the way to some of the biggest money you ever saw in your life. Play ball with me and you'll make a million."

"Why not? I can use a million."

BIG JOE SILVA joined them at the bar. He looked at Rudd and made a slight motion with his head indicating that he wished to speak to him alone.

"You can talk in front of Smooth," said Rudd. "What's on your mind?"

"We just picked up a call from Hoegy Bright. He says

---

* Carriage trade means wealthy customers. Snow birds are narcotic addicts.

he's goin' to send again in ten minutes—a message for you. Want to hear it?"

Rudd nodded, took Smooth by the elbow and followed Silva through a narrow hall that led into a room at the far end of the penthouse. Silva closed the door and locked it. Rudd seated himself at a desk beside which was a new model all-wave radio. He pointed to a chair close by and indicated that Smooth should sit down and say nothing. Silva swung a heavy set of drapes across the windows and stood beside Rudd.

The noise of the gambling room came to them as a faint murmur, deadened by the heavy door and walls. Smooth watched Rudd closely as he made a slight adjustment of the dials and saw him glance at his wrist watch and hold it out to Silva.

"When does he send—on the even hour?" he asked.

"Yeah—ought to be comin' in now."

Rudd turned to Smooth and jerked a finger toward the radio.

"Bright's on the *Roulette,* about twelve miles off Toms River on the Jersey Coast. When he wants to shoot me a message he sends a few signals so the boys can locate me. He ought to be—listen—"

Smooth heard a rhythmic hum drifting from the loud speaker. The code letters B-G-R were repeated five times and after a pause of three minutes they were again repeated. Smooth smiled to himself when he realized that once more his months of training as a student in the department were proving themselves well spent. He had begrudged the hours of study he had put into learning code. When, he had asked, would an agent be called upon to use Morse, International or any other code?

He was getting his answer now.

Silva and Rudd were leaning forward, listening intently to the stuttering hum. The sender was a speed merchant and he was ripping it out in bursts. And now Smooth saw Rudd grab a pencil and write quickly on a pad. Deliberately Smooth turned a shoulder to the desk as though not wanting to see the message.

"C IN JAM." The sender repeated this as though for emphasis. "NOT FS MAYBE HJS N REPORTS C DOWN AM SHIFTING TO MP."

There was a long hum and once more the message came through. But Rudd was not listening. He had thrown the pencil petulantly to the floor and his fingers were twisting and interlocking above the pad. Silva was cursing low voiced and steadily and he stared at Rudd as though awaiting orders.

"**DID YOU GET** that, Smooth?" barked Rudd.

"It's Greek to me," lied Smooth. "Dots and dashes don't talk my language."

"Yeah? Well, you're gonna learn 'em. That was Hoegy Bright singin' a swan song." He glanced at the pad. "He says the *Cigarette* is in a jam. She's a fast little boat I use to contact the *Roulette* and bring in the junk. I told that mug not to operate tonight—too much moon. But the wise guy thinks he's a jump ahead of me and he sends out the boats. Next, he says it's not Federals but maybe it's hijackers. Nice, eh?"

"Tough," said Smooth. "But she might get away."

"Not a chance! The last part of that message said the

Cigarette is down—sunk! The other boat, the *Nicotine*, imported that. And then Bright says he's shifting his position from the Jersey Coast to Montauk Point. I'll shift him—the fool! For a dime I'd burn him!"

"Aw, anyone can make a mistake," said Silva. "Take it easy."

"Not in this racket, they can't!" said Rudd slowly. "The *Cigarette* was a fast little number and she was carrying plenty. That mistake sets me back damn near a hundred grand and I don't intend to let Bright make another."

"We ain't got a man to replace him," protested Silva. "Be a good guy, Rudd. Give him a break."

"Oh, all right." Rudd unlocked the door and motioned to Smooth, "You stick around, Joe, and listen for some more headaches. We're goin' to the bar."

Dorothy and Gilda were seated on stools, sipping cocktails, when Rudd and Smooth joined them. There appeared to be an armed truce existing between them and they were laughing at the exaggerated antics of a bartender who was shaking a drink. Gilda looked once at Rudd and lifted her eyebrows in an inquiring gesture to Smooth. He winked and ran a forefinger about the rim of his collar in a manner that meant, "He's hot."

Dorothy had caught the little byplay and was clever enough to let Rudd cool off before she spoke to him. The bartender had set a tall glass of milk on the bar and she slid it before the gambler and smiled.

"You girls had enough of this place?" he asked.

"More than enough," smiled Dorothy. "Gilda's broke and I won two hundred." She slid a pile of chips toward him. "Here's the stake you gave me. Thanks for the fun."

"Keep it," he said. "I'm glad somebody's lucky around here tonight."

"I'm not complaining," laughed Gilda. "Every day isn't a holiday—and I had my luck with me in California. Didn't I, Smooth?"

"Let's get out of here," said Smooth. "Cash your chips, Dorothy—it's the end of the night." He turned to Rudd and touched his arm. "Want me to roll a hack tomorrow?"

"Yes. Meet Tout Ender in front of the Cadillac Hotel about four o'clock. I want him to show you around. Then stop in at my place after supper."

"Fair enough—let's scram."

MULLANS SAW THEM coming from the doorway and lifted his hand to signal a cab. There was a moment's wait and Smooth grinned when he saw Lucky Carmine swing in before the marquee. He handed Mullans a bill, winked to Lucky and started to help Dorothy into the cab.

"Smooth, you take Dorothy home, like a good fellow," said Rudd. "I'll grab another cab and drop Gilda off on the way. She lives on the East Side near my place."

"Oh, I get dropped, do I?" laughed Gilda. "Well, a gal can't always be lucky. Goodnight, Dorothy—and you too, Smooth darling."

Smooth stepped into the cab, gave Dorothy's address to Lucky and leaned back against the cushions. A high pointed heel came down upon his instep and he jumped. When he turned to face Dorothy she was looking out the window, waving to Rudd.

"Why the kick in the shins?" he asked.

"Oh, did I kick you, Smooth, *darling?*" she mimicked Gilda's voice and the inquiring lift of her eyebrows.

Suddenly her manner changed and also her voice. "Why shouldn't I? I've heard nothing but, 'When we were in California—' and 'Smooth said this and Smooth did that, the dear'—and I'm sick of it. Who does that dame think she is?"

"You big baby!" laughed Smooth. "She's kidding you and you sizzle every time she hands you a burn. Grow up, Dorothy."

He caught her hand and held it between both of his. For a moment she stared at him and he saw that her eyes were wet. Then her head was against his shoulder and his arms were around her and she was whispering foolish words against his chest.

When Lucky turned into West End Avenue, Smooth caught his eye in the mirror and nodded toward the Drive. Lucky swung west and rolled across to the waterfront. The meter clicked steadily as they swept north along the bank of the moonlit Hudson but Smooth didn't hear it. When they turned and started downtown again he had told Dorothy for the twentieth time that she was the only girl he had ever loved—that Gilda meant nothing to him— that there never was a blonde who could compare with a brunette—and all the other things a man in love can tell a girl in the back of a taxi.

LUCKY COUGHED AS they neared Eighty-third Street and Dorothy pushed Smooth away and glanced a little shamefacedly at her wrist watch.

"Smooth! It's almost morning," she gasped. "Oh, tell him to take us home."

"I'll never forgive him for that cough," said Smooth. "But you're the boss."

He tapped on the front window and Lucky circled the block and drew up before Dorothy's apartment. Smooth helped her from the cab, walked with her through the dimly lit foyer and stopped near the elevator. The elevator boy was perched on a stool, his head resting against a wall of the car, and he was sleeping soundly. Smooth pointed to him and held a finger to his lips. He asked for another kiss.

Twenty minutes later he whistled his way across the sidewalk, reached in and pulled Lucky's cap over his eyes and cuffed him playfully on the ear.

"What do you think of the future wife?" he asked as he climbed into the back of the cab.

"Grand number," answered Lucky. "Got more class than the blonde, but what does Gilda think?"

"Guess you're wondering what it's all about, eh, Lucky?"

"Me?—say, I never wonder about nothin'. To me it's all a lotta tripe. But, feller, you're sure travelin' high, wide and handsome. If I was you I'd slow down on the corners."

"I guess you got me spotted as one of Rudd's men," said Smooth quietly, "so I'll give you the setup. I took a quick hop to the coast and knocked off Spanish's outfit. But why not? He pulled a squeeze on me when he talked me into the job. If I'd a said no—his mob would've left me in an alley. It was a case of sign up, or else—"

"I ain't holdin' it against you, Smooth. Spanish was nothin' to me—I even coppered my bets when he asked me about you. If you guys want to battle—fight it out amongst ya! Me, I'm in the clear. Theresa would knock hell outta me if I got mixed up with a mob."

"That's what I told Rudd when he asked about you. You're in the clear. But I figure you were close enough to

Spanish to know most of his men. Some of them are still on the loose and when they catch up with me—I burn. Any idea who they might be?"

"I wouldn't know," said Lucky quietly. "Where do I drop you off?"

"Old Closemouth, eh?" laughed Smooth. "All right, pal—have it your way. But swing east at the corner. Eleventh Avenue is too damn empty for a guy in my trade."

21

TAKEN FOR A RIDE

LUCKY SHRUGGED AND slowed to make a left turn. As the cab wheels thudded over the cobbles, a dark sedan cut in to the left and jerked to a stop, blocking the taxi. Two men leaped from the rear of the car and headed for the cab. One held a Tommy gun slung beneath his right arm and the muzzle never wavered from Smooth's head.

It would have been suicide to go for his gun and Smooth lifted his hands and kept them up. He noticed Lucky sat quietly at the wheel and stared directly ahead. It was none of the little hackman's business what happened in the back of his rig and Smooth knew he did not intend to get mixed up in it.

The man with the Tommy gun opened the cab door and prodded Smooth to the far side of the seat. He jerked up a drop seat, got in and sat facing Smooth. The other man held a low voiced conversation with Lucky and then seated himself beside Smooth and lifted the gun from beneath his armpit.

Smooth saw the driver of the sedan make a quick turn and streak up Eleventh Avenue; Lucky swung the cab and fell into the wheel marks, and Smooth tried to remember a few prayers to pass away the time that was left before the Tommy gun started to stutter. He remembered having seen the man with the gun at the bar in the Trocado and he realized that at last Spanish's mob had caught up with him.

Well—that was the breaks. Sometimes you win and then comes the upset that evens things. He had no complaint. When his luck was in he had forced it and now it seemed to have run out. McNeary would need a new agent and Rudd would get a new lease on life, for a time at least. Dorothy? He didn't want to think about that. He watched the street lights wink past and decided the man beside him was one of those who worked out of town for Spanish—he looked like it—too damn healthy looking.

Lucky took the curve that led onto Riverside Drive, stepped down harder on the gas and settled in his seat. They were passing Eighty-first Street when Smooth caught sight of another car burning the road behind them. He forced a grin. It was quite an honor to have such elaborate plans laid for his last waltz. A Tommy gun—a car ahead—and now another car behind. Quite a parade!

WHEN THEY REACHED the Nineties, Smooth saw the rear car swing wide and pull alongside. The man beside him cursed and started.

"Hey, Joe!" he barked suddenly. "Looka that crate out there! Who is it?"

Smooth tensed and drew a deep breath. So that car wasn't part of the job! It looked as though there might be fireworks in a minute and he set his feet firmly against the floor.

"I don't make it!" said Joe and turned the gun slightly away from Smooth's chest. "If they don't scram quick, I'll give 'em a burst—serve 'em right, the punks!"

Lucky's foot was tight against the floor boards and the taxi was pounding the pavement, swinging from side to side and lurching over the slight rises in the roadbed. The driver of the other car flicked his wheel and crowded the cab hard against the curb. Lucky cursed! He slammed on the brakes and the cab went into a screaming slide.

SMOOTH WAS LIFTED from his seat by the sudden stop. He lashed out at the barrel of the Tommy gun, grabbed it and held tightly as a short burst of slugs ripped through the taxi floor.

The man beside him had slammed against the forward section of the cab and the gun in his hand had shattered the window.

Curses dribbled from his lips as he yanked his slashed hand free of the glass and turned the gun on Smooth.

"Hold it—rat!"

The voice was hard and it meant business. A man was standing at the cab door, a Tommy gun pointed just over Smooth's head at the man beside him. The cursing stopped and Smooth twisted, crouching to keep out of the line of fire. He took his own gun from the slashed hand above him, bent lower and backed from the cab.

He wanted to shout—laugh—give vent to his pent up emotions in words, but he compromised by swinging the barrel of his gun across the jaw of the man who had held the Tommy gun against his chest.

"Thanks for the surprise party," he said to his rescuer. "I don't make you—but thanks again."

"That's okay—glad to do it." He held the gun steadily on the men in the cab and spoke to his partner. "Take those bums, Garison. Put 'em in the back of the rig and keep an

*The machine gunner
was gaining on Smooth*

eye on 'em—keep two eyes on 'em!" He drew Smooth to one side. "How about the driver—he in on this?"

"He's clean," said Smooth. "But who t'hell are you?"

"McNeary sent us. I'm Ted Wade, an old-timer in this division. The lad I just spoke to is Frank Garison and the driver is Bill Duffy—both of 'em new men here in New York. What about the car up ahead? Think we can catch him?"

"Not a chance. He's only some two-bit punk, anyway. But how did you manage to pick me up here on the Drive? McNeary said he was going to have some of you guys keep tabs on me, but I asked him not to."

Wade laughed silently and nudged Smooth in the ribs.

"When the Chief decides one of his agents needs protection, he can't seem to hear suggestions. We've been tailing you ever since you left Rudd's place. And what a merry-go-round! We saw that car pick you up outside Silva's joint and we tagged along behind. I thought you'd ducked out a side door of that apartment house when you took Miss Manning home, and we were just about to leave when you came out."

"Yeah?" grinned Smooth. "I was saying good night."

"After the joy ride along the Drive I figured that might be the case," smiled Wade. "Boy!—that would have been a laugh from a plane. I'd have spent a week's pay to see it. You leading the procession in a cab—these punks tailing you—and us right behind them. It must have looked like a funeral."

"It damn near *was* one," said Smooth. "Ask McNeary to keep those bums away from a telephone. Don't turn 'em over to the cops for a few days. And now there's one more trick you can pull for me, if you will."

"Glad to oblige. What is it?"

"Walk over to the cab with me and follow my lead. I don't want the word to spread that I'm a Fed and the hackman is all ears."

"Sure thing. But why not let us take him in too?"

"He can do me more good on the street. Besides, he's a pal of mine."

GARISON HAD BUNDLED his prisoners into the rear of the Federal Agent's car and was facing them with a gun tucked under his arm. Duffy, the driver, leaned against the wheel and Smooth noticed his eyes were steady upon Lucky Carmine. The hackman was sitting quietly in the driver's seat of the cab, his eyes staring out into the night and an expression of utter disinterest on his face. It appeared as though he were merely waiting for a rider to decide what destination he wished to go to, or as though Lucky were bored with the whole affair.

He turned when Smooth and Wade walked to the taxi door and stared at both of them blankly.

"Well, much obliged, pal," said Smooth and extended his hand to Wade. "Tell Rudd his guess was better than mine."

"Yeah, we'll tell him," said Wade. "But later!"

"Oh, don't hurry. Take those two punks for an airing before you burn them. And make a clean job of it—especially that bird who had the Tommy gun. Six in the chest and six in the skull—as a favor to me, eh?"

"It's a pleasure," grinned Wade and climbed into the car.

"Guess that takes care of everything," said Smooth to Lucky as he seated himself in the taxi. "The angels were sure close that time. But now those other mugs can sweat a little."

"That's the way it goes in the racket," agreed Lucky. "You're runnin' in luck to be workin' for a guy like Rudd. He must like you to be savin' you like that."

"He needs me. Don't kid yourself about that liking bunk. He'd dump me in a second if he didn't."

Lucky drove silently across town to Broadway and pounded south to Forty-fourth Street. He stopped at the corner and swung open the door for Smooth. Then he glanced ruefully at the meter, grunted and tossed up the flag.

"What's the clock say?" asked Smooth.

"Nuts!" growled Lucky. "That job's on the arm.* I heard you give me an okay to that bird with the Tommy gun. He was a greedy bloke, too—just achin' to have me join those

---

* On the arm means a call done without payment.

other two stiffs. Thanks, Smooth—maybe I can do the same for you some day."

"Aw, that's the old bilge water," protested Smooth. "I'll bet you ain't got two pounds done all night. And there's a busted window to explain to the boss. Here?" He handed Lucky one of the bills that Rudd had given him earlier in the evening and he saw Lucky's eyes widen. "That cover it?" he asked.

"A double sawbuck! I was beginnin' to forget what one looked like. Thanks, sucker."

A COLD OCTOBER drizzle had turned the streets to black glass when Smooth left McNeary's office and headed toward the garage. He lifted up his coat collar, hurried across Times Square and kept close beneath the theater marquees on his way to Ninth Avenue. The Chief had said little about the affair of the previous evening but had listened with interest to Smooth's report.

Both were agreed upon one point: The Spanish mob was just about wiped out. Their supply and distribution organizations had been disrupted and they were no longer operating as a unit. But the "brains"—the man who had built the huge drug business into a smooth running concern—was still at large.

McNeary was inclined to believe this man was not to be found amongst the gangsters. His moves had been too well thought out—too cleverly planned for a mobsman. The Chief argued that a person of this mentality would hardly allow himself to become actually associated with a crowd of gunmen. And if he were located, it would be in the president's office of some large corporation or financial institution. McNeary reminded Smooth that bank officials had supplied backing to the bootleggers during Prohibition and it was reasonable to suppose their habits had changed little with the arrival of Repeal.

Smooth could not agree. And as he threaded his way through the rain-swept streets, he again checked over his reasons. Luck had played a major part in his success to date. True, he had been ready to accept the breaks when they came his way, and he had made the most of each. But hardly had he made a move before a counter move had been started. That little party last night had been no coincidence! Someone had tipped the "brains" of the Spanish mob that Smooth was at Silva's place. Whoever had passed the word along was not seated in an office. Far from it! He must have been in close contact with the few remaining members of the mob. He was with them—one of them. And even now he might be watching and planning his next move.

Smooth shrugged and hoped for the best. There was no use worrying about it. If the breaks were with him, he'd come through—if not, all the cleverness he possessed would help little. He turned in off Ninth Avenue and started up the garage ramp. Old Squint was squatting on the concrete runway, mumbling and scratching and staring blankly out at the rain. Smooth tossed him a dime.

"Thanks, Smooth," he grunted. "There was some guys here lookin' fer you a while ago."

"Yeah? Who were they?"

"Aw, I dunno! A coupla close-mouthed lugs what wouldn't slip me a jit. I told 'em you didn't work here no more."

"Good for you, Squint. Let me know if they come back and I'll buy you a drink."

He tossed the derelict another coin and walked into the garage. McNeary had kept him talking longer than either realized and it was after four o'clock. The huge ham-like structure was empty save for one cab near the mechanic's bench and another close to the office. Smooth looked through the open door but saw no one inside but Harry Tone. Evidently his visitors had accepted Old Squint's statement and looked elsewhere.

SMOOTH REALIZED HE was asking for trouble by driving a hack in Manhattan. The Spanish crowd were out to get him and were making the rounds of the garages. Well—it was his job to clean them out and it would save time if they were both anxious for a meeting. But he hoped he would be the first to get a gun clear when the crash came.

Harry Tone looked up when he stepped into the office and the ever-present cigar again turned around and around. He looked back at the cards before him and said nothing.

"Does that mean I'm in the dog house?" grinned Smooth.

"The voice is familiar but I don't place the face," growled Tone and kept on with his figures. "Did you ever work here before?"

"Quit clowning. I been sick—the measles. Be a good guy and let me roll out one of those relics of yours. I'll probably book five pounds tonight."

"Listen, Smooth—if I wasn't stuck for a driver, I'd screw you out of this joint plenty fast. Where you been all week?"

"I told you I was sick," repeated Smooth. "How about it—do I roll?"

"Oh, all right. Take that lump that's outside, and by the

way—throw your hat in before you come up the ramp in the mornin'. You had visitors today and they might come back."

"Why, Harry!" laughed Smooth. "You don't think anyone would want to hurt me, do you? I'm playin' it legit, now."

"It ain't my business to think," said Tone. "I checked back on you and the cops give you a clean bill. That lets me out. You always used to be a good kid with a decent record. If you made a mistake—that's your business, and I'll bet you paid for it, plenty. I'm givin' you a chance to make a decent livin' and the least you can do is treat me right. G'wan roll the shekels and keep your snoot clean. I'm busy!"

22

A BAD MISTAKE

SMOOTH TOOK A blank card from the desk, checked the meter readings and drove down the ramp. Tone was a good sport. He was in a business that gave him little return for his investment and like other fleet owners he was constantly fighting to make both ends meet. He was forced to carry liability insurance but could in no way protect himself against the damage done to his own rolling stock. A few bad crackups would put him out of business, yet his cabs must always be spotless and mechanically perfect. Yes, it was a tough game for both owners and drivers, and Smooth realized only too well that Harry Tone was proving a good friend when he let him take out a rig.

He swung east to Sixth Avenue, doubled back to Forty-third Street and Broadway and found Tout Ender standing on the steps of a hotel. He threw the flag, opened the door for Ender and they swung north on Seventh.

"What kept you?" asked Ender irritably. "Don't you know we gotta keep a schedule?"

"Yeah, I know," said Smooth. "I was talkin' to the guy that owns this crate. He says there was a bunch of visiting firemen lookin' for me at the garage. They're probably still lookin', and if they catch up with us—wham! Want to call off the party?"

"Rudd *would* send me out with a guy that's hot," growled Ender. "Here I am, mindin' my own business and deliverin' decks of junk like a gentleman, and he slips me a driver that's practically a clay pigeon. Poisonally, I think it's the bunk. All this shootin' and stuff is gettin' me jumpy. I don't like it."

"Don't let it throw you, pal. The first hundred shots are the toughest—after that you get used to bein' a target. Now where do we go?"

Ender directed him to a small café on upper Eighth Avenue and Smooth made a note of the address. A rat-faced little sneak met them at the curb, grinned slyly at Ender and stepped into the cab. Smooth watched them in the mirror and saw Ender deliver a package of narcotics and accept payment. He stopped when Tout signalled and their passenger got out.

"Who was that creep?" asked Smooth.

"Whatja expect? A polo player?" snapped Ender. "You take what you get in this racket, and that little chiseler puts out plenty of junk, even if he is crummy lookin'. His name is Weesly—or Wowsley, or somethin' like that, and he hangs out in that joint back there. Now bounce over to Ninth."

FOR THE REST of the afternoon Smooth rolled up one avenue and down another. Rudd's distributing system was a web with strands that led through every section of the city. The poorer localities each had a tight lipped runner to accept his supply from Tout Ender and pay off in cash. At times there were arguments that were always won by

Ender and in some neighborhoods they had to circle the block a few times waiting for the policeman on duty to move on. Each contact was eventually made and each was silently noted down on the back of Smooth's trip card. He asked for and was told the name of the various runners and smiled to himself when he thought of the look of astonishment that would come over McNeary's face when he read this report.

It was a complete index of Rudd's New York trade, and Smooth knew the gambler had not as yet started to widen his ring. He was solidifying his position here in Manhattan, wiping out the remnants of the Spanish mob, and then, when the field was clear, he would move on. The web would spread until it touched every key city in the country and Rudd would be at the center, supplying the dope and collecting the profits.

Yes, it was a nice little racket, thought Smooth. It was starting like dozens of other rings and when McNeary was ready to make his move, it would fold the same way. The Bureau of Narcotics was a branch of the Treasury Department seldom heard of—an old, smooth running outfit that did its work with little fuss and no publicity. The newspaper boys had missed it—ignored it completely in their excitement over the Department of Justice. And that was as the Bureau wished. Smooth remembered the first bit of advice he had received when his application had been accepted: "Keep your mouth shut and keep out of the spotlight!" It was good advice and he had profited by it. As a result, one of Rudd's men was supplying him with a complete list of jail prospects—and with evidence that would stand up in any court.

They stopped for a light supper in a white tiled lunch room and then rolled up through the Negro district. Lenox Avenue and One Hundred and Thirty-seventh Street added another name to Smooth's list and still another when they swung across to St. Nicholas Avenue. Two sleek colored youths, dressed in the exaggerated splendor of the Harlem dude, stepped from narrow hallways and hurried across the rain-swept sidewalks to the cab. Each turned over a roll of bills and received a supply of narcotics in return. There were a few words, white toothed grins, and they were gone—hustling through a dripping alley to some back-yard tenement.

"We got one more stop at Broadway and a Hundred and Twenty-fifth," said Ender. "That winds up my day and, feller—I'm glad! I got enough money in my pants to pay for a dozen knock-offs and the sooner I pass it along to Rudd the better I'll feel."

"Want me to get you a motorcycle escort?" laughed Smooth. "The coppers'd be glad to oblige."

"Feelin' funny, eh?" grunted Ender. "Well, Smart Gee, take a look over your shoulder and get a load of the rig behind us. It's been sittin' on our tail all afternoon."

"*What!* You screwy punk. You mean someone's tailin' us and you just cracked wise? Which rig is it? Show me!"

"Aw, cool off," said Ender. "I may be wrong, but it seems like that white cab is stickin' close to us. I thought I spotted it when we were on Ninth Avenue and again in Harlem. But them cabs all look alike. Yeah—maybe I'm wrong."

SMOOTH SWUNG WEST on One Hundred and Forty-fifth Street, turned down the side window and leaned from the taxi. He watched a half dozen cabs hurry across the

intersection and finally a white car made a left turn behind
him. They were on a sharp incline leading up to Amsterdam Avenue and Smooth dropped into first speed and
crawled along between the trolley tracks. He kept an eye
on the mirror and noticed that the white cab seemed to
have difficulty in making the grade. Two cars swung in
ahead of it and Smooth twisted his wheel and spun north
on Amsterdam. He stopped at the corner and waited to
see if the white taxi would also make the turn.

The traffic lights changed and a sudden flurry of cars
blocked his view. He rolled again and cut over to Broadway. Swinging south, he hugged the curb and within a few
blocks he picked up the white cab.

"You ain't wrong, Tout," he said. "That mug's on our tail.
Why t'hell didn't you chirp up before?"

"I tell ya, I wasn't sure! Ever since I been in this junk
racket I been seein' a million guys follerin' me. Cripes! It's
givin' me the heebie-jeebies. Fer a dime I'd tell Rudd to go
to hell and quit. The profits are swell, but when I think of
doin' a bit in Atlanta—"

"Yaller, eh?" said Smooth. "You punks are all alike. You
get a crack at big money and it throws you. When you're
in the clear you see a regiment of coppers behind you. And
when something real is on your neck, you go blind on me.
Now get this! At the next traffic light, hop out and scram
into a doorway. Grab a good look at that bloke behind
us—spot him right—get his number! I'll loop the block
and pick you up again. Get it?"

"Aw, t'hell with him. I don't feel like playin' hide an' seek
in the rain. Besides, I'm heavy with dough—too heavy to
be wanderin' around loose in the dark."

Smooth stopped for a traffic light and swung to face Ender. His lips were thin and his right hand was toying with his tie. He stared at the runner and jerked his head toward the cab door.

"Out, bum! Do as I tell you or I'll scatter your ribs all over the floor. Scram! I'm givin' the orders around here!"

Tout Ender cursed slowly and steadily but he opened the door and ran toward an apartment entrance that fronted on Broadway. The rain had increased to a steady drive and the lights of the store fronts were dull yellow loops that extended part way across the sidewalk. The wet swish of automobile wheels filled the air with a steady, sibilant whine. Pedestrians hurried from a near-by subway exit and ran to shelter in the nearest stores, waiting for the downpour to subside. A wind whipped in from the Hudson, howled through the narrow canyons leading up from the river and swept twisting torrents of rain before it.

SMOOTH ROLLED DOWN a sharply inclined street leading to the Drive, drove north for two blocks and doubled back onto Broadway. He wondered if Tout had been correct in thinking that white cab had been following them. It might have been coincidence. A sudden thought brought a grin to his lips. Suppose McNeary had kept a few men on his tail? He had agreed to call them off when Smooth said it would make him conspicuous. But the Chief was a peculiar sort of a chap. It was hard to guess what he really had in his mind and that square jawed face told no secrets.

If there really were two men from the Bureau of Narcotics in that cab, Smooth would certainly have the laugh on his boss when Tout reported to him with a complete description. On the other hand, if they were two members of the almost extinct Spanish mob, a word to Rudd would send a dozen killers out after them. Smooth realized that McNeary would hardly approve of a move of that description. But this was a killer's racket, and Smooth intended to take advantage of any help he could get.

He drove slowly along Broadway toward the apartment into which Tout Ender had run. When he reached the corner, he noticed a crowd milling about the entrance in spite of the pouring rain. A radio car splashed to the curb and an officer elbowed his way past the crowd and hurried into the hall. Smooth drove past the entrance, parked his cab and mingled with the people in the street.

"What's up?" he asked an excited storekeeper at the edge of the crowd.

"A keelink! I look from de front from mine store and—blowie! A shot goes off! I run out—I look wid astonishment, und as I liff und breed, it comes anodder shot. Blowie! Such a business is dis. Two guys mit refolfers desh oudt—dey desh to a keb and phoff! Dey is gone! Dat dees could happen on Brotway—yiiiii!"

"You mean a guy was just killed in there?" barked Smooth.

"Saay! What's de metter? You don' talk Eengleesh? Soitintel—of coss he is keelt!"

For a moment Smooth stood motionless. He had tried an old hackman's trick when he sent Tout into that hallway. It was the best possible way of checking on a following car and one not likely to be caught by the average gangster. He was sure the traffic had covered Tout's exit from the taxi—that the white cab would follow him around the block while Ender looked from the hallway and spotted the trailers. But the men behind had outsmarted him. He realized it must have been the hack driver; the passengers could not possibly have spotted Tout. And that meant he was fighting another taxi driver—a man who knew as many tricks as did he.

He squirmed his way through the excited throng and walked into the hall. Another group blocked the entrance but Smooth got past them and stood behind an officer who was leaning over all that was left of Tout Ender. The killing had been the work of a professional—two shots, one in the stomach and the other squarely between the eyes. Tout was finished.

"Wadda you want, Nosey?" barked the officer. "G'wan—get outta here!"

"Yeah—I'm goin'," said Smooth.

His eyes were on the other officer who was methodically searching through Tout's pockets. A gun, a few small bills, the usual assortment of papers and envelopes—and a single paper of narcotics; the killers had left a perfect setup to send the police running in circles. Smooth saw the officer look at the cocaine and grin. He held the paper toward his partner and grinned.

"Aw, just another junkie—a small time rodman that ran with the wrong mob," he said. "There's about twenty bucks on him, so it wasn't robbery. Better give the house a ring and tell 'em to send down a homicide man."

SMOOTH EDGED BACK through the crowd. And as he walked to his cab he realized that mistakes cost plenty in this game. Tout Ender had been carrying not less than ten thousand dollars when he stepped into that hallway—a nice little take for the sorely pressed Spanish crowd. Tout had lost the ten thousand and had lost his life along with it, not through any fault of his own—simply because Smooth had made a mistake. But for the breaks of the game, it might have been Smooth lying crumpled in that hallway.

He shrugged, drove south to Times Square, and parked his cab in Forty-fourth Street. He entered a small hotel in the middle of the block, hurried to a phone booth and called Rudd. While he was waiting for the connection, he silently rehearsed the lie he must pass along to the gambler, and he smiled grimly when Rudd's suave voice came over the wire.

"Smooth talkin'," he said quietly. "Tout's through—a washout. They got him cold a few minutes ago."

"Yeah? Let's have it."

"We stopped at a Hundred and Thirty-sixth and Broadway to make a delivery. No one showed up and Tout scrammed into an apartment to look for the guy. He was—"

"*Where was that?*" barked Rudd.

"Hundred and Thirty-sixth," repeated Smooth. "You'll read it in the late editions."

"The rat! He must have been pullin' a phony—that spot wasn't on his route. Well—go on!"

"I pulled to the corner and waited. I heard the music back there—two quick ones—but I stayed put. The place was hot—there was a thousand peasants scramblin' for a look and I mixed in. The cops figure it a regular knock-off because there was a few bucks in his pockets,"

"A few bucks! That's a laugh," said Rudd. "Did they get much stuff?"

"Only a few decks—we were just about finished. So now what do I do?"

"Come up here in about an hour. I want you to take me to Brooklyn. G'by!"

Smooth dropped the receiver on the hook and leaned back against the wall of the phone booth. He lit a cigarette, thought for a moment and then called McNeary at his hotel. There was no answer and he then tried him at his office.

"Working late, eh, Chief?" he said when McNeary's "Hello" sounded in the receiver. "Get a report on that job at a Hundred and Thirty-sixth?"

"Yes. Tout Ender, wasn't it?"

"Right. And I was driving. I got a perfect route list for you and if you'll send a man to meet me, I'll pass it along."

"Nice work, Smooth. But who pulled that job?"

"Yeah—who killed Cock Robin—how would I know? Big Spanish must have a few boys left on the streets and they need money. Well, they got a chunk tonight."

"Does Rudd know about it?"

"Sure. I just told him. He wants to see me later but I'm not sure what's up. Wish me luck."

"You seem to have plenty. Meet Ted Wade at Forty-second and Sixth in a half hour and give him that list before your luck runs out. I need it."

"That's a pleasant thought," laughed Smooth, and he flipped the receiver onto the hook.

23

INVADING BROOKLYN

HE DROVE TO a Forty-second Street cafeteria regularly frequented by hackmen, ordered coffee and rolls and seated himself at an empty table in the rear of the restaurant. It was a little after ten—lunch time for the night drivers, and the place was crowded with them. He saw Lucky Carmine at another table near the rear wall and waved a roll at him. Lucky nodded, walked to the counter and ordered the inevitable second cup of coffee, and seated himself beside Smooth.

"Watcha got done?" he asked, and twisted his face into a knowing grin. "You oughta be rollin' plenty in the rain."

"Oh, I can't kick," said Smooth. "I'm close to two pounds. Not bad, eh?"

"Quit stallin'," laughed Lucky. "All the hackin' you been doin' you could stick in your eye and never find it. You got a grand racket, pal—I wish Theresa would let me grab a few quick dollars. But she's a straight little broad and everything's gotta be strictly on the level to suit her. But that's the way it goes when you go overboard for a dame, eh?"

"She's smart, Lucky," said Smooth seriously. "This may sound goopy comin' from me, but take my advice and play it Theresa's way. Fast money ain't the kind that sticks in your pocket. And between the two of you, you must have a nice little sock put away toward that farm. When d'you expect to go rural?"

"Well—things ain't so good just now. Theresa lost out when the Trocado folded and she didn't hook up with a job yet. As for me—you know what I can grab. Maybe twenty plunks a week, tops."

"I didn't know the Trocado closed. How come?"

"With Spanish in jail, things didn't go so good and the backers wrapped the joint up. I understand he was backin' that show the Manning girl was in, and that's foldin' up, too. Didn't she tell you?"

"Not yet—I don't think she knows. But I'll ask her about it later."

"You goin' to meet her after the show?"

"I don't think so," said Smooth. "I gotta do a job over to Brooklyn in a few minutes."

"Where abouts?"

Smooth grinned and shrugged his shoulders. He hadn't meant to tell Lucky that. He had learned long ago that it was safer to keep his mouth shut about his movements. But it had slipped out. He stood up, stretched indolently and turned up his coat collar.

"Well, I gotta go out in the dewdrops and shove the crate around. Say hello to Theresa for me and tell her I'll be up for meat balls and spaghetti one of these nights."

"Good enough, Smooth. I'll do that little thing. And Theresa can sure cook a mean dish of macaroni. I'll be seein' ya."

SMOOTH DROVE EAST on Forty-second Street and when he reached Sixth Avenue, Ted Wade stepped to the curb and hailed him. Smooth opened the cab door, threw the flag, and continued on toward Fifth Avenue.

"You're just the kind of a guy," said Wade, "who would drag me out in a rainstorm. What's on your mind?"

Smooth handed him his trip card, on the back of which was noted the name and address of each of Rudd's runners. Wade glanced at it and whistled. He folded the card, put it in his pocket and reached forward to pat Smooth on the shoulder.

"What a clean-up!" he said. "Keep it up like this, Smooth, and you'll be District Supervisor within a year."

"Thanks, Ted, but I wouldn't want McNeary's job for all the pennies in the Treasury. It's always easier to take orders than to give them. Now, where can I let you out?"

"Oh, just drop me at Grand Central. I understand you're on your way to Rudd's place."

Smooth swung in to the curb at Vanderbilt Avenue, tossed up the flag and opened the cab door.

"Thirty cents, mister," he grinned. "And us hackmen usually gets a dime tip in the rain."

Wade laughed and spun him a half dollar, turned and disappeared in the crowd. Smooth rolled north on Lexington, swung east, and left his cab before Rudd's apartment. Simpson answered the door and escorted him to the library.

"Mr. Rudd's been expecting you," he said.

"Well, here I am, wet and dripping."

"Yeah, here you are," said Rudd from behind the Queen Anne desk. "Sit down, grab a drink, and tell me the misery. Gilda's coming up in a few moments—I was foolish enough to let her know I expected you and she insists upon meeting her former husband. All right with you?"

"Sure—if Dorothy isn't comin' too."

"I'm afraid Dorothy has deserted me, now that you're in town again. But I don't hold it against her." Rudd laughed and ran a hand through his graying hair. "We can't stay young forever, can we, Smooth?" The smile left his face and his eyes were like small round pebbles as he looked at Smooth. "Tell me about Tout!"

THE STORY THAT Smooth told was the same in substance as he had reported over the phone. He insisted that Tout's death would in no way be connected with Rudd's narcotic outfit and seemed puzzled as to why Ender had made the stop at One Hundred and Thirty-sixth Street.

"That's not hard to guess," said Rudd. "Tout wasn't used to big money and I guess ten G's was too much for him. He probably spotted a few of his pals in the hallway and expected to get away with a phony stickup. Then he'd come back here and bellyache about being robbed. But the gag back-fired and his pals decided to get rid of one cut. Served him right."

"Don't you figure it might have been Spanish?" asked Smooth.

"Spanish? The Feds have got that guy and just about all his mob sewed up tight. Oh, I'll admit they missed the brains, but whoever the wise guy is, he's been left holding the bag with no money and damn few men. There's no doubt but what he'll try to get organized again, but when he makes a move I'll spot him."

"Maybe this is the first move," protested Smooth. "Ten thousand dollars isn't exactly chicken feed."

"I've thought of that, but it doesn't stand up. If a car had followed you, caught you up an alley and pulled a stick-up, that would have been different. But when you tell me that Tout insisted upon stopping at One Hundred and Thirty-sixth Street, where he had no right to stop, it simply means he expected to meet someone. Don't you see, Smooth, it couldn't possibly be Spanish's mob."

Rudd's reasoning was sound, and Smooth wondered if he had not made a mistake in the weaving of his story. The newspapers would undoubtedly mention the fact that the killers had used a taxicab to make their getaway. Of course he could deny this and explain to Rudd that it was probably a distorted version handed out by an excited shopkeeper. There was just a chance that someone might have taken the license number of the taxi and Smooth knew that it would be a stolen car, picked up purposely for the job. Later, it would be found abandoned on the streets, and if a report of this was made by the newspapers, Rudd would certainly become suspicious.

There was nothing else Smooth could do. He couldn't tell Rudd the truth and admit it had been his mistake— that he had sent Tout Ender to his death. Rudd was not the type of man to overlook an error that had cost him ten thousand dollars. And, to date, his faith in Smooth had apparently been wholly justified. Why change things?

"Well," said Smooth, "it won't do any good to sit here and weep about it. What's on for tonight?"

"Take your time," said Rudd. "First, do you think you could break a new man on Ender's route?"

"Sure I can. Tomorrow if you want."

"Good for you. I'll send Yitz Cohen around with you tomorrow afternoon. We'll see him tonight—remind me of it."

SIMPSON ANNOUNCED MISS Garland and Rudd smiled and lifted an eyebrow toward Smooth. He nodded to the butler and then leaned back in his chair.

"Hello, darlings," said Gilda. "What a break on a rainy night—a nice apartment, good liquor and good company. What more could the little girl ask?"

"Hello, Gilda," said Smooth. "Don't you know enough to stay in out of the rain?"

"Rain makes the flowers beautiful," she laughed. "So t' hell with it—let it rain on me. It might have the same effect."

"Sorry, honey," said Rudd. "The beauty parlor seems to have taken care of that. Drink your little drinkee, say hello to Smooth and find a good book. We're going out on business."

"Be nice, Rudd. How do you expect me to romance the lad if you're going to drag him out in a blizzard? Won't the business wait?"

"Not a chance," said Rudd. "We've been wishing for this rainstorm."

"Oh, I get it," said Gilda wisely. "The boats, eh? And that reminds me, you've been promising me a look at that yacht. When do I see it?"

"In a few days," said Rudd. "I'll let Smooth take you for a moonlight ride."

"Not if I know it!" protested Smooth. "She was hard to handle in an airplane but she'll probably be worse on a yacht."

GILDA REACHED UP and caught him by the ear lobes. She stared into his eyes and grinned. Smooth was standing beside the desk and when he tried to back away from

Gilda he almost upset the decanter. He caught her by the wrists and forced her hands to her sides. Rudd laughed and extended a hand to steady the glasses.

"If you two want to wrestle," he said, "I'll try to get you a match at the Garden. Behave yourself, Gilda—suppose Dorothy caught you pinching Smooth's ear. Think she'd like it?"

"Not as much as Smooth does. But all jokes aside— wouldn't you like to have me come along with you tonight?"

"I'm sorry, Gilda," said Rudd. "We won't have time to look at the stars this evening. But the weather reports promise a clear sky for tomorrow night. Will that be okay with you?"

"That's a bet."

"All right, I'll call Dorothy and ask her to come along too. Or maybe *you'd* rather do that, Smooth?"

It was obvious to Smooth that Rudd was playing one girl against the other. McNeary had been right in his estimate of the man. This gambler was quick to take advantage of any human weakness and turn it to his advantage. By pitting the girls against each other he would make allies of both. Each would keep an eye on the other and be only too ready to report any irregularities to Rudd. It was a clever move and Smooth tossed a mental bow to the gambler.

"Yes, I'll ask her to come along, if you want me to," he said. "What's it going to be—a party?"

"It *would* have been," said Gilda coldly. "But now it will probably be a free-for-all."

Then she turned to Rudd and frowned. "Just what has this Manning girl got that makes her so popular?"

"Smooth might help you out there," laughed Rudd. "Why not ask him?"

"You can both go and take a running jump in the lake," said Smooth. "Leave me out of this."

"Aaah! He's weakening," smiled Gilda. "One more trip to the coast and he'll be shopping for a wedding ring. Wouldn't you, Handsome?"

Rudd rang for the butler and Simpson brought him a gabardine topcoat and dark felt hat. He put them on and waited while Smooth slipped into his overcoat and finished his drink. Gilda ran a thumb along the rows of books in a near-by case and lifted it to her nose when Rudd suggested a book of Indian love lyrics. She held out her hand to Smooth and when he grasped it, she leaned forward and kissed him lightly on the lips.

"That's for luck," she said. "Be careful, lover—I'd hate to lose you—even to a brunette."

They hurried to the elevator and Rudd was grinning broadly as they crossed the foyer and stepped out into the rain. He seated himself in the back of Smooth's cab, turned down the front window and lit a cigarette.

"Know anything about Brooklyn?" he asked. "The Bay— for instance?"

"A little. I used to hack there. Where do we go?"

"Yitz Cohen is waiting for us at the end of Emmons Avenue. The *Nicotine* was to bring in a load from the *Roulette* tonight, and I want to see how the boys are working. But don't hurry—we're early."

24

TAXI RACE

THEY ROLLED DOWN Fourth Avenue, over the Manhattan Bridge and out Ocean Parkway. The rain had settled down to a constant drizzle and the roads were empty canyons that glistened with the yellow rays of the street lamps. Occasional hurrying figures darted across at the intersections, and splashing taxis spun past them with their homeward bound loads of theater-goers. Smooth settled comfortably in his seat and kicked the car along at a steady rate that would eat up the ten-mile trip in a little over a half hour. There was a chill in the air, and he kept both forward windows closed.

"Is that a sure date for tomorrow night?" he asked when they had cleared the traffic and were rolling along the outer stretches of the Parkway.

"Yes, we might as well have the girls out for a little party. It'll do us all a lot of good—take the curse off. It hasn't been a picnic getting this organization started, and we both need a little relaxation. Besides, I want you to see the *Roulette* and get a line on her. If you're going to be as much help to me as I expect, I want you to know all the angles."

"That suits me. The more I learn, the more I'm worth.

But I'm not anxious to run south on the *Roulette*—one trip across the line was plenty."

Rudd laughed. He seemed to derive a great deal of amusement from the mistake that Spanish had made when he sent Smooth to the coast. It was one of the little vanities common to most smartmoney men that they enjoyed the other fellow's mistakes and exploded away their own. In Rudd's estimation, Big Spanish had acted like a sucker and had deserved the double cross that had been handed him. He said as much, and Smooth agreed with him definitely.

"But there's one thing I don't get," Smooth said. "Why do you always use cabs? In your spot, I'd travel in a nice bullet-proof sedan with glass an inch thick. It's safer than a hack."

"Don't kid yourself," snapped Rudd. "A private car puts you on the spot—makes a target of you. Within a week every mug in town would have it spotted. But a taxi is just a taxi—there's thousands of 'em on the streets, and I might be in any one. And as for that bullet-proof guff—nuts! Show me a piece of glass that a Tommy gun wouldn't make a sucker of. Those babies could eat their way through it in one burst. T'hell with it."

They drove along the old waterfront that edged Sheepshead Bay, and Rudd directed him to a group of bungalows near the end of the street.

There was a police booth near by, and Smooth pointed to it and looked inquiringly at Rudd.

"So what?" said the gambler, and grinned. "We're not expecting a truckload of whisky. Our stuff comes in a suitcase—a small one at that. I'm no hog. I learned my lesson when the *Cigarette* was sunk. There was quite a bit of stuff on that boat—too much to lose. So now I make Hoegy Bright send in a little at a time. It's slower, but it costs less when a knock-off comes."

"That's smart," agreed Smooth. "And by the way—what did you do about the *Cigarette?* Any idea who took her?"

"I'm not sure, although I think it was that wise guy who's running Spanish's mob. He was stuck for junk—had to get some in a hurry to keep what little trade he's got left. Some fool in my outfit talked too much and tipped him off to the boat racket. But that's just a guess."

"Think he'll try it again?"

"I hope he does," said Rudd quietly. "And I hope he's in the boat when it happens. The boys have some high powered artillery on the *Nicotine*—enough to put up a swell scrap with a battleship. And they're aching to try it out."

"Won't that be fun," laughed Smooth thinly. He glanced through the side window and saw a man watching them from the porch of an empty bungalow. "Is that Cohen, over there?"

"Yeah, that's him," said Rudd, and tapped lightly on the glass.

COHEN SPLASHED THROUGH the puddles, crossed the road and seated himself in the rear of the cab. He was drenched, but seemed not to mind the rain at all. He winked to Smooth, stamped his feet against the floor boards and asked Rudd for a cigarette. When it was lighted, he jerked a thumb toward the police booth and grinned.

"Mr. Cooper wanted to know why I was hangin' around in the rain. I told him I was expecting a couple of saps who wanted to go fishin'. How about it? Wanna fish?"

"We're a little early to catch anything," laughed Rudd. "And Smooth forgot the bait. We'll roll down the avenue and maybe Flatfoot will feel the urge for a cup of coffee. I don't want him stickin' his beak in when the *Nicotine* hits the dock."

"Good idea, boss," agreed Cohen. "That guy just came on duty at midnight and along about twelve-thirty he's goin' to get sick of countin' raindrops. This joint is a morgue."

Smooth stepped on the starter and swung the wheel. They cruised slowly along Emmons Avenue and doubled back through Voorhees. Rudd glanced at his watch occasionally and at length nodded when he caught Smooth's eyes in the mirror. They turned back along the waterfront and as Cohen had predicted, the officer had left the booth when they arrived.

They left the cab and walked along a narrow boardwalk that led out to a small dock. The night air was colder when it swept in off the ocean and the rain whipped against their faces like hail. A heavy sea thundered around the lip of Oriental Point, but spent itself in the open water. Back in the dip of the bay the waves were small and choppy. They lapped against the dock and sent up a damp odor of seaweed and marshgrass. An occasional squeak sounded from a protesting dock timber, and at times a door slammed in one of the empty bungalows at the water's edge.

Rudd and Cohen had turned their backs to the drive of the rain, but Smooth leaned into it and studied the black expanse of water before him. Suddenly he heard the steady throb of a boat's motor. It grew in volume and a dark shape loomed out of the spray.

A sleek lined boat lifted high as she swung into a wide

circle and headed toward the dock. Smooth saw a man studying the group through a pair of night glasses and Cohen turned and lifted one arm. The motor was cut and the boat slid quietly to the dock.

Chick Binder and Bert Lovette stepped out onto the stringpiece and waved a salute to Rudd. Smooth recognized them, despite the fact that they were grotesque figures in their oilskin coats and southwesters. Their faces were raw from the lash of the wind and rain, and they proceeded to curse the off-shore trade in thorough and explicit language. Binder handed Cohen a small suitcase and then pointed to the boat.

"ANY OF YOU gents like to go for a little spin?" he asked.

"Nuts to you, feller," laughed Smooth. "I'll stick to my hack. There ain't so much southern exposure there as you get in a wave hopper."

"We'll be out tomorrow night," said Rudd. "No business—it looks as though we're going to have a clear night."

"That's what you think," growled Lovette. "Me—I expect this rain to last forever. And cripes—it's cold stuff."

"Aw, stop weeping," barked Rudd. "Augie and Little Tommy are a damn sight colder on the bottom of the Atlantic Ocean. Or maybe they're hotter, where they are now—who knows?"

"You're tellin' us?" said Binder. "We're the ones who found the *Cigarette* just before she sank. Those boys had enough lead in them to keep them down forever. Hell! They were a mess. Whoever did that job is one sweet gunner. He ripped a slash along the waterline with one long burst, then swung back and sprinkled slugs all over hell. Augie was just a smear—ugh! Little Tommy was damn near cut in half and he seemed to be noddin' at me when the *Ciga-rette* stuck her tail in the air and dove."

"All right, all right!" snapped Rudd. "I know it's tough, but what t'hell you think I'm payin' you boys heavy money for? A ballet dance? Forget it! And if that same bird shows up again, do a little chopping yourselves."

"It'll be a pleasure," growled Lovette. "A positive pleasure to see how much lead that lug can hold without leakin'."

"That's okay with me," said the gambler. "Now you guys chase back to the *Roulette* and tell Bright to dress the scow up nice for tomorrow night. We're going to have ladies aboard, and I want things neat. Make a trip in tomorrow and pick up some wine." He handed Binder a few bills. "This ought to cover it. Now scram."

The *Nicotine* lifted on her step and roared off into the night, and Rudd started up the dock. Yitz Cohen followed him closely, carrying the suitcase, and Smooth walked beside him. They noticed that the police booth was still empty as they picked their way through the wet street to the cab. Cohen set the bag on the floor, got in behind Rudd and closed the door. Smooth stepped on the starter, swung the wheel and was about to drive along Emmons Avenue when he noticed a cab standing a few hundred feet further along the road.

"Any of the boys following us?" he asked Rudd.

"What do you mean—following us? Of course not. Why?"

"I thought you might've told some of them to tail us in another rig and keep an eye on us. But if you didn't—get ready for a party."

"What t'hell's eatin' you?" asked Cohen.

"See that cab over there? Well, it don't make sense! All these bungalows are empty this time of the year. And even if one copper fell for that hokum about a fishing party—I don't! What would a cab be doin' here this time of night?"

"Anyone in it?" snapped Rudd.

"I think so. Looks as though a guy was pikin' us off through the back window—I can't be sure. The motor's running; I can see the exhaust. And the way he's heading, he's on the wrong side of the street. So what does it add up to?"

"It adds up to one dead chump!" said Yitz Cohen quietly. "You guys sit tight while I bounce across the road and feed a clipful of hot ones into that dope's chest."

HE LIFTED AN automatic from a shoulder holster, leaned forward and opened the cab door. He had put one foot on the running board when Rudd grabbed his arm.

"Sit down—fool!" snapped the gambler. "Use your head! That mug isn't squatting in the back of that cab with a rod—not a chance! It's a thousand to one shot that he's got a chopper lined on us right now. Swell break you'd have against that!"

"Think so?" asked Cohen nervously.

"Why not?" said Smooth. "He's got us bottled up in a dead end street—he let us get into the cab so there'd be no chance of us scattering—he's sitting pretty, waiting for us to try to pass him. Then comes the blast. Sure, he's got a chopper."

Rudd's lips were tight. He leaned forward and stared intently at the other cab. Smooth glanced back and was surprised to see a half smile on the gambler's face, and he noticed that those white hands were still—resting lightly against the window. At least Rudd had guts. When his number went up he didn't snivel and whimper like Cohen was now doing. The thin-faced gunman was snapping his head from one side to another, casting about like a cornered fox for a way out. His eyes were constantly in movement and his fingers were twisting and doubling against the palms of his hands.

Smooth looked at his own hands. They were tight on the wheel, and he wondered if they would tremble if he released his grip. He fumbled through his pockets for a cigarette and match. Bending below the windshield so the flare of the match would not make a perfect target, he lit the butt and dragged a deep breath of smoke into his lungs. He heard Rudd's mirthless chuckle and turned to face him.

"Grabbin' a last one, eh, Smooth?" smiled the gambler.

"Looks like it," he answered. "I'm tryin' to guess a way out, but no dice, so far. The best I can offer is a quick break. I'll duck out the front, you take one door and let Cohen try the other. If we scatter, there's a chance he won't nail all of us—but what a lousy chance!"

"Nix!" squealed Cohen. "I ain't goin' to try to outrun a slug—not me. I'm sittin' tight—somethin' might happen."

"You're damn right something's going to happen," grinned Rudd. "That bird is going to get sick of waiting, and he's going to drop a burst into this rig. If he don't, he's dumb."

"See you in hell, Rudd," said Smooth, and twisted the door handle.

He slid one foot through the partly opened door and was about to lunge forward when he saw a dark shape splashing toward them through the downpour of rain. He jerked back, grinned, and turned to face the men in the rear of the cab.

"Hold it, you guys!" he snapped. "I think we get a break." He pointed to the lumbering form in the darkness. "See that?" he asked.

"Yeah," said Rudd "But I don't make it. What is it?"

"A bus. There's a bus line here that operates from the subway station, and this is the end of the line. The driver'll make a turn here and start back. If that lug with the chopper holds off for just a minute, we may grab a pass."

THEY WERE SILENT. Each man crouched low in the cab and their eyes held steadily to the huge bus as it wallowed through the puddles toward them. It passed the cab on the far side of the street, swung into a wide turn and stopped. Smooth saw the bus driver lean back in his seat and stretch. There were no passengers, and the driver dipped into the crown of his uniform hat and took out a partly consumed cigarette.

The bright lights in the interior of the coach made of it a stage upon which a single actor performed. All unknown to him, he was watched by the most intent audience ever assembled. Three men crouched in one cab, their eyes steady upon the bus driver, and each repeated endlessly, "Roll, fool! Roll!" as though to hurry the driver by mental persuasion. In another cab a cold-eyed killer crouched above a sub-machine gun and waited for the bus to clear his line of fire.

The driver finished his butt. He opened the door slightly and flipped it into the rain, stretched again and examined his face in the mirror. He felt his chin stubble with the back of his hand, and rubbed his eyes. Each movement brought a curse from Cohen or a chuckle from Rudd. Smooth stepped down on the clutch, slipped into second speed and touched the gas throttle lightly. The driver yawned, blew his nose lustily, glanced at the meter readings and rolled.

Smooth let in the clutch and sent his cab alongside of the bus. As the huge coach gathered speed, Smooth ripped into high and kicked at the gas. He jockeyed forward, crowding between the bus and the curb, and almost crashed when the driver swung right to avoid a bump in the road. They were past the other cab now, and Smooth fed gas hard. He swung out in front of the bus, careful to keep it as a screen from the other cab, and raced down Emmons Avenue.

He glanced in the mirror. Rudd and Cohen were kneeling on the rear seat, their eyes to the window, and each held an automatic ready at hand.

"How's it look?" Smooth asked.

"Step on it, kid!" barked Rudd. "You got company! That bird is comin' like the hammers of hell!"

"Knock out the back window and try for his tires! All he needs is one crack at us with that chopper."

"Great idea," said Cohen. He swung his gun, and the crash of breaking glass followed the movement.

There were three quick shots and Smooth heard Rudd cursing. Smooth twisted sharply to the left to avoid an obstruction in the street that was the result of a road repair job. Another shot flatted against the night air and Cohen yelped.

"Lug!" barked Rudd. "Watch that gun. You damn near ripped my ear off."

"You don't need to knock out a tooth, do you?" howled Cohen. "I slipped."

"Hang on, customers!" shouted Smooth. "We're goin' around a curve!"

He heaved at the wheel, slammed down on the brake and went into a half spin that carried the cab into Haring Street. It was a dark alley leading from the waterfront to the back roads, lined on either side with small bungalows and low-roofed wooden houses. The street lights were widely spaced, and the road was paved with an uneven macadam surface. He swerved past a treacherous looking puddle, fought the wheel and fed gas.

FROM THE DISTANCE he heard a stutter of shots and instinctively he ducked. The front tires bounded high over a hidden ridge and the wheel spun from his hands. Another rattle of fire drowned out a closer sound that hummed past the cab like a swarm of hornets. Smooth grabbed the wheel, heard the front right fender fold against a street light and saw a running board curl around the pole like a cruller.

"Ride 'im, cowboy!" laughed Rudd as he bounced against the roof.

"Know any good prayers?" yelled Smooth. "That fender's binding on the wheel. When it burns through the rubber we stand on our ear."

"Why bring that up?" yelped Cohen. "Just get this load on smooth ground fer a second and I'll spot that bum at the wheel. Yooow!"

Another burst ripped from the following cab and Cohen dove at the floor boards. Smooth was using all the strength in his arms to overcome the drag of the wheel. He braced himself, swung along Voorhees Avenue and then turned into a narrow road that led through the marshes. It was part of an old real estate development that had long since been abandoned to the weather. The pavement was good in spots, but at intervals there were stretches of uneven ground that sent the cab into a waddling dance.

It took skillful driving to pound along through that stretch of back road, and Smooth realized he was up against a driver equally skillful as himself when he failed to gain an appreciable lead on the cab behind. He doubted that an ordinary gangster could have made the grade—there was a possibility that one of the mob who had once handled a booze truck might have done it. But when another hum of steel jacketed hornets proved that the following gunner was coming into closer range, Smooth was willing to bet the few remaining moments left to him that the driver was a hackman.

"If you guys don't nail that driver before we hit a good road," he cried, "the party's over. There's a smooth stretch just ahead—try hard!"

"Whatta you think we're doin'?" howled Cohen. "Snipin' at ducks, or somethin'? I ain't no rodeo rider, and it's as easy shootin' from the back of this crate as it would be jugglin' a feather on a basket of snakes."

"Stop snappin' your mouth and give that gun a chance!" barked Rudd. "You're supposed to be a gunner—well, gun, damn it!"

Cohen emptied the few shells left in his clip and Smooth knew he had missed when he saw the steady approach of a pair of headlights in his mirror. Rudd made his last play and hurled his empty gun through the back window in a final gesture of defeat. Smooth's hands were locked around the wheel and he dared not release them to reach for his gun. He shouted to Cohen, and the little gunman reached across Smooth's chest and lifted his automatic.

Another blast from the sub-machine gun hurried Cohen's aim, and he emptied the clip in desperation at the oncoming cab.

"Washout!" said Rudd. "This bum shoots like I swim—lousy! It's up to you, Smooth. Any out for us?"

"A Chinaman's chance!" snapped Smooth. "Rip out the back seat and slide it through the rear window. When I yell, drop it and hope like hell that it don't bounce."

He heard them pulling at the cushion and a low curse from Cohen when his wrist ripped over a pointed piece of glass in the window sill.

"Yeah—that's a great idea," yelled Cohen. "But it won't work—we can't get the seat through the window—won't fit!"

"Shove it out the door window, dummy! Pass it around to Rudd—hurry!"

A DEPRESSION IN the road a few feet distant had formed a wide-spreading puddle, and as the front wheels spewed the water aside in twin black cascades, Smooth slowed.

"Drop it!" he yelled.

He heard the splash as the seat landed, and had his fingers not been clamped tightly about the wheel he would have crossed them for luck. A moment later Rudd's cry blended with a howl from Yitz Cohen. Then there came the sound of screaming rubber and a crash.

"It got 'im!" cried Cohen. "He clipped it and piled up! Look at the bum—he's doin' a barrel roll and a nose dive—wow!"

"Grand thinking, Smooth!" said Rudd. "That was one for the book. How'd you guess it?"

"Think I shoved a hack for a livin' without learning to keep alive?" grinned Smooth. "That was a gift—from one hackman to another."

"How come?" asked Rudd.

"No one but a hackman would've shoved that rig along behind us the way that bird did. Wanna go back and sort out the pieces?"

"Like hell, I do! The gunner *might* be alive, and he *might* be cuddling that chopper. No, thanks! We'll keep rolling. Get us over to civilization where we can grab another cab. We'll drop this load in a back street and scram home."

"No good!" protested Smooth, "You grab another cab, but I gotta roll this clunk into the garage. It belongs to a friend of mine, and he needs it. And before you go, slip me a few dollars to pay for the seat and glass."

"Once a hackman, always a hackman," laughed Rudd, and handed Smooth some folded bills. "Okay, drive it in and give me a ring on the phone tomorrow."

Smooth stopped at an intersecting avenue, hailed a passing taxi, and watched Rudd and Cohen climb in and shut the door. Cohen held the suitcase across his knees, patted it lightly and threw a kiss to Smooth.

" 'Night, sweetheart," he laughed. "Thanks for the buggy ride."

"Chirpy little bird, ain't he?" said Rudd, and put the palm of his hand against Cohen's chin and pushed. "But he hummed a different lullaby when the music was hot."

Smooth grinned, saluted gravely, and turned to look at the taxi. He found a light stick of timber on the road and pried the fender away from the wheel. The rubber was badly worn, but it looked as though it might carry him to the garage. He climbed in behind the wheel, headed for Ocean Parkway, and settled down for a half hour drive.

25

DOUBLE CROSS

ALTHOUGH IT WAS well into the morning when Smooth drove up the garage ramp, his was the first cab in. The washers were playing rummy with the night man, and they looked up in surprise when Smooth came into the office and stamped the rain from his shoes.

"Sunny weather driver?" asked one.

"Oh, I'm not hungry,"* laughed Smooth. "I got mine, and I'm leavin' some for the other feller."

He scribbled his name across a blank trip card, folded four twenty-dollar bills in it and fastened them together with a clip.

"Here," he said to the night man. "Give this to Harry and tell him, 'Thanks for everything.' The rig needs a new rear window and seat—the front fender's got a wrinkle in it, and the tire's chewing-gum. Outside of that—she's ready to roll. Have fun, fellers, and good-*night*."

A chorus of emphatic curses followed Smooth to the office door. The night mechanic was looking ruefully at the battered fender and swinging an open-end wrench thoughtfully in one hand. He looked hard at the bridge of

---

* Hungry—A driver greedy for work and money.

Smooth's nose and seemed to be measuring the distance, but his eyes widened when Smooth tossed him a five-dollar bill and pointed to the group in the office.

"Whack it up amongst you," said Smooth. "A gift from Cinderella to the big bad wolves."

He chuckled happily as he walked down the ramp and headed toward Forty-second Street. Checking over his day's work, he decided he was due for a pat on the back from McNeary. And he hoped Dorothy would be on hand in the morning when he made his report. It was getting near the time when McNeary would be able to crack down and wrap up the case. There was a chance that he would rate a promotion if the Chief was pleased with his work, and he had definite ideas as to what he intended to do with the additional pay.

His nerves were still jumping, and now that the excitement of the chase had worn off he was chilled to the bone. He decided against a cab ride to his hotel and a hot shower, and turned into the hackmen's favorite cafeteria on Forty-second Street. A few drivers were huddled about the tables, totaling their calls and filling in imaginary trips to take the place of those which had been omitted during the rush hours. Smooth recognized none of the men, and when he had ordered his coffee and buns, he went to an empty table at the rear of the restaurant.

The hot Java made his soaking clothes a little more bearable, and soon chased the chill from his system. He dawdled over a second cup, smoked a cigarette, and tried to see Dorothy's face in the smoke that curled from the butt. He had partly succeeded when another face intruded. He drowned the cigarette, looked again and saw Lucky

Carmine, sodden and mud-stained, standing at the counter and reaching for a cup of coffee.

When the hackman turned and saw Smooth, he grinned and started toward him. The light from a wall bracket threw his face into sharp relief against his upturned coat collar. And Smooth saw that Lucky's cheek carried a strip of adhesive tape that ran from temple to chin. There was an ugly bruise beneath his eye, and his coat sleeve was ripped at the elbow. When he walked he limped slightly, and Smooth noticed he was having difficulty holding the plate and cup.

SUDDEN DOUBT SENT Smooth's hand to his shoulder holster. It closed about the empty leather and he remembered that Yitz Cohen had not returned his gun. Lucky caught the movement, and for an instant it seemed to Smooth that he hesitated. Then a broad grin creased his features and he limped to the table.

"I know I look like a bad dream," he smiled. "But that shouldn't send you reaching, feller. Why the quick grab?"

"Where'd you collect the bruises?" snapped Smooth.

"In a crack-up," answered Lucky easily, and seated himself opposite Smooth. "Why? Does that make me hot?"

A definite suspicion was crystallizing in Smooth's mind. Earlier in the night Lucky had asked him where he was going. And when he had mentioned Brooklyn, the little hackman had again questioned him. Remembrance of other coincidences came to life in an instant. That talk of Spanish's, at the Trocado—Spanish apparently asking Lucky for instructions—the cab that had followed him earlier in the day and resulted in the death of Tout Ender—the stickup on the Drive! All these things seemed to revolve about Lucky Carmine! In some way he had been connected with each.

"A crack-up, eh?" he said slowly. "Where'd it happen?"

He did not withdraw his hand from beneath his coat and he noticed that Lucky's eyes were held steadily upon it, and that he was careful to keep his own hands in plain view on the table. He knew Smooth packed a gun, but he did not know it was not in its holster tonight. It was the one ace Smooth held, and he had to make it stand up. If Lucky was, what he now thought him to be, one of Big Spanish's gunmen—it was going to be tight going—for the next few moments.

"Aw, I was loopin' it down the Concourse," said Lucky, "and a balkie* dope spins out of a side street. I went into a skid tryin' to miss him and wrapped up the wagon. Nice, eh?"

"The Concourse? Sure it wasn't in Brooklyn?"

"Look at the sheet," said Lucky, and passed his trip card to Smooth. "There's only one soldier** on it—the rip that took me to the Bronx. Naw—I ain't been in Brooklyn tonight."

Smooth pushed the card back to Lucky and grinned.

"Nuts with the card," he said. "I don't read fairy stories this year. And I'm tryin' like hell to believe you, Lucky. I *want* to believe you—see? I like you. But there's an awful sour smell about this setup. A guy gunned me in Brooklyn tonight and I had a tough job duckin' him. Had to spin him in a ditch to get clear. And that bird was one sweet driver—a hackman, or I'm crazy. Could it be you?"

---

* Balkie—Unskilled driver.
** Soldier—A call for more than a dollar— *i.e.,* the figure 1.

Lucky lifted the cup to his lips and blew into the steaming coffee. Smooth saw there was not a tremble—that his wrist was steady. And the grin never left Lucky's lips when he sipped the hot Java.

"Behave, Smooth," he said. "Why should I wanta burn you? I'm legit—you know that. Don't get yourself all jumpy over a few bursts and start suspectin' your pals. I'm your friend, feller." Smooth knew it was a lie as the words left Lucky's lips. The little hackman had tripped up on one word—*bursts!* Smooth had made no mention of sub-machine guns—he had simply said he had been shot at. In the jargon of the mobs, pistol fire was never referred to as "bursts." That was the term reserved for a Browning or Thompson gun. And Lucky had used the wrong word.

FOR A MOMENT Smooth said nothing. The coffee had soured in his stomach, and he was cold. He was used to the double cross—expected it in his dealings with the mobs. But Lucky and he had spent many hours over the coffee cups in the old days, discussing their troubles and telling the endless tales of the hackmen. They had worked out of the same garage many times, and once had thought of buying a cab and working it on shares. It had been a peculiar friendship—one confined to their working hours, save for an occasional trip to the Polo Grounds or the Yankee Stadium. But Smooth had always counted Lucky as a friend, or at least as a pal who could be depended upon to come through when the going got tough.

Now they were enemies. And for the past three days Lucky had been tracking him down—systematically trying to kill him. Less than two hours ago this same hackman had slashed through the wet streets, hunting him, eager for the kill. And even now, as he smiled across his coffee, he was probably waiting to follow Smooth into the street and finish the job.

Smooth checked back over the facts. The evidence that linked Lucky to Spanish's mob was purely circumstantial, and Smooth had learned through his years of training in the Bureau of Narcotics that it was one thing to make an arrest and quite another to get a conviction. It seemed that the courts delighted in making it difficult for this particular branch of the Treasury Department to function. They demanded ironclad proof of guilt, and innumerable times had released prisoners who were, as McNeary put it, "Guilty as hell and twice as hot."

There was no doubt to Smooth's mind as to Lucky's ability to clear himself in court as matters stood at present. And Smooth was somewhat surprised to find that he was glad this was so. Lucky was clever enough not to put up a fight if Smooth showed his credentials and attempted to arrest him. But McNeary was having trouble enough keeping the rest of Spanish's mob bottled up until the Bureau was ready to close the trap. Obviously, the thing to do was to stay in his role of gunman for Rudd and let Lucky slide out. He leaned across the table and stared into the little hackman's eyes.

"QUIT STALLIN', PAL," he said quietly. "You and I are workin' for different bosses. You're not kiddin' me any with that stuff about the Concourse. I know the street and the spot where you went into your waltz, and I'm the guy that spun you. Right?"

"Smart feller," grinned Lucky. "So what do we do? You're sittin' pretty with your hand on your roscoe—why talk?"

"Maybe I don't want to kill you," stalled Smooth.

"Maybe you're smart," added Lucky. "Listen, pal, I figure you're fast with that cannon—but no matter how good you are, I expect to get in *just one slug*. And I'm goin' to try to make it count—see?"

"Would you think I was yaller if I called it a draw?" asked Smooth.

"Hell, no! I'd know you were smart—and I might tell you to scram out of town for the good of your health. Things are goin' to happen in this burg—big things, pal."

"Thanks for nothing," said Smooth quietly. "Now take a receipt. It's a smart mob that knows when it's licked. And the Spanish outfit is through—for keeps. Pull out, Lucky—get to the clear while you can. If that guff about the farm wasn't the old hoopla, buy it tomorrow and spend the rest of the winter milkin' cows. Theresa will look swell in a sunbonnet—much better than she would in black. Give her my best, and don't buy any wooden ducks."

He kicked back his chair, backed around the edge of the table and walked to the cashier's counter near the door. He did not hurry, and his eyes were upon Lucky every moment of the time. It required a little manipulation to get some change from his right coat pocket with his left hand, but Smooth managed it, and did not take his right hand away from the empty holster. It was his only out—a bluff that must be played through. For he knew that Lucky Carmine was a killer—and hot.

Once outside the cafeteria he ran quickly along Forty-second Street until he found a hackman who was just pulling away from the curb. He opened the door of the taxi, jumped inside and crouched down on the seat.

"A short one, feller," he said. "Just drive over to Forty-fourth near the Claridge."

The driver grunted, threw the flag and bumped across the car tracks. Smooth glanced from the rear window, saw that he was not being followed, and drew his first easy breath since the time he had met Lucky in the restaurant.

26

WELL LAID PLANS

SMOOTH PHONED McNEARY before eight o'clock in the morning and caught him at his hotel. The Chief agreed to wait for him, and Smooth dressed quickly, smoked an extra cigarette as a substitute for breakfast, and hurried to McNeary's suite.

Some of the worry seemed to have left the Chief's face, and he smiled happily when Smooth dropped into an easy chair and hooked his legs over the arm.

"That was a nice job you did yesterday, Kyle," he said. "A real pleasant surprise after a week of headaches. Anything else on your mind?"

Smooth told him briefly of the events of the previous evening, and McNeary damned the mobsmen thoroughly when he heard of the attempted killing. He listened to Smooth's explanation about Lucky and made a note of the name. Then he paced restlessly about the room until Smooth had finished.

"You have an unhappy faculty for getting into trouble," he said at length. "I suppose you know without me telling you what your next job is to be."

"I could guess," grinned Smooth. "But I'd rather hear your setup."

"Very well, here it is. We can't wait any longer to present our case against Big Spanish and the men of his mob. Those that aren't decorating a slab in the morgue are sure of a long vacation in Atlanta or Alcatraz when we go to trial. Your evidence is a very necessary link, and I want you to dictate a complete report to a stenographer in a few minutes. I'll have it witnessed and notarized—just in case."

"Yeah, in case I'm not around when the trial comes up, eh? And that sounds as though Mrs. Kyle's little boy is going to get bounced right into a mess of trouble—quick."

"You've asked for it," said McNeary wearily. "You wanted to play this your way, and you seem to be the only man who can approach Rudd. He's the big catch now. I'll admit we've missed out on the brains of the Spanish outfit, but I don't think we'll catch up with that gentleman any sooner by stringing along with Rudd. Your friend the gambler seems to be as much at sea as our outfit. So we'll let that angle wait and crack down on Rudd."

"How do we stand on evidence?" asked Smooth.

"Almost enough to clean house completely. We've located his source of supply, and that list you turned in takes care of the distribution organization. We want the gang on the *Roulette* and the *Nicotine*. And that's your next job."

"I thought so," laughed Smooth. "Just a pleasant little evening's work."

"Oh, I know it's not going to be easy. But you might be interested to know I've put through a recommendation for promotion for a fresh faced kid in my district. If he cinches this case for me, I don't think the Bureau will have the heart to disapprove of it."

"Thanks, Chief," said Smooth earnestly. "But it would be worth losing it if I could stay in your district."

"Yeah—well, just wait until you make a mistake and then we'll see if you sing that tune. And now, what about tonight?"

"Rudd's throwing a little party on the *Roulette* with me as the guest of honor. He wants Dorothy to come, too, but that's out."

"I'm not so sure about that," said McNeary thoughtfully. He turned to the phone and put through a call.

Smooth started to protest when he heard the number, but McNeary waved him aside.

"That you, Dorothy?" he said into the instrument. "Good morning, young lady… I'd like to see you for a few moments… Yes, he's here… All right, we'll wait." He put down the receiver and turned to Smooth. "She'll be right up. I want her to hear this."

"I can't see where she fits in tonight," protested Smooth, "If we crack down on that outfit there's going to be fireworks. Why mix her up in it?"

THE CHIEF SMILED and fingered a menu that was stuck in the corner of the desk blotter. He glanced at Smooth and pointed to the card.

"Had your breakfast?" he asked.

"Oh, t' hell with it. I'm not hungry. You killed my appetite when you dealt Dorothy into this mess."

McNeary studied him quietly, turned to the phone and ordered a meal to be served in the room. He paced restlessly for a few moments and then seated himself opposite Smooth again.

"Let's figure things out," he suggested. "You've told me

the *Roulette* was anchored somewhere off Montauk Point,
That's rather indefinite—she might be anywhere within a
radius of a few hundred square miles. Not much chance
for us to find her, is there?"

"Why not? I'm going out to her tonight, and I'll pass the
approximate location along to you."

"How?" snapped McNeary.

"By radio—she's got a sending outfit."

"And just how do you expect to get away with that?"

"I don't know," admitted Smooth. "It's a gamble—but
I'll put it across somehow or other."

"Yes—with Dorothy to help you. That girl is smart as a
whip. Between the two of you, I expect to clean this case
up tonight. You can't possibly do it alone, and there's no
one else who could get on the *Roulette*. Be sensible—give
Dorothy credit for at least as much sense as you have. She'll
know what to do, and she'll know how to keep out of trouble. And that seems to be more than you can manage."

"But how about the fireworks?"

"There won't be any until after you leave the boat. If
Rudd plans this as a little party, he's probably given orders
to the *Roulette* to move into Long Island Sound. Her usual
position must naturally be outside the twelve mile limit
beyond Montauk Point. Think it over, Smooth. If your
party drove out to the Point it would take hours of riding
to get there—it's well over a hundred miles. No—she's
not out there."

"Oh, I agree with you on that," said Smooth. "Hoegy
Bright will run her down the Sound a way—probably to a
spot near Port Washington, the boys will pick us up in the
Nicotine, run us out to the *Roulette,* and drop us somewhere

along the North Shore after the party. But how does that fit in with your plans?"

"When you learn her approximate position, I expect Dorothy to keep the party amused while you slip through a radio call to me. It's a thousand to one shot, but if it doesn't click, we can copper our bets later. Break away from the crowd—tell 'em you're sick, or anything—and get to a phone as soon as the *Nicotine* puts you ashore."

The waiter arrived with the breakfast, and Smooth busied himself with the food for a few moments before he answered McNeary's suggestion. In substance, McNeary's ideas matched his own, but he had not intended to include Dorothy in the plan. He was forced to agree that it would be a good deal easier to put it across if he had the help of a partner. But it worried him to think of Dorothy on the *Roulette*.

THEY WERE STILL discussing the many angles of the plan when she arrived. She smiled at sight of the breakfast table and helped herself to what coffee was left in the pot.

"Such hours!" she laughed. "I don't think I'd have been quite so anxious for this job if I'd known it would get me up in the middle of the night." She looked sharply at Smooth and frowned. "You look as though you'd been pulled through a wringer," she said. "Don't you ever get any sleep?"

"Not much," admitted Smooth ruefully, and pointed to McNeary. "The old slave driver is swinging the lash hard this morning."

McNeary laughed and sketched out the plan to Dorothy while Smooth leaned back in his chair and smoked a cigarette. When the Chief explained the part Dorothy was

to play, Smooth noticed that her eyes widened with pleasure. She was eager as a child, and her utter disregard of the
danger involved sent a chill through Smooth that made his
stomach contract. He knew she would play this through as
though it were a game. And for an instant there came to
his mind a picture of Tout Ender, crumpled in a hallway
with a red smear covering his face. He heard the whine of
those steel-winged hornets that had flown past his head
in Sheepshead Bay, and he remembered Chick Binder's
description of Little Tommy in the *Cigarette*—"cut in half
and noddin' at us."

"No dice, Chief!" he said suddenly. "I don't want Dorothy to make the trip. I won't have it, I tell you! *She's out!*"

"Take it easy, Smooth," said the Chief quietly. "Dorothy
is an agent in the Bureau of Narcotics—and so are you. I'm
the District Supervisor, and I give the orders—understand?
I say she goes and that settles it."

"Oh, don't be such a baby, Smooth!" smiled Dorothy.
"You know very well the Chief won't let me get hurt. And
you know you couldn't possibly get into the radio room
without someone to help you. Don't be selfish and try
to grab all the glory. I *want* to go." She walked to the
window and stared out into the morning sky for an instant.
"And besides," she said quietly, "I want to be with you if
anything—"

"That's it!" interrupted Smooth. *"If!—if!—if!* There's
always an if in this racket. But by God, I'll burn down
Rudd and his whole mob if anything goes screwy tonight."

McNeary nodded and spread a map upon the desk. He
marked off a dozen spots along the North Shore, and next
to each he wrote a number.

He motioned to Smooth and pointed to each spot in turn.

"Make a list of these towns along the coast and the number against each of them. It depends upon how much time you have in the radio room as to what you can send. If you're in a hurry, just rap out the number nearest to the anchorage and we'll try to locate the *Roulette*. We'll wait until your party leaves and then take her before Bright runs up the coast and outside the twelve mile limit. If you have time, be more explicit—send: Five miles north of number 12, or whatever the case may be. Get it?"

"I understand," said Smooth. "Where will your contact point be?"

"We'll hook up with the police at Northport. It's a central location, and we'll sit close to the radio until we hear from you. If you have to use the phone, call this number." He passed Smooth a slip of paper. "Anything you don't understand?"

"Only one thing," said Smooth. "Why can't we leave Dorothy out of it?"

"Because, darling," she smiled, "neither the Chief nor I trust you with that fuzzy headed blonde. You might be counting stars or watching ripples over the bow and forget you were working for the Bureau."

McNeary laughed at the expression that came to Smooth's face and he tapped the point of his pencil against the list of runners that comprised Rudd's distributing system.

"How about these birds?" he asked.

"Shall we make a day of it?"

"Might as well," said Smooth. "If this is the blow-off,

we've got to work fast and careful. I'm taking Cohen with me this afternoon to break him in on the route. Any ideas on how you want to work the job?"

"If you follow the same routine as you did yesterday I don't think we'll have any trouble. I'll detail men to cover all the stops, and when Cohen makes his delivery we'll pick up the runners. We'll be damn sure none of them gets to a phone to pass the word along, and Rudd won't realize his outfit is wrapped up until he meets them in court."

"Good enough. But don't touch Cohen. He'll probably go back to Rudd's place with me and we can get him later," said Smooth.

"Naturally," agreed McNeary. "Well, I guess that takes care of everything. What time do you start?"

"Four o'clock from Forty-third and Broadway."

"And when do I meet you?" asked Dorothy.

"I'll pick you up at the theater at showbreak," said Smooth. "And if you're not there I won't be sorry. That's one standup I could take with pleasure."

"I'll be there!" she promised.

"You're just the type," he snapped, and rubbed his cigarette out against an ash tray. "And if you two don't mind, I'm going back to my room and catch up with a little shut-eye."

27

THE TRAP IS SET

YITZ COHEN WAS standing on the hotel steps when Smooth rolled up to the curb. He grinned, climbed into the back of the cab and slammed the door.

"Ah—take me for a drive in the Park, me good man," he said. "Mind the bumps—me kidneys are weak."

"I'll bounce 'em outta your ears if you don't quit clownin'," snapped Smooth. "Got the stuff with you?"

"My word! What a saucy driver. I'll report you to my friend the commissioner. Such insolence from a cabby, no less!" He turned up one of the drop seats, crossed his feet on it and leaned back in a corner.

"Soitinly, Smooth, old ducky-wucky—I got the junk. In fact, I'm a walkin' supply department. An' just so I don't get the same deal that was handed to Tout Ender, would you mind doin' a few buck and wings through the traffic so we can lose any visitors that might be on our tail?"

"Good idea," said Smooth. "And, by the way—gimme my gun."

Cohen folded a newspaper about the automatic and handed it to Smooth, who dropped it into the holster and settled back in his seat. He doubled back and forth through the side streets, looked for traffic jams and threaded his way

Cohen screamed as he fell

through hundreds of closely packed cabs, and at length was satisfied no one was trailing them. He cut across town and made his first stop at Eighth Avenue. The same mouse-faced individual who had eased from a restaurant and slid into the cab the previous day repeated the routine. He was a little surprised to find Cohen in the rear of the cab, but recognized him as one of Rudd's men and accepted the decks of cocaine.

Smooth drove slowly, knowing McNeary's men were waiting for the drop off. When the transaction was completed he stopped, opened the door and saw Ted Wade and Frank Garison follow the runner into a hallway. He smiled and stepped on the gas. Those two hard-boiled agents of the Bureau of Narcotics would waste little time with Mouse Face. A few doses of knuckle treatment and he would be hustled along to the central collection depot arranged for by McNeary. Then Wade and Garison would hurry to a point further along the route to repeat the performance.

Smooth saw Duffy and Levine, two more of McNeary's men, pick up the trail of the next runner to be contacted at Ninth Avenue, and when he drew away from his fourth stop, he grinned when he caught a glimpse of Wade and Garison back on the job again.

"Feller—I'm beginnin' to like this racket," laughed Cohen as they swung across the Park and headed for Harlem. "We deliver a little snow and in return we collect heavy sugar—nice, eh? Can y'imagine how the Feds'd burn if they knew what suckers we were makin' of them?"

"Never mind the Feds!" snapped Smooth. "The less I hear about them the better I like it."

"Aw, don't get hot. Bet-a-Grand Rudd'll always be one jump ahead of those birds. Why—I'll bet we been deliverin' this junk smack under their noses. D' y' know, I wouldn't be surprised if there was Federal men walkin' right up and down those sidewalks out there." He pointed leisurely out the cab window at the throngs of pedestrians. "Yes, sir! Just walkin' up and down, and what good does it do 'em?"

"I wonder," grinned Smooth. "Sometimes, Yitz, I begin to think you might have a brain."

"Aw, I'm smart—plenty smart. You'll get to appreciate me when you know me better. How many more stops we got?"

"Only a few. This route is just about wrapped up now."

"Glad to hear it," said Cohen. "Speed—that's what I like. A nice snappy job, no lost motions, everything under control—and we swing into the home stretch way out front and breathin' easy. Yeah, a nice snappy job."

"Oh, it was a snappy job, all right," repeated Smooth. "And we're headin' for the long stretch now."

"*Home* stretch," corrected Cohen. "Ain't you ever been to the track?"

"Never had time. I'll take a week off and try it, soon."

IT WAS AFTER ten when he dropped Cohen off at Rudd's apartment and headed for the garage. A bright moon and myriad stars were lighting the side streets with a dim reproduction of the glare of Times Square. He rolled past the many cafeterias where the night drivers stopped for their evening meals, but at none of these did he see Lucky Carmine. Ever since the showdown of the previous evening Smooth had kept a wary eye on the taxis that swept past him on the night streets. And he promised himself when this case was completed he would start a search for the little hackman that would put an end to this game of hide-and-seek.

It seemed that New York wasn't big enough for both of them now, and when Lucky learned Rudd's mob had folded up, he would certainly spot Smooth for a Federal. Before this happened, Smooth wanted to have a little talk with Lucky, and he wanted to be speaking over the sights of his own gun when it took place. He had decided to run the little hackman out of town—or at least give him one more opportunity to crawl out from under before he put on the pressure. If Lucky would not take the offer—some one was going to get hurt.

He swung the front wheels of his cab over the curb and started up the ramp, when he saw Old Squint waving to him from his usual position among the refuse barrels.

Smooth stepped down on the brake, tossed a coin into the outstretched hand and grinned.

" 'Lo, Squint. Kinda late for you to be around."

"Yeah, kinda late," agreed Squint. "Here—a little bloke gimme this fer you. I missed you goin' out."

He passed Smooth a note and lurched off in the darkness toward the smoke joint on the corner. Smooth unfolded the paper and spread it against the wheel.

I TOLD THERESA ABOUT LAST NIGHT. SHE THINKS YOU COULD HAVE PLUGGED ME AND DIDN'T WANT TO. SHE SAYS THANKS AND TAKE A NIGHT OFF.

Smooth crumpled the note, stuck it in his pocket and rolled into the garage. He drove to the wash stand, checked his meter readings, and walked toward the office. The first part of the note was easily understood, but Smooth wished Lucky had been a little more explicit with his warning. There was no doubt but that Theresa and Lucky were trying to give him a break. Their advice to him to take a night off evidently meant this evening, as Lucky had given Squint the note early in the day.

He thought for a moment, could figure no way in which Lucky could fit into the scheme of things tonight, and dismissed the note with a shrug. Harry Tone, the fleet owner, was still at his desk, and he looked up in annoyance when Smooth stepped into the office.

"Now what?" he barked. "You're the screwiest damn driver I've ever hired. Why so early?"

"Oh, just callin' it a night," said Smooth. "I'm givin' you two pounds for your end—and quitting."

"Whatsa matter? You gone nuts?"

"No, Harry—just movin' on. I may stop in to see you in a few days and tell you all about it. But I can't tonight. If any one asks for me, tell 'em I'm still rollin', will you?"

"Gimme the money and goodby," barked Tony. "You're a swell kid, Smooth, and I like you. But all this hocus-pocus is putting a curl in my hair. Last night you roll in with a folded up rig and eighty bucks. Tonight it's something else. So long, feller—write to me when they drop you in the clink. I'll send along some cigarettes."

SMOOTH GRINNED, TOSSED him the money and the trip card, and left the garage. He hailed a cab, drove to his hotel, and changed into fresh clothes. He glanced at his gun, saw the clip was full, and dropped it back into the holster. Something made him pause when he was about to leave the room—some fleeting idea that he had forgotten or neglected a duty. He glanced about, opened the top bureau drawer and, hardly conscious of the action, he dropped a few additional clips into his coat pocket. He shrugged, left the hotel, and taxied to the stage entrance of the Clinton Theater.

A few musicians of the pit orchestra were grouped about the alley, and as Smooth waited he found himself comparing this night with that other when he had rolled through the street on the front end of a hack, and had been hailed by a frightened girl standing in the shadows. It was hard to believe that had been less than two weeks ago. He had been detailed to his first big assignment—a new man in the district, out to make a name for himself. Now the Chief had put through a recommendation for his promotion. And better still, Dorothy was—

"Hello, darling. Keep you waiting long?"

He looked up and saw her standing beside the cab. She was smiling and beautiful, and Smooth climbed from the taxi and stood silently admiring her. He liked the way her hat tilted over one eye, and the silver fox collar of her coat made a frame for her face. He caught her hands, held them for a moment, and helped her into the cab.

"Sure you want to go through with it?" he asked.

"Of course I am—silly," she smiled, and leaned toward him. "Think I'm going to let Gilda have you?"

Smooth directed the driver to Rudd's apartment, turned up the front window and swung to face Dorothy.

"Would it make much difference?" he asked.

"Sometimes I think little boys only grow up on the outside—inside they're always *just* little boys with very little sense. Maybe these girls with a direct attack know more about men than we give them credit for. Maybe their way is the right way—let's see."

SHE SLIPPED ONE arm around his shoulder, drew him to her and kissed him firmly on the lips. For a moment she held him and then kissed him again.

"*Now,*" she said. "Does that give you any ideas—or courage?"

"When do we get married?" he blurted.

"*Mister* Kyle! This is *so* sudden!" she laughed. "Would next Saturday afternoon at about three o'clock be all right? I'll have the afternoon off now that the show is closing."

"Stop clowning, Dorothy," he said. "I'm—I'm on the level. Oh, I know I'm a washout as a Romeo—but—but—"

"So am I, Funny Face," she whispered. "I'm on the level with you—so much that it hurts. I love you, Smooth."

"That's swell. I was going good the other night on the Drive, and sort of hoping I'd work up enough nerve to propose. But this morning in the Chief's room, you acted as though I was two other guys. Naturally, I—well—"

"Did you expect me to bounce into your arms with McNeary as an audience? Say—he'd have tossed us both out, and I don't intend to start housekeeping on nothing a week. Be sensible, darling."

"That's a tough order with you around," he grinned. "But now that I'm practically the lord and master—how about you taking an order?"

"What sort of an order?"

"I'll drop you off at your place and tell Rudd you couldn't make the party. Tomorrow I'll square things with McNeary and—"

"Nothing doing!"

"Wow!" cried Smooth. "I start off with two strikes on me, eh? One word from me and you do as you please. And I thought brunettes were easy to manage. When do I get some obedience?"

"Whenever you ask the right questions," she laughed. "But this is business, dear, We've got to go through with it."

"Yeah—a hell of a business, if you ask me."

He paid off the driver and escorted Dorothy across the foyer and into an elevator. His teeth were clamped tightly and two little lumps of muscle twitched at the base of his jaws. The elevator boy smiled a greeting and Smooth growled at him, and when Simpson opened the door he growled again.

"Snap out of it, darling," whispered Dorothy, and pinched his arm. "Smile—it's a party."

"Nuts!" growled Smooth as he helped her out of her wrap.

Gilda was seated on the corner of Rudd's desk, holding a glass into which the gambler was pouring champagne. She waved a greeting to Dorothy, threw a kiss to Smooth, and pointed to other glasses on a silver tray near by.

"Bubbles for the ladies," she called. "Ruddy, old dear, is throwing a party as is a party. Warm up your tummies before he takes us out on the deep, dark ocean."

"Thanks, Gilda," said Smooth. "I was just saying to Dorothy it was a bit cold for a yacht party." He turned to Rudd. "Why not call it off tonight? We could bounce up to Silva's place and have more fun."

"Don't listen to him," protested Dorothy. "The moon is beautiful, and it's not a bit cold. I've never seen a more perfect night for a sail."

"Or a murder," added Smooth.

"What's the matter, Smooth?" asked Rudd. "Change your mind?"

"We won't let him," said Dorothy. "If he spoils our party we'll toss him overboard."

"I can swim," laughed Gilda. "Toss us both over—I'd enjoy the company."

"You're wet now, sweet," said Dorothy coldly to Gilda. "Why add to it?"

"I think Smooth's right," said Gilda. "It *is* cold tonight. I felt the chill when Dorothy came in."

RUDD WAS LAUGHING heartily, and he seemed regretful to end the quarrel. But at length he rang for Simpson and the butler brought the girls' wraps. While they were putting them on, Rudd caught Smooth by the arm and drew him aside.

"We won't stay long," he said. "Yitz Cohen will drive us out to the landing. He's hired a car, and should be waiting for us at the door. I want you to have a look at the *Roulette*, because I might have to send you out to her sometime. You're going to be a big man in my organization, Smooth, and I've got some great plans for you. The sooner you learn all the angles the sooner we can branch out and take over the other large cities."

"Oh, I don't mind going out to the *Roulette*," said Smooth quietly. "I'd be glad to go alone. But I've never known it to fail, when two women stick their noses into things— blowie! Trouble!"

"Don't be a pessimist. We'll have a fine time, and we'll probably remember this as one of the first of many pleasant evenings."

"I'll remind you of that tomorrow," promised Smooth.

The girls were standing at the door, and Gilda waved impatiently as Simpson helped Rudd into his overcoat.

"Come on, slowpokes," she called.

They found Yitz Cohen seated behind the wheel of an expensive seven-passenger car, and the little gunman seemed quite proud of his duties as driver. When the doorman handed Rudd and his party into the car, Smooth waved him away with a flutter of hands and closed the door himself. Yitz crawled back into the driver's seat and sent the car swiftly across town and over the Queensboro Bridge.

"How far out do we go?" asked Smooth.

"I told Hoegy Bright to bring the *Roulette* down the Sound and anchor off Bayville. Chick Binder will pick us up at Sea Cliff with the *Nicotine* and run us out to her."

Smooth remembered that Bayville was one of the points McNeary had checked off on the map. Its number was six, and it was less than twenty miles by water from Northport. The Chief had come close in his guess as to where Rudd would place the *Roulette*—much closer than Smooth had figured. He had expected the boat to be at least fifty miles further along the Sound and was surprised at McNeary's accuracy.

"You brought her quite a way in," he said. "Any particular reason?"

"Why not?" laughed Rudd. "When you see the *Roulette* you'll realize the little lady is like Caesar's wife—above suspicion. She's a dream of a boat, and if I have the time I think I'll cruise south in her next month."

The traffic thinned out when they swung into Northern Boulevard, and Cohen kicked the car along at a good rate. When they passed Little Neck, and left the city limits, he glanced into the mirror, saw there were no State Troopers behind them and jumped the speed again.

Smooth managed to glance from the rear window occasionally without attracting any attention, and as they skimmed along the open road he had a growing conviction they were being followed. A pair of headlights behind them lost their anonymity—they ceased to be one of a great many sets of twin beams and took on an individuality. A slight outward cast of the right lamp had distorted the focus, and Smooth was able to identify them from the many other lights that swung into line at their rear.

FOR A MOMENT he thought of telling Rudd and suggesting they swing off into a side road to lose the trailer. But there was a possibility McNeary had changed his plans and sent a car along behind them to locate the contact point. He watched when they swung north at Roslyn and headed toward the waterfront at Sea Cliff.

Less than a half mile behind, the twin beams flared around the turn and straightened out to follow.

"By the way, Rudd," Smooth said quickly. "I hope you learned something last night. I mean about loud music."

He said it lightly, and tried to get his question across without giving the girls any idea of the seriousness of it. Rudd smiled and winked, and made a slight gesture toward Cohen.

"I'm way ahead of you, Smooth," he answered. "Yitz has decided to take violin lessons and he brought his fiddle along. It's in that leather case on the seat next to him."

"Yeah?" said Smooth. "I always wanted to play a fiddle. It's soothing to the nerves. Mind if I get in front and have a look at it?"

"Not at all. But is there any reason for your nerves to need soothing just now?"

"No-o-o—not particularly. But I'd feel better."

Rudd leaned forward and instructed Cohen to pull to the side of the road. When Smooth changed to the front seat, he saw that the following headlights had also stopped.

"Would you gentlemen mind talking English for a while?" said Gilda when the car rolled again. "Fiddle playing! Are we all going nuts around here?"

"Oh, no," said Rudd suavely. "Yitz Cohen expects to entertain us later this evening, and Smooth is probably one of those nosey individuals who has to see a thing to be convinced. Right, Smooth?" he added.

"Absolutely," agreed Smooth.

He bent forward, opened the case against the floor of the car and lifted out a Thompson sub-machine gun. He fitted the drum into place, set the muzzle against the floor and gripped, the stock between his knees. Yes, Cohen had brought his fiddle, and it was ready to play a tune if Lucky Carmine happened to be in that car behind them.

"I think it's a Stradivusy," said Cohen. "You know— one of them expensive makes. If I stick to me practicin' I might grab off a job like Rubinoff or Ben Boiney. Y' never can tell."

"If you try to stroke that cat tonight," warned Gilda, "I'll bend it around your ear. Of all the lunatics I ever met— you and that patsy we met in San Diego take the marbles."

SMOOTH WAS AWARE that Dorothy had said nothing, and he was sure she understood Rudd's guarded conversation. When they reached a small landing at the water's edge in Sea Cliff he caught a worried look from her and smiled in assurance. Cohen climbed out from behind the wheel and helped the girls from the car. But Smooth made no move to get out. He turned and watched the back road and nodded when Gilda called to him.

"Go ahead—I'll be along in a moment," he said, and turned to Rudd. "You folks go out to the end of the dock. I'll stick around—just in case."

"All right, Smooth," said Rudd. "Come along as soon as you're satisfied. The *Nicotine* is waiting for us." He pointed to the small runabout moored to the dock end.

"See her?"

Smooth nodded and waved him away. He waited until the party had seated themselves in the *Nicotine,* saw that the headlights had stopped at a bend of the road, and unlimbered the gun. He packed it in the case, grabbed the handle and sprinted down the dock.

The *Nicotine* was a trim little craft, about seventeen feet long and fitted with a double cockpit forward of the motors. Rudd and the girls were crowded into the rear seat and Chick Binder grinned at him from behind the wheel and motioned toward Cohen to make room for Smooth in the front seat. When he was comfortable, Chick idled the boat away from the dock and swung out into the Sound. She lifted smartly when he gave her a full throttle and Smooth judged they were skimming along at better than thirty-five miles per hour.

"Nice little number, ain't she?" asked Chick.

"A beauty," agreed Smooth, and turned to face Rudd. "This little honey wouldn't have been much good back in the old days. We needed plenty of boat to carry booze and a pair of engines that could drive weight."

"Them days is gone forever!" sang Rudd, and laughed. "It's a pushover, now, compared to the rum-running racket. We could carry all the stuff we need in a canoe. And I'd like to see any tub the Fed's could get to run this baby down. As a matter of fact," he grinned, "I'm afraid Chick might get a yen to become another Gar Wood and quit me. He's a sucker for these fast hoppers."

"They ain't so hot in a storm, Rudd," complained Chick. "A night like this is aces, but when it starts to blow, this baby tries to pound herself to pieces if I don't take it easy."

"Aw, stop bellyachin'," said Cohen. "Me—I go fer this Barnacle Bill stuff in a big way. Give 'er the gas, pal!"

28

MACHINE GUN

CHICK SWUNG THE wheel to catch a series of short waves that rolled toward them from a passing boat. The *Nicotine* banked sharply and flatted against the waves in a series of short, choppy jumps. Cohen yelped and grabbed Smooth by the arm as they banked again and straightened out on their run.

"Nix, pal!" he cried. "Don't take me serious—it was a gag, see?"

"What's that town over there to the right?" asked Dorothy, pointing to a few lights along the shore.

"Bayville's in there some place," said Chick. "Back a little from the beach. And that strip of land out there is Rocky Point. Those lights over to the left—just ahead of us—that's the *Roulette*."

"Nice sailin', sailor," said Cohen. "Now let's see you make a landing without sinkin' us."

Chick cut the motor and they glided in beneath the boom of the slim-lined yacht. Smooth judged her to be at least one hundred and twenty feet over all, and built for both speed and comfort. Bert Lovette waved to them from the deck and pointed to colored lanterns strung about the boat.

"All dressed up and waitin' for you," he shouted. "Come aboard and make yourselves at home."

"Now isn't that a hell of a way for a deck hand to greet the owner?" laughed Rudd. "You'll have to admit that this racket certainly makes for a community spirit amongst the boys." He pointed to the ladder leading over the side. "Up you go, ladies."

When the party had gone aboard, the *Nicotine* was moored to a boom extending outward from the starboard beam. Yitz Cohen took his "violin" from Smooth, glanced about the deck and winked.

"I understand all these scows is equipped with saloons," he said. "How's about a little drink?"

"G'wan, find it yourself," said Bright. He turned to Rudd and saluted smartly. "Ready for inspection, Admiral."

Rudd laughed, introduced the girls and they started forward.

"Hoegy used to be a cook in the Chinese navy," he said. "The sea's in his blood—makes him very nautical at times."

"Never mind that Chinese stuff," grinned Bright. "Durin' prohibition I was the pride of the off-shore fleet. I brought in more good booze in a week than all the bootleggers in town could cut and spoil in a month." He pointed to a small engine mounted well forward and covered with canvas. "Now that's the anchor engine. Everything's up to date and shipshape aboard this gondola. And behind you, them windows look out of the saloon, only it ain't the kind of saloon Cohen thinks it is."

"Aw, I knew there was a catch to it," grunted Cohen, and glanced through one of the ports. "It looks like a dining room to me."

"Right above it," continued Bright, taking no notice of Cohen, "is the pilot house where the skipper hangs out." He cupped a hand to his mouth. "Hey, Cap! Come down here!"

A tall, gaunt figure opened the door of the pilot house and stared down at them. His hair was gray and flew in untidy snarls about his face. Three inches of white cuff extended below the sleeves of his coat, giving to his arms the appearance of dangling, ape-like appendages. He was tall, but stooped, and a smouldering cigar was clamped in one corner of his mouth.

"Wadda you want?" he barked.

"Pleasant little feller, ain't he?" said Bright to the girls. "That tramp carries a master's ticket for any ocean, and when he's sober he's a crack sailor. But he's practically never sober. He used to work with me in the rum fleet—name's Cap Hartson." He waved his hand disgustedly toward the pilot house. "G'wan back in your coop,"

HE SHOWED THEM through the saloon and then went on a tour of inspection through the staterooms and galley. Dorothy insisted upon being shown the refrigerator and electric stove, and complimented Bright on his cleanliness. Gilda was bored and did not take the trouble to conceal it. And when Bright suggested a trip to the engine room to see his prized Diesels, she flatly refused.

"I came here for amusement, not a course in seamanship," she protested.

Rudd grinned and led them back into the saloon. He turned on the radio and a Jap mess boy opened champagne. The party got off to a flying start when Yitz Cohen decided to give an impersonation of Pat Rooney and landed on his ear in the middle of a double bell. Bert Lovette came in to say hello, and later Rudd introduced Smooth to Bill Oler, an additional member of the mob.

"This must have set you back aplenty," said Smooth when Rudd and he were alone. "You'll have to put out lots of junk to cover expenses."

"Oh, not so much," said Rudd. "The rich playboys had to get rid of their yachts when they became un-rich. These things are selling for a song now. And I know the song." He stood up and took Smooth by the arm. "Let the kids amuse themselves for a while. I want to show you something."

He led Smooth back through a narrow passage to a stateroom that had been equipped with the latest make of sending apparatus.

"Nice little radio outfit, eh?" he said. "That's the baby that brought us the bad news at Joe Silva's place the other night. Think you could learn to make it talk?"

"In about ten years. Who sends for you now?"

"Hoegy Bright. He's fast as hell, but he sends stuff that's hard to take sometimes. Understand?"

Smooth knew Rudd was referring to the loss of the *Cigarette,* and he realized this suave gambler intended to get rid of Bright at the first opportunity. He nodded wisely, and seated himself at the key.

"Maybe Bright could show me the tricks," he suggested.

"Why not?" grinned Rudd. He stepped to the door and called Bright. When the gunman arrived, Rudd pointed to the set. "Smooth wants to see the wheels go round. Show him how it works. I'll go back and amuse the ladies."

Bright nodded and took Smooth's place at the key.

"First you gotta learn code," he explained. "It ain't hard, and you can practice with spoons on restaurant tables."

"Okay, pal," said Smooth. "Let's try the numbers for the first lesson. Let's see—six is my lucky number. How do you send six?"

"Aw, that ain't the idea," protested Bright. "You might just as well start at the beginning. Learn the alphabet in Morse and International and then work on through the rest."

"I know—I know," said Smooth. "But let's hear what six sounds like."

Bright rapped out the numeral and repeated it again and again until Smooth said he had enough.

"And that goes bouncing all over hell, eh?" asked Smooth. "Anyone this side of China can hear it?"

"Not much!" grunted Bright. "I'm workin' a dead key. You can't go splashin' code around—the government would raise hell."

SMOOTH NODDED AND figured his next move. The set was different from any he had seen, and it was going to take some clever questioning to learn its operation. Bright was wise and suspicious. He had no intention of teaching Smooth, and was merely stalling for time. Distrust was part of the racket, and he had not been fooled by Rudd's casual request.

"What makes the set talk?" asked Smooth.

"We'll get around to that later. How about a little drink?"

"Swell idea, Gorgeous," said Gilda from the doorway. She was holding a brimming glass of champagne in one hand and she extended it to Bright. "Take this and go look at the stars."

"Oh, I get it," laughed Bright. "You wanna have a talk with Smooth, eh?"

"Goodby, Hoegy. You're too smart for one little boy."

"Well—I'd like to give you a break," smiled Bright. "But you'll have to find another place to vamp the guy. This radio shack is outta bounds. It's one spot I don't allow visitors—see?"

Smooth would cheerfully have tossed Gilda through a port if he could. Whatever chance he had of getting off a signal to McNeary had gone glimmering when that blonde decided to go on the hunt. He tried to smile, but it didn't work, and when Hoegy ushered them both to the door, Smooth helped Gilda over the sill with enough force to send her sprawling against the opposite bulkhead.

"Darling! Have you gone cave-man on me?" she yelped.

"A love-pat," he grunted, and started back toward the saloon.

"Wait," she said, and grabbed his arm. "Come out on deck and let the moon soak some romance into your system. Please."

He took her arm and led her to the stern and leaned against the rail. The music of the radio drifted out to them and he heard Dorothy singing. At the end of the number there was a furious burst of applause from the men in the saloon, and Smooth wondered if she would miss all this attention when they settled down in a three-room flat.

"Does she always bounce that contralto at the ceiling?" asked Gilda coldly. "It must get monotonous after a time."

"That was a number from her show," said Smooth absently. "Boy—how she slays them with that."

"We were talking about the moon," said Gilda quickly.

She rested her forearm on Smooth's shoulder and leaned against him. "I wonder what's become of it. The stars are gone too. But that's all right—maybe they're being considerate and want to leave us alone."

Smooth glanced up and saw a heavy bank of clouds had rolled in across Long Island and spread a mantle of darkness over the Sound. The shore lights were distant pinpoints of fire, and the water had become jet, like wet pavement in a dark alley. He was scarcely conscious of the fact that Gilda's arm had slipped around his shoulders and he stared off into the blackness, wondering just what sort of an idiot McNeary was calling him when the signal failed to come through.

THE FAINT THROB of a motor came across the water, and in a moment it grew in volume. A speed boat, probably the same type as the *Nicotine,* was pounding along the shore line, and although Smooth could see no moving lights, when the whir of her motors increased he realized she was coming toward the *Roulette.* For a moment he wondered if it might be McNeary searching for him. It was late, and he had been unable to contact the Chief. Possibly this was a Federal boat.

"Why so silent?" asked Gilda.

"Huh?" grunted Smooth. "Oh—yeah, it's a swell night, isn't it?"

"What a lover!" she laughed. "Stop staring at nothing and tell me I'm beautiful."

"Yeah, you're beautiful," said Smooth, and the words were empty in his ears as he listened to the throb of the motors.

He remembered the *Nicotine* had been equipped with

a powerful spotlight that had sent a dancing ray ahead of the boat as they drove out to the *Roulette*. He looked for a like beam, but found nothing but a wall of darkness that seemed to draw closer as the clouds piled heavier in the sky. He felt Gilda's hair against his cheek and suddenly the roar of the motor swung closer.

Was it McNeary? The Chief had promised not to start any fireworks until the girls were off the yacht. And Smooth found it difficult to mistrust his boss. But when the speed boat turned and circled the *Roulette,* and then came tearing under the stern, his doubts grew to an over-powering conviction.

He tried to force his sight through the darkness and spot that boat. But Gilda had twisted in front of him and was staring into his eyes. She kissed him and he grinned foolishly.

"Thanks, Gilda," he said. "But if it's all the same—"

Crimson flame leaped out into the night. A spitting line of fire drew a jagged line across the black water. The white beam of a spotlight flooded the stern of the *Roulette* and the *rat-tat-tat* of a sub-machine gun chattered again.

"Get down!" yelled Smooth.

He caught Gilda by the shoulders and threw her to the deck. She screamed, and instinctively started to get up. Smooth was beside her, one arm holding her down and the other pointing toward the passageway.

"Crawl in there—quick!" he snapped. "That burst was high—the next might be right."

The light from an opened door splashed a yellow triangle on the forward deck. It was marked with shadows as the group in the saloon poured out and ran to the rail.

"Get back—hurry!" yelled Smooth.

The words had hardly left his mouth when another burst of gunfire smashed out of the darkness. A man screamed—high and thin, and it ended in a curse. Smooth saw Hoegy Bright bow grotesquely as though he were curtsying to Death. He sprawled, and behind him Smooth saw Bill Oler, his hands tearing at a throat that was ringed with a scarlet necklace.

"Close that door!" cried Smooth. "Kill the light, you fools! Get down before you get burned down!"

THERE WAS NO doubt in his mind now. That wasn't McNeary out there in the darkness. The Chief would never make a move of that sort. No, the man squeezing the trigger of that Tommy gun was probably a thin shouldered hackman who smiled a twisted grin as he sprayed those steel-jacketed slugs. It was Lucky Carmine—out to collect a debt.

Gilda had crawled over the sill and into a passage leading to the saloon. Smooth followed her, lifted from his knees and sprinted ahead. The lights were still burning and he glanced quickly about for Dorothy. She was close to the door, crouching against a bulkhead and peering out into the night.

Smooth caught her by the arm and dragged her into the passage. She looked at him and smiled faintly, and nodded when he gestured toward the deck.

"And stay down!" he ordered.

Rudd had switched off the lights and a silence hung over the *Roulette*. Smooth heard the throb of the speed boat's motor, and by the sound he judged it was turning in a wide circle.

"Gimme that chopper, Cohen!" he cried. "You wanted music, feller—you're gettin' it."

"Yeah—but who do we shoot at?" yelped Cohen. "I didn't think there was anybody mad at us."

"As long as Spanish has got a punk left on the street," said Rudd, "we're goin' to be targets. What's your guess, Smooth? Think it's the Spanish mob?"

"Of course it is," said Smooth. "I thought I saw a car tailing us from the city. Now I'm sure! That mug saw us leave Sea Cliff, doubled back somewhere and grabbed a speed boat. Now he's out there shooting us to pieces."

"Let's get outta here!" yelled Cohen. "Hey, Captain—Admiral—somebody get up the anchor and let's scram."

"Great idea," barked Rudd. "Hoegy and Olin are through, but there's enough men on this tub to take her down the Sound."

"Not a chance," said Smooth. "That boat can run circles around us."

"I know it," said Rudd. "But it's a gamble. If we can get out to open water there may be a wind. We'll get away." The door opened and Captain Hartson walked slowly into the saloon. His gaunt figure was faintly outlined against the sky, and he stood, hands on his hips, peering into the room.

"Now what t'hell?" he growled. "What's all the shootin'?"

"Get the anchor up and let's run down the Sound," said Rudd. "Have you got anyone in the engine room?"

"Yeah—my first engineer is down there with a bottle. I'll go down and have a talk with him."

He stalked off through a passage, and Cohen cursed him eloquently. Smooth located the Thompson gun, fitted a drum into place and crept toward the door.

"What happens?" asked Cohen.

"C'mon up forward with me," said Smooth. "We might be able to get that hook out of the mud."

"And how!" yelled Cohen. He crept out onto the deck, and in his eagerness to get the *Roulette* under way, he sprinted toward the anchor engine. "Just watch Yitz the sailor," he shouted.

29

LONE WOLF

SMOOTH HAD NOT heard the speed boat's motor and he hoped Lucky might be having engine trouble. He flopped down, looked out over the water and cuddled the gun under his arm. As though Cohen's words had been a signal, the white beam of a spotlight flared over the bow. It lighted Cohen's figure and made of it a sharp silhouette.

"Down!" yelled Smooth.

He was an instant too late. The submachine gun stuttered and Cohen screamed. It was as though a giant hand had swept him across the deck and hurled him against the rail. He spun and dropped and Smooth swung his gun along the beam and squeezed.

The spurt of flame from the muzzle blinded him, and the spotlight winked out, leaving the water a black void. The motor of the speed boat throbbed steadily, turning in a wide circle that brought it off the port beam. Smooth ran across the deck and followed the sound with the gun. It was useless to shoot into a wall of darkness, and it looked as though he would need all the slugs left in that drum. He hurried back to the saloon and found Dorothy and Gilda seated on the deck with Rudd.

"Where's Chick and Bert?" he demanded. "I could use a little help around here."

"They'll be back," said Rudd. "We got a nice outfit stowed away in one of the staterooms. Take it easy."

There was a sound of footsteps along the passage, and Smooth saw two dark figures crawling toward the saloon. He heard the clink of metal, and suddenly a match flared. Chick was jamming drums into place in two sub-machine guns and hurrying to complete the job before the match burned out.

"Now that's something," said Smooth. "I'll take the stern, you get up to the bow, Chick. Bert can bounce around here and cover whatever side that mug out there decides to come in on."

"Yeah—but don't get careless," warned Binder. "See what he done the last time? He cuts his motor and drifts in close, and when he gets something to shoot at—wham!"

"All right—don't give him anything to shoot at," said Smooth. "Come on—let's get goin'."

He crawled aft, keeping close to the deck house and taking advantage of the deeper shadows cast by a canvas awning stretched above the after deck. He listened but could hear nothing above the gentle slap of the waves against the sides. He slipped the muzzle of the gun forward, drew a coin from his pocket and threw it against the deck house bulkhead a few feet away.

As the silver tinkled the spotlight flared again. It swung quickly along the deck and caught Chick Binder flat-footed in the bow. The motor roared into life and with it came the chatter of the gun. Smooth emptied a drum at the moving light and saw it wink out.

He listened, waiting for his ears to pick up the sound of the motor. The staccato crack of his gun had deafened him for the instant, and when he was again able to distinguish other sounds he heard the motor roaring off into the night. There was another sound, too. One that was closer and even less pleasant. Chick Binder was crying—low, broken sounds that sounded like a child in pain.

SMOOTH CRAWLED FORWARD and found him huddled against the anchor engine. He looked once and turned away. Chick wasn't playing in this game any more. He was finished.

A figure beckoned to Smooth from the saloon door and he crawled toward it. Lovette was crouched on the deck, his gun tight under his arm and a worried frown on his face.

"Think you hit 'em?" he asked.

"I might have put a crease in the boat," said Smooth. "It's like peggin' at a firefly. That baby must be doin' better than thirty an hour, and every time the gunner lets go a burst, the guy at the wheel swings. The odds are against us—plenty!"

"What t' hell happened to that rumpot skipper?" asked Lovette.

"How do I know? Why don't you go and dig 'im up? If we don't get outta here quick *we ain't goin'!*"

Lovette nodded and crawled to the ladder leading down to the engine room. Smooth heard him curse and saw a flare of light come from the doorway when Lovette snapped on the switch. He lifted his gun and waited for the burst that he thought would follow that light. But it did not come, and Smooth wondered if his shots had been better than he imagined. A moment later there was a muffled crash of a sub-machine gun. Smooth looked quickly over each beam but saw nothing. Then he realized the shots had come from below.

Lovette joined him and the gunman's face was hard. He nodded toward the engine room and laughed at Rudd.

"Nice crew you got, boss," he growled. "They needed a little rum to steam up their nerve and didn't know when to quit drinkin'. They were stiff—blind drunk and shiverin' on the deck."

"And you—" said Rudd quietly.

"I sung 'em a lullaby—the lice!"

"Not so good, Bert," snapped Rudd. "How do we move this barge if the coppers decide to come out and investigate?"

"Aw, them bums down there wouldn't 'a' been any good for two days. If we could get in to Sea Cliff I know where to dig up a guy to sail this boat."

"Yeah—if!" said Rudd. "With that gunner buzzin' around in the dark, our chances are lousy."

"Hey—that's not a bad idea," said Smooth quickly. "Rudd—why don't you let Bert take you and the girls ashore? You can outrun that other boat and I'll stand 'em off till Bert brings out a few guys to help me."

"Horatius at the bridge, eh?" grinned Rudd. "That's a nervy play, kid. We might put it across at that. But how do we get away in the boat without collecting a dose of lead poisoning?"

"And why don't you come, too?" asked Dorothy suddenly.

"Oh, hello, baby," grinned Smooth.

"Thought you and Gilda were asleep."

"Sleep hell!" said Gilda. "We're just keeping out of this

rose carnival and letting you smart boys find the answer. The sooner I see the last of this tub the better I'll like yachting."

"We could all get away together," insisted Dorothy. "There's no reason for you to stay, Smooth."

"Me—I like it here," said Smooth. "And when you gals hear another speed boat slamming past the old *Roulette*, you'll be glad Uncle Smooth is sitting pretty with a chopper to cover your back. No, I'll hang around a while."

"It's your party," said Rudd. "If you want to slip us an easy out, it suits me."

"Good! Now hold everything while I see if we have visitors."

HE CREPT OUT onto the forward deck and made his way ahead until he found what was left of Chick. He took the gun from the limp hands and stretched out behind the anchor engine. The night was quiet and the clouds were low flung and even darker than previously. He searched over the narrow limits of surface visibility but could see nothing. Again he tried to attract attention by a flung coin. Nothing happened and he got to his knees.

A spotlight flared in the darkness and Smooth dropped. He flattened himself against the deck and pressed his face to the boards. A long, even burst came through the darkness, and Smooth forgot to breathe. There was another splash of fire from the speed boat and Smooth knew the gunner was painting narrow strips along the deckhouse bulkhead with a brushful of lead.

Suddenly the light died. The boat roared off in a wide circle and Smooth sprinted to the saloon.

"Come on! Get goin'!" he said quietly. "Scram into the

Nicotine and head for the beach before that bird completes his circle."

Bert leaped down the ladder and swung the *Nicotine* in from her mooring at the boom. He turned and helped the girls into the rear seat as Rudd shook hands with Smooth.

"Goodby, sucker," said Rudd. "If you pull this job, I'll cut you in even on the take."

"That's swell," said Smooth. "Tell me more about it later." He turned to Dorothy. "G'by, Sweet—keep your feet dry."

"Smooth! Please—"

Lovette started the motor and the *Nicotine* lifted on her step. Smooth caught a glimpse of Dorothy's face turned toward him and he grinned. Then the speed boat roared off into the night. He heard another motor throbbing in the darkness and flattened against the deck. A beam washed the side of the *Roulette*, held for an instant on the empty boom, and was suddenly snapped off.

"Smart people," grunted Smooth.

If Lucky Carmine was shoving that boat around he certainly knew what he was doing. The odds had been reversed, and even though Rudd knew little about a submachine gun, his chances of making a hit were about the same as Lucky's. It would be anybody's fight out there in the darkness, and if Lucky played around with that spotlight, he was just asking for trouble.

Smooth hurried to the radio room and switched on a small desk light. His fingers had been aching to get at the key ever since the fight had started. But had he made a play of this kind with Rudd aboard, instant suspicion would have turned a gun at his chest. He studied the set and had about decided upon its operation when he heard the roar of a speed boat.

"Now what!" he grunted, and switched off the light.

The boat was circling the *Roulette*, each loop brought her nearer, and at length the motor was cut. Smooth went silently on deck and hoisted himself up onto the canvas awning. It bulged slightly beneath his weight and he realized that a good thick piece of steel would offer a better protection to sub-machine gun bullets, but this at least gave him a vantage point of height. And, he decided, no one would be apt to look on top of an awning.

A spotlight swept along the deck below him. It started at the bow and moved slowly along to the stern.

"You're a prize chump!" said a woman sharply.

30

THE LAST LAUGH

SMOOTH STARTED AT the voice that came out of the night. Remembrance came to him instantly. It was Theresa—Lucky's dark-haired girl friend from the Trocado Club. He eased off the trigger, not from any timidity or squeamishness about sending a burst at a woman. Far from it. That little lady had helped to burn down half of Rudd's crew, and he could hardly consider her a shrinking violet. But curiosity and a belated realization that he was an agent in the Bureau of Narcotics held his fire. McNeary wanted a few prisoners to show for his night's work, and at the rate things were going, Smooth wondered just where those prisoners were coming from.

"Aw, they're all gone!" Lucky's voice was low and filled with disgust. "They couldn't take it."

Smooth was glad Theresa was not speaking to him when she had called some one a prize chump. For an instant he had an idea she was talking over a gun sight that was pointing in the general direction of his chest. Now he realized her words were for Lucky. He drew his first breath in sixty seconds.

"That guy Smooth wouldn't run out," insisted Theresa. "He's a wise egg. Plenty smart!" Smooth nodded and thanked her silently. "I spotted him for a wisey the minute I saw him at the club," she added, "and if you'd listened to me he'd never have reached the coast to ruin things for us. I told you to knock him off."

Smooth withdrew his thanks and listened with growing interest.

"Yeah—you knew!" said Lucky. "I been after that mug for days, and could 'a' had him cold at the garage this mornin', only you said to lay off."

"Sure I did. He had you *right*, in the restaurant last night. That guy would never have let you get a gun clear—he just went soft on you. But what's that got to do with this set-up?"

"Nothin', only you keep jabberin' about him. I tell you he ain't on the boat. If he was, he'd been peggin' at us already."

Smooth rested the tip of his chin on the awning pole and looked down at the water. The light was off, but he made out the dim outlines of the speed boat as it drifted toward the *Roulette*. Soon he saw Theresa was at the wheel, and next to her Lucky Carmine stood, with a submachine gun pointed at the deck house.

"I'm goin' aboard," said Lucky. "There must be a load of junk on that scow. And it's goin' to be a pleasure to grab it and send her to the bottom when we get done unloadin'. You know—a present from Lucky Carmine to Bet-a-Grand Rudd, with love and kisses. I hope t' hell I loaded that louse plenty with one of those bursts."

"All right, stupid," snapped Theresa. "Make up your mind. If you're going to be a fool, hurry up and get it over with. Those birds will be back with the army and navy in about ten minutes. Let's get doin' something!"

THE BOAT WAS rubbing alongside the *Roulette,* and Theresa had grasped the mooring line. She held it while Lucky started up the ladder, the gun under his arm and a grin of anticipation on his face.

"Comin' aboard?" he asked.

"Maybe I better," she said. "Keep your eyes on the deck, and if anything moves, don't ask questions—smear it!"

She climbed up beside Lucky, and they stood silently for a moment viewing the deserted decks. Smooth twisted the muzzle of his gun on a line with Lucky's chest and tightened his finger slightly on the trigger.

"Put it down!" he barked. "Down, Lucky—drop the gun or I'll spread you like a fried egg!"

Lucky started and the gun lifted automatically. But Theresa was quicker and grabbed the barrel. Lucky nodded his head silently and let go his grip on the stock. The gun clattered to the deck.

"You rat!" he grinned, and looked up at Smooth.

"That's only one of his names," said Theresa. "And now—is he smart?"

"Thanks, pals," said Smooth, "If you kids will sprawl face down on the deck, I'll climb from my perch and have a drink with you. Face down, please," he repeated. "I trust you—but let us be sensible. And Lucky—kick that chopper out of reach before you take the nap."

Carmine moved the gun along the deck with his foot and stretched out on the deck beside Theresa. It took Smooth five minutes to maneuver his way down from the awning without getting out of position for a quick burst if Lucky should happen to change his mind and try for the gun. At length he was standing above them, and he leaned down and lifted a small caliber automatic from Lucky's shoulder holster. He looked at Theresa and could think of nowhere a gun could be hidden, but remembering Gilda had once surprised him with a sleight-of-hand trick in Mexico, he decided to make sure.

"Strictly business," he said as he searched and winked at the name Theresa muttered in his ear. There was no gun, and he backed away a few feet. "Stand up, folks, and let's talk it over."

Lucky helped Theresa to her feet and Smooth was glad the little hackman could take it with a grin. He had seen so many would-be gunmen go sour when they looked into the wrong end of a gun that he had begun to think there was no nerve in any. He saw that Theresa was deathly pale, but she, too, tried for a grin and her hands did not tremble when she asked for and received a cigarette from Lucky.

SMOOTH CAUGHT WITH one hand the butt that Lucky tossed him and flipped it into his mouth. He fumbled for a match, but lifted the gun muzzle a trifle when Lucky stepped forward to offer him a light.

"No thanks," he said. "I'll manage. And now how about exchanging secrets, eh? I'm a Fed—got a swell job with the government. What's your racket?"

"*I knew it!*" snapped Theresa. "I wasn't sure until you held back on that trigger when you spotted us. But then I figured you right. One of the Narcotic boys, eh?"

"That's right," said Smooth. "And maybe we can still make a deal. This little party you staged tonight could mean the toaster* for both of you. I'm not promising, but I might

---

* Toaster—electric chair.

be able to throw you a pass* if you talk. The Chief's anxious to know who's supplying the brains for Spanish. If you know, and talk pretty, maybe we could strike a bargain with McNeary. You'd be doin' it all**—but what t' hell, that's the breaks."

"Thanks for nothing," laughed Lucky. "I was on the level when I told you my lungs were shot to pieces. I'd last about a month in stir. No—a deal won't help me, Smooth, I play it all or none. But that stuff about the farm wasn't hokum. Theresa has a spot all picked out, and if you say you'll try to get her a light one, I'll play ball."

"Shut up!" cried Theresa. "Don't you know better than to make a deal with a Fed?"

"Aw, Smooth's a pal of mine," laughed Lucky. "He wouldn't cross me." He turned to Smooth. "Listen, chump—I'm the Spanish outfit—see? All the time you been learnin' to be a good boy, I been takin' over the Big Town. Big Spanish is just a punk for me. I been supplyin' the headwork for the organization and takin' the profits. Theresa and me decided the hack would be a grand front. What t' hell—who'd go lookin' for a big shot on a cab seat? It gave me a legitimate front and she stacked away the marbles in a safe deposit box while I clowned around on a taxi. Nice, eh?"

Smooth whistled and shook his head. And again he was glad his finger had not tightened on that trigger. Here was a break that would wrap up the case for McNeary and draw at least three lines of praise from the Treasury Department in a formal letter of recognition.

---

* Pass—commutation of sentence to life.
** Doin' it all—life sentence.

"So we were both usin' the old hack racket for a front," he said. "And all the time I was chasing around town after the brains of the Spanish mob, he was looking at me over a cup of coffee. Well, I'm the champion idiot of the world!"

"Yeah, but a lucky one," said Theresa. "The boy friend is carrying the wrong tag. It ought to be Unlucky Carmine. So now that's over—where do we go?"

"You and Lucky have been wantin' to take me for a ride," grinned Smooth. "Here's your chance. McNeary's waiting for me at Northport, and he must think I've gone on a vacation. Rudd left to collect some boys to fill up the gaps you shot in his outfit and he'll be back soon. So I guess Theresa will have to drive us into Northport and I'll ask the Chief to arrange a welcoming committee for Rudd's mob."

"It'll be a pleasure," said Theresa. "I'm tryin' to hate you, Smooth—but I can't. You're a swell kid, even if you are on the wrong side of the fence. But as for Rudd! Bring on the Feds, Honey—and bring plenty."

LUCKY HELPED HER into the speed boat, and seated himself beside her. Smooth watched them from the deck and was careful not to let his gun swing away from them when he eased over the side and dropped into the back seat.

"What 'd you name this runabout?" he asked when Theresa swung the wheel and headed for Northport.

"*Late Money,*" grinned Lucky. "I picked her up at a bargain this morning. After I tailed you chumps down to Sheepshead Bay in the rain, I figured Rudd was bringin' in his junk with boats. So I hadda compete."

"You did a swell job," grunted Smooth.

He noticed Theresa was using but one hand on the wheel

and had the other about Lucky's shoulders. She pulled the little hackman toward her and turned to kiss him.

"Hey!" shouted Smooth. "Save that till later. I know you love that egg, but keep both hands on the wheel."

"You don't know the half of it, dearie," said Theresa. "I love this guy so much I can't even think about him goin' anywhere alone. Why—he'd even be lonesome in hell without me. Poor Lucky—he tried so damn hard to make a million for me, and he came so damn close." She shook Lucky's chin and kissed him again. "I won't leave you, honey—ever!"

The spotlight swung in a graceful arc as they turned in toward the lights of Northport. It flickered across a tide marker that leaned sharply with the current. The boat straightened out, whirled forward through a smother of spray and drove straight at the bobbing pole.

"Look out!" cried Smooth. "Theresa! Look out for that pole! You'll crash!"

"I expect to, Smooth," she said.

Smooth leaned forward to grasp the wheel, but Lucky knocked aside his arms. The next instant the *Late Money* jammed her bow against the pole. There was a sound of tearing wood, a scream of metal as the motors tore loose, and Smooth hurtled through the blackness. He smashed against the water and felt the gun leave his hands. For a second he was stunned, his mind a whirl of clashing thoughts. He fought his way to the surface and saw a few bits of wreckage twisting in a smother of white water. He swam toward them, the weight of his coat and trousers slowing his movements.

"Lucky!" he called. "Lucky—Theresa—where the hell—"

"That's the spot—hell," said Theresa.

He turned and saw her with both arms around Lucky's neck. A jagged cut had marred the whiteness of her cheek, and Lucky's eyes were closed. She seemed to be supporting him and keeping her mouth above the surface with difficulty. When Smooth started toward them she smiled and shook her head.

"S'long, Smooth," she gasped. "Hope you make it to the beach—not far. Lucky and I are goin' places. We couldn't stick it out alone because—"

The black water closed over their heads and Smooth cried out in horror. His clothes hampered his movements, and the bitter cold waters of the Sound cut into him like a knife. He tried one foolish dive, nearly strangled when the coat wrapped about his head, and then came gasping to the surface. A kapok cushion bobbed slowly past, and he reached for it. His hands were numb, and the fingers had no substance. He jammed the cushion beneath his chest, lifted his head and yelled.

A MOTOR THROBBED near the shore line and came pounding toward him. He yelled again and waved an arm. The effort twisted him from the cushion and he sank below the surface. His ears were filled with a steady roar when he splashed up into the night and the white shaft of a spotlight blinded him.

The motor stopped, and hands reached down from the boat and pulled him from the water. A violent chill shook him and he looked stupidly about at his rescuers. McNeary was supporting him by one arm, and on the other side Ted Wade grinned and thumped him on the back.

"Quit it," he gasped. "Look around—quick. Lucky and Theresa were with me."

"Sorry, Smooth," said McNeary. "You're all alone—just you and a cushion."

"Somehow I'm not sorry," said Smooth quietly. "What a swell kid she was—what a sticker!"

McNeary helped him out of his wet clothes, and Ted Wade rubbed him vigorously, alternating the rubs with hearty thumps on his chest and back. Smooth briefly outlined the events of the night through teeth that chattered and shook. The boat was speeding toward a landing and they hustled him into dry clothes donated by Wade and the men who comprised the crew of the speed boat.

"We'd just about given up hope of any word from you," said McNeary. "Ted Wade got impatient and we walked down to the dock, otherwise we'd never have heard that crash. Thought I'd lost an agent when I did hear it."

"It was close enough," said Smooth. "How about the *Roulette*—will you send a few men out to take her?"

"Yes. Garrison and Duffy are here. They'll go out with Wade and form a reception committee for Rudd's mob. I'll go to the city and drop in to see Rudd at his apartment. It's a job I've been anxious to do for a long time."

"Yeah?" grinned Smooth. "But what about me?"

"You?" repeated McNeary in amusement. "Oh, you can call it a night. I'll drop you off at the hotel and you can crawl under the blankets."

"Like hell! Gimme a break. Chief—I wanna take that guy. Besides—Dorothy is probably at his place, and if Rudd saw you there might be shooting. Why not wrap it up nicely?"

"How do you figure that?"

"Rudd won't be surprised to see me. In fact, he'll be expecting me. I can take him before he knows what it's all about. Be a regular—let me have one little laugh before the party breaks. So far I've been on the receiving end all the way through."

The boat had run alongside the dock and McNeary and Wade stood grinning at the picture Smooth presented. The trousers were too long, and he had rolled them into bulky cuffs at the bottoms. Wade's coat was tight across his shoulders and Smooth had been unable to button the shirt. One of the crew had donated a pair of canvas topped shoes that flapped along the boardwalk like paddles. His hair was plastered over his eyes and he was shivering, and his lips were blue. Still, he persisted.

"How about it—do I take Rudd?" he demanded.

"All right, hungry," laughed McNeary. "Get in that car and try to get warm. I'll let you play it through—but if you muff this deal I'll wring your neck."

SMOOTH GRINNED AND thumbed his nose at Ted Wade. He climbed into a sedan parked near the waterfront and waved to the other Federal men who were laughing at him from a distance. McNeary got behind the wheel, and after a few hurried instructions to Wade, he started toward New York.

Smooth curled into a knot on the back seat, rubbed his ears and blew on his hands. The car rushed along the night roads, ignoring the traffic lights and taking each turn in a screaming slide. They raced over the Queensboro Bridge and McNeary drew to a stop a half block from Rudd's apartment.

"Here you are, son," he said, and handed Smooth an automatic. "You may need it, and that gun of yours might not behave after the ducking. Now go up and take Rudd!"

"Yes, *sir!*" said Smooth, and paddled along the street.

The doorman was off duty, but the elevator boy's eyes opened wide in astonishment at Smooth's appearance. He said nothing, but stopped at Rudd's floor and Smooth heard him laughing as the door closed.

Simpson, the butler, had evidently gone, and it was Dorothy who answered when Smooth rang the bell. She stared at him silently for an instant, and then her arms were around him and she was crying.

"I was frightened," she whispered. "So frightened. We've been waiting and waiting—and when we didn't hear from you—I—"

"Take it easy, sweet," said Smooth. "Here—what's the idea of the tears?" He dabbed at her eyes with his fingers and drew her to him. "Everything's all right now. Stop crying—I'm not hurt. It's the same Smooth under this cockeyed outfit." He held his lips close to her ear and spoke quietly. "Stay out of the way when I take him—get it?"

She nodded and he felt a nervous tremor run through her body. A moment later her head went up and she smiled—a forced, twisted smile that called for another kiss. Smooth shook her chin lightly, and suddenly grew cold. Theresa had done that to Lucky Carmine—just before they died.

"Where t' hell did you get those clothes?" laughed Rudd from the doorway.

He slipped an arm through one of Smooth's and led him into the library. Gilda was seated on the corner of the desk and beside her was the leather case in which Rudd kept his diamonds. She looked up from the stones and grinned when she saw Smooth.

"Don't tell me," she laughed. "I'll guess in a minute—now let's see—you're going to a masquerade—that it?"

"Never mind the smart cracks," said Smooth, and reached for the decanter. "I'll explain them away when I have a drink."

HE POURED HIMSELF a generous drink, lifted it to his lips and downed it when Rudd seated himself behind the desk. Dorothy was standing near the door, her hands rigid at her sides and her eyes steady upon Smooth. He moved back a step, set down the glass and grinned at Rudd.

"It's a long story," he said. "But that was Lucky Carmine behind the chopper. He's dead now. That winds up the Spanish outfit, because Lucky was the brains."

"Well, I'll be damned!" snapped Rudd.

"Maybe," said Smooth. "And now that you're the Big Shot in the dope racket—my boss wants to have a little talk with you."

"Your *boss?*" said Rudd, and his eyebrows lifted in surprise. "I don't get you, Smooth. Who's your boss?"

"A guy by the name of McNeary," said Smooth. His gun was in his hand and it was steady on Rudd's chest. "He's the District Supervisor of the Bureau of Narcotics. Ever hear of him?"

Silence was heavy in the room. It seemed a live thing that beat against the walls. Rudd was leaning forward, his hands flat on the desk top, and his eyes were glinting like little black beads. Beside him, Gilda was rigid. One hand was resting on the stones and the other had lifted to point at Smooth.

"A copper!" she cried. "Smooth Kyle—a *copper!*"

And then she laughed.

"Steady, beautiful!" snapped Smooth. "Get off that desk and lift your hands a bit. That's the girl. Now, Rudd—be a good boy and take it like a gambler."

"You fool!" said Rudd quietly. "I would've made you rich—a millionaire! Shove that gun back under your arm and listen to reason—you dumb bunny. What can the government offer you that I can't double? *Double?* Hell— I'll raise the ante a million. Act smart—hackman! I took you off a hack—a midnight taxi that crept up alleys looking for nickels and dimes. I gave you a crack at big money. And now, you fool, you want to kick it all to hell."

"Yeah—so they tell me," said Smooth. He motioned to Dorothy with his left hand. "You'll find a rod on Gilda's chest—take it."

Dorothy walked around behind Smooth, crossed to Gilda and took a small automatic from her. Gilda stared at Dorothy in disgust and her lip lifted in a sneer.

"Hell—another copper!" she said. "The place is cluttered up with Feds tonight."

"Save it," said Smooth. He looked at her and grinned. "I know how you feel, but—"

"Look out, Smooth!" cried Gilda suddenly. "Rudd's a gambler—he'll—"

Rudd's hand had dropped into the open desk drawer. It came out with a gun that flipped up over the desk top and leveled at Smooth's chest.

"Sucker!" said Smooth, and tightened his grip on the automatic.

THREE SLUGS CAUGHT Rudd in the stomach. The

gambler's head pounded against the desk top. His body slid in a loose heap behind the desk.

"Thanks, beautiful," said Smooth to Gilda. "I never figured he'd try a long shot like that. Hell—the odds were a thousand to one against him. Bet-a-Grand Rudd, eh? They named him right."

"Not a bad guy when you got to know him," said Gilda.

"Yeah—but why do I get a break from you? I thought I was poison,"

"You're a hard guy to stop liking," she said quietly, and turned to Dorothy. "And you're a little slow, honey. You better learn to take better care of your man if you expect to keep him. All men are stupid—and the nicer they are the dumber they act."

"So I've noticed," said Dorothy.

"Remember it," said Gilda. She ran a finger through the diamonds spread upon the Queen Anne desk. "And to think I had just earned another of the pretty things. Oh, well—"

"They're all yours, beautiful," said Smooth. "Pick 'em up. And I hear that southern France is a swell place to spend the winter. There's swimming and gambling, and—well, there's even a title floating around if a gal is smart enough to marry the right guy. How's about it—wanna go?"

Gilda turned and scooped the stones into her purse. She snapped it closed, crossed to Smooth and kissed him lightly on the lips. She walked to the door, turned and stared at Dorothy.

"You're getting a grand guy, damn you!" she said. "Lord, how I envy you!" She smiled at Smooth. "Spend your honeymoon in Cannes—I promise to make it interesting."

When she had gone, Dorothy looked at Smooth and her eyes were soft and very wise. She smiled when he put an arm around her and asked for understanding.

"Don't let's tell McNeary," he said. "He might not agree."

"I won't tell him—anything," she answered.

Nor did she remind Smooth that he had fired only two shots at Bet-a-Grand Rudd. The first had come from her gun—the one she had taken from Gilda. And her shot had been inches nearer to the gambler's heart.

She kissed him and waved a warning hand to McNeary, who stood smiling at them from the doorway. The Chief clasped his hands above his head and shook them. He might have been human, too.

ABOUT THE AUTHOR

AFTER BEING SUCCESSFULLY born in New York City, I managed to struggle through a very normal and uninteresting seventeen years of life. Then someone started a war, and that put an end to a prep school education, as well as to normal and uninteresting years.

In 1917 I enlisted in the U.S. Navy, and made ten trips to France on an ammunition carrier. During the first year of my enlistment I became a gunner's mate at least a half-dozen times, but I never held the rating more than a few days. Whenever they let me out of the brig I did quite a bit of boxing, losing about as many fights as I won (I don't talk about the ones I lost).

To come back to prep school seemed a rather dull prospect after the war, and so I decided to become a bantam-weight champion of the world. Half a dozen professional fights settled that. Oh, I won some of them—well, two at least. Then I went through the usual routine of the service graduate—stock clerk, salesman, insurance, etc., etc. None of it any good, and I wound up driving a taxi in New York.

With prohibition going strong, I decided to put my Navy training to some practical use, and became an "off shore man." In other words, a member of the rum fleet in good standing.

However, the boys played too rough, and I've never liked machine guns, for which reason I went to a job in the ship yards, and then had a try at road construction. I worked as a rigger and iron-worker for a while, and then I went sand-hogging. I started on a shovel in the Holland Tunnel, working on up to hydraulic super on the succeeding jobs.

When I tried writing about it, one day, I discovered it was much nicer to tell the story of a flooding tunnel than to be in that same flooding tunnel. Seriously, I have tried to tell of some of the things the boys actually go through under pressure. They're a swell gang, all of them. It goes without saying that in recounting their experiences I have been forced to trim them down a bit. If I wrote the whole truth it would be called exaggeration.

When Hollywood bought "East River," I bounced out to the Coast to lend a hand. I told the Powers That Be that it might possibly be a good idea to have a few of the real boys come out and work as extras. "Nuts!" said they. "They can't act." So they shot a picture of sand hogs, and my heroes held their shovels as though they were paint brushes!

I had promised my real sand hogs that we'd all see the picture together. Then I caught a quick look at the preview, and ran in the other direction.

www.ingramcontent.com/pod-product-compliance
Lightning Source LLC
Chambersburg PA
CBHW031151020726
47499CB00002B/331